Welcome to Lightning Creek Ranch, nestled in the foothills of Montana's majestic Bitterroot Mountains, home to the strong-willed Brody family. Life isn't always easy on the Lightning Creek, but challenges are nothing new to the men and women who live and work here.

And there's something about the ranch, something in the beauty and solitude that works a kind of magic on those in need of a second shot at life...

Dear Reader,

When I wrote The Brodys of Lightning Creek miniseries, I saved the eldest sister's story for last because, unlike her siblings, Allie Brody has no great love for the family ranch. She lost her father on the Lightning Creek and her marriage imploded there. She'd have been quite happy to never set foot on the property again, but, of course, she doesn't get her wish. I sent her home to make peace with the ranch and face her problems—one of which turns out to be her former high school nemesis, a recently retired professional football player who doesn't put up with Allie's prickly ways.

After retiring from professional sports, local football legend Jason Hudson quickly realizes that his athletic career has in no way prepared him for the next phase of his life. Despite this obstacle, he knows what he wants to do and he'll find a way to do it—just as soon as his difficult father convalesces from a heart attack and he's free to leave the Eagle Valley.

Allie and Jason had me going in circles for a time. They were two of the most stubborn characters I've ever created and it wasn't easy making them realize that their carved-in-stone attitudes and plans were not the best attitudes and plans. Now that I'm done, I love their story and their happily-ever-after, and I hope you enjoy it, too.

Best wishes,

Jeannie Watt

JEANNIE WATT

To Court a Cowgirl

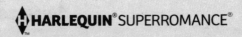

HARLEQUIN® SUPERROMANCE®

Recycling programs
for this product may
not exist in your area.

ISBN-13: 978-0-373-60998-7

To Court a Cowgirl

Copyright © 2016 by Jeannie Steinman

Printed in U.S.A.

www.Harlequin.com

Jeannie Watt lives in Montana's beautiful Madison Valley, where she and her husband help manage the family cattle ranch. When she's not writing, Jeannie enjoys sewing, shopping for vintage patterns, reading and making mosaic mirrors. To find out more about Jeannie and her books, please visit her website at jeanniewatt.com.

Visit the Author Profile page at Harlequin.com for more titles.

CHAPTER ONE

"DAD, I'M NOT going to work for Uncle Jim." Jason Hudson didn't have all the answers regarding his immediate future, but he had not quit football to become a salesman. End of story.

"But Jimmy's your biggest fan," Max Hudson protested.

"I thought you were my biggest fan," Jason replied dryly.

"Immediate family notwithstanding." Max leaned forward in his chair, the Dobermans sleeping on either side of him each opening a sleepy eye as the recliner squeaked. "You haven't even talked to him. You wouldn't be selling," his father assured him. "You'd be managing."

Because he had so much experience in that. No, he'd be smiling and glad-handing the people that came in to see the curiosity. Him.

"My degree is in physical therapy."

"You have no experience with that, either." Jason cocked an eyebrow and his dad's mouth shifted sideways. "On the giving end, I mean. Let's visit this later, okay?"

"I'm not a sales guy." He was a former professional athlete heading into a new phase of his life earlier than expected. His original plan, subject to the whims of team management and performance stats, had been to play until he was up for free agency, but an injury-plagued season followed by his father's massive heart attack had changed that plan, and now here he was. Sitting in his dad's living room, being counseled on his future—which was not going to be in sales.

"You're staying in the area, though, right?"

"For now." He didn't want to stress his dad and trigger another heart attack, but he wanted to be as honest as he could. Max wanted him nearby—perhaps so that he had someone besides his daughter, and Jason's sister, Kate, to boss around, and in the long run that wasn't going to work out. Jason and his dad had a relationship that at times bordered on adversarial, but he couldn't imagine life without the old man, so he'd come home to help his sister care for him while plotting a course for the next phase of his life.

"Then contact Ray Largent. Ask him about that property down the street. It'll sell fast, since it overlooks the lake."

Jason smiled at his dad and got to his feet. The houses in their area were big and pricy and practically stacked one on top of the other. Not the way he liked to live. "I got a couple things to do. Kate's going to hang out with you."

"See Ray," his father called after him as he left the room.

Jason blew out a breath and grabbed his keys off the hook. Kate was due in fifteen minutes and his appointment with Ray Largent was in ten. According to the doctor, his dad didn't need a full-time caretaker but he did need someone close by, so Jason and Kate had decided that at least one of them would be there for the majority of the time. That didn't sit well with Max. He wanted his kids close. Very close. But not watching over him. No, he was supposed to be watching over *them* and since his illness, his need to intrude into their lives had increased markedly. Thus the visit to Ray, although not entirely for the reason his father had suggested. He wanted a property where he could disappear when he came back home; close enough to town to easily spend time with his dad, but not so close that they ended up at each other's throats. Like they always did.

Hopefully Ray could help him with that problem.

ALLIE BRODY NEVER in a zillion years imagined herself moving back to the Lightning Creek Ranch, yet here she was, lugging her suitcase up the front steps of her childhood home. The place where her father died, the place where her marriage imploded.

She should have her head examined.

No. She should toughen up. Her relationship with the Lightning Creek had never been easy, but it was time for her to make peace with the family ranch, especially since her little sisters were hell-bent on living there, or nearby in the case of Dani, whose husband owned the Staley house a mile to the north.

Allie set down her suitcase on the newly painted porch and dug out the key from her pocket—the same key her mother entrusted to her seventeen years ago, after her father's untimely death from a heart attack, when she'd become second in command of the family. She drew in a breath and pushed open the door.

The house had been practically empty when she'd moved out after her divorce two years ago— what her ex-husband, Kyle, hadn't claimed as his own she'd sold to help pay her college expenses— but her sisters Dani and Jolie had once again filled the rooms of the house with furniture and bric-a-brac. Well, Jolie more than Dani. Her middle sister had been quite comfortable with one chair and a bed, pouring her money into savings for the giant indoor arena that now stood next to the larger of their two barns. But now Dani was on the other side of the country and Jolie was on the other side of the state. Mel, the second oldest of the four sisters, was in New Mexico, and Allie was right where she swore she would never be—on the ranch, trying to hold things together yet again until her sisters returned to take up the reins.

For a moment she stood near the door, wondering if she could do this.

Loss.

That was what this ranch, this house, represented to her. Deep and painful loss.

Allie put her hands to her temples. She was strong. She could do this. Take back this house. As she saw it, she had two choices—move into the Staley house and visit the ranch twice a day to feed and care for livestock, or man up, pour herself a shot of whiskey, toast the past and head into the future here. In this house. Her unwanted birthright. Her sisters had made peace with the ranch. In fact, they'd all thrived there. In the place where she'd lost her husband, they'd all three found theirs.

Allie walked into the kitchen, opened the cupboard next to the refrigerator and, sure enough, there was a bottle of Jameson right where she had left it during her brief Christmas visit. Her sisters were beer and wine women, but on the occasions she imbibed, she was whiskey all the way, and right now only one small thing stood between herself and toasting the past. A shot glass.

After a few minutes of futile searching, Allie reached for a water tumbler. A glass was a glass and all that really mattered was the amount of alcohol poured in. Granted, a toast to the future in a water glass lacked the panache of tossing back a shot, but one had to work with what was at hand.

She carried the bottle and glass into the living room and set them on the sideboard beneath one of her more colorful oil paintings—a painting that had been stored in the attic with several others until Jolie moved home. Truth be told, Allie wasn't wild about having her artwork back on the walls, but kept her mouth shut because she didn't live at the ranch permanently and her sisters viewed her artwork differently than she did. Maybe it was good to have it up—another way to face the past, acknowledge and move on.

She opened the bottle and had just started to pour when the sound of footsteps on the front porch startled her, causing her to slosh a healthy amount of liquid both into the glass and onto the table.

What the hell? Or rather who the hell?

The Lightning Creek was not on the road to anywhere, except for the vacant Staley house, so anyone who was at the ranch had come for a specific purpose. She only hoped it was a friendly one.

Allie set down the bottle and crossed the living room, tamping down stirrings of apprehension. She paused at the window to peer out through the crack between the curtains, then took a quick step back. The guy on her porch was, in a word, big. He also seemed oddly familiar, even though Allie was fairly certain she didn't know anyone that tall. Then it struck her.

Jason Hudson?

No. Way.

But when she peeked through the curtains again, it was indeed the hometown hero on the other side of her door. She'd just seen him on TV a few days ago in a campy commercial, doing the wide-receiver thing, catching pizzas thrown by his quarterback. So what was he doing on her porch?

It had to be a lost dog or something.

She unlocked the door and pulled it open, tilting her head back to meet Jason's gaze. He smiled at her. "Hi, Allie. Jason Hudson. I assume you remember me?"

She did. She remembered him using that crooked smile and charming expression to get pretty much anything he wanted after he and his wealthy California family had arrived in the Eagle Valley at the beginning of her junior year—including the valedictorian scholarship that should have been hers. She no longer held a grudge, but at the time she'd been outraged that when their GPAs had tied, he'd been given the top spot and she'd received salutatorian. She'd done a lot more extra curriculars...but he'd

helped them win the state football championship. Sports topped good work.

"I do," she said. Who in this town didn't?
Their big claim to fame—a professional football
player. She took hold of the edge of the door as
she gave him a once-over. He was taller than she
remembered and solidly built, which was to be
expected given his profession. He was also better looking than he'd been back in the day. His
face had developed some fascinating planes and
angles and his once blond hair had gone dark,
which only seemed to make his eyes seem bluer.
A charmer and a looker. Allie was no longer
impressed by either description, but that didn't
mean she wasn't affected by the guy's sheer mas-
culinity. It was all she could do to keep from
swallowing dryly.

"What can I do for you?"

He cocked his head. "Any chance I could talk
to you for a few minutes?"

"Sure." She stepped back and let him come
into the living room, figuring it was unlikely that
a recently retired football player was there to do
her bodily harm. Besides, they had once been in
chess club together—not that he'd ever deigned
to speak to her. They had traveled in different
social spheres, with the exception of chess club.

"Nice place," he said, looking around.

She shrugged and said thank you, even if

it was all her sisters' doing. "What was it you wanted to talk about?"

"Your ranch, actually."

The first red flag popped up. "What about it?"

"I, uh…" He frowned a little as one corner of his mouth quirked. Allie followed his gaze straight to the glass with the splash of amber liquid in the bottom sitting in a puddle of whiskey next to the bottle itself. She looked back at him, raising an eyebrow, daring him to say something. Anything. Like "wow, that's a giant whiskey glass."

He did not. Not on the subject of the whiskey anyway. "I heard that you've recently considered selling the ranch."

Allie's chin slowly rose as her eyes narrowed. "Where'd you hear that?"

"Ray Largent."

Her insides went cold at the mention of her ex-father-in-law. "The ranch isn't for sale," she said abruptly. How many ways could her ex-in-laws come up with to try and get this place away from her? And how was Kyle going to cash in on this?

"I understand that."

"Then why are you here?" she asked, no longer caring about politeness or the fact that he was even hotter than he'd been back in the day.

"To let you know if you decided to sell, I'd be interested."

"All right," she said in a clipped voice. "If we decide to sell, I'll let you know."

"I appreciate that." He shifted his weight. The silence stretched, then he said, "I'm moving back to the Eagle Valley to be closer to the family. My dad had a pretty serious heart attack."

Was he making small talk or playing the sympathy card? Either way she wasn't biting.

"I'm certain you can find a suitable acreage to buy."

"No doubt. This ranch is close to Dad's place, but not too close, if you know what I mean."

Dad's place. One of those monstrosities overlooking the lake at the center of the valley. Allie lifted a shoulder. "Sorry. And not to be rude, but I was in the middle of something."

His eyes strayed to the bottle and Allie felt her color rise, even though she told herself she owed him no explanation. "Then I won't take up any more of your time."

She saw him to the door, closed it behind him, waited until she heard his car engine start before she headed back to her whiskey. After putting the stopper in the top, she took the bottle to the kitchen and resolutely stowed it away on the shelf. Then she returned to the living room, lifted the glass from the puddle and sipped the small amount of liquid in the glass—not as a toast to the past, but to still her nerves.

She didn't know what was going on here. How

the Largents and the Hudsons were involved, but once again the Largents were after her ranch and she wasn't going to put up with it. And to send the golden boy…

She tossed back the rest of the whiskey.

"THANK GOODNESS YOU'RE HOME." His sister, Kate, spoke in a low voice as Jason came in the back door. "I need someone to distract Dad."

Jason smiled even though he didn't feel much like smiling. There was something about his conversation with Allie Brody that stayed with him—something beyond being told no, the ranch wasn't for sale. "That's what you're here for."

Kate blew out a breath. "My life has just been thoroughly evaluated—for the third or fourth time this month. Your turn now."

"I already had my turn today."

"That you, JD?" his father called.

Kate gave him a push toward the living room. "Go and get counseled."

Jason went to the fridge and pulled out a beer. Paternal counseling, especially for the second time in one day, went down easier with alcohol. He popped the top, tilted the can at his sister with a wry smile and then headed to the living room. Behind him he heard the fridge door open again and another top popping.

"Hey, Dad."

"You were gone awhile. Any luck with Ray?"

Jason shook his head and sat on the leather sofa across from his dad's recliner. "He'll keep looking, though."

"What about the house around the corner that overlooks the lake?"

"I want something with more privacy."

Max frowned deeply as he sat in his recliner. "Maybe right now, but as time goes on, people are going to get used to having you around. They won't be gawking."

"I know," he said patiently. Once upon a time he and his dad triggered each other by merely walking into the room, but dealing with more than one megalomaniac coach had taught him a thing or two about thinking before reacting. "This is more about me wanting a place where I can have privacy because I like privacy."

His old man frowned, seemingly confused by the concept. "Since when?"

Always. He'd always liked privacy. Jason shrugged rather than giving an answer and took a pull on his beer.

"It's like I don't know you anymore."

Jason laughed at that. "Right."

Max leaned forward in his chair, resting his forearms on his knees. "What are your plans if you won't go to work for Jimmy? What will you do to fill your time?"

His father was of the school that believed if a person wasn't working, they were either going to become depressed or get into trouble. He had no concept of taking a few months off to let things fall into place. He'd never done that, so why should anyone else?

"I'm looking at options, Dad. Trust me—I'll come up with something."

"Here."

"For now."

Max narrowed his eyes and Jason met his father's stare dead-on. He wasn't going to lie. He'd stay here until Max was back on his feet and then he would start phase two of his life…although his dad was right about the fact that if Jason didn't find something to do during Max's convalescence, he was going to go stir-crazy.

"Wherever I land, it'll be close enough to come home for long weekends and such."

"I think you should talk to Jimmy."

"I'm not a salesman, Dad."

Max gave a snort. "It's getting late. I need to get to bed."

"Have you taken all your meds?"

Another sharp look. Max didn't like it when people tried to control his life, which was why Kate looked so tired.

"Yes." Max got up out of the chair, moving a bit slower than usual. Jason didn't like seeing that. He waited until he heard the bathroom door close before he went back into the kitchen, where Kate was just finishing her beer.

"Pop is going to turn us into alcoholics."

Jason smiled humorlessly as he took a seat across the table from his sister. "His own life is out of control, so he needs to control ours. Gives him a sense of security."

Kate eyed him darkly as she set the can on the table in front of her. "Thank you, Dr. Freud."

Jason shook his head and leaned back in his chair. "Tell the truth, you probably haven't done this much life analysis in a long time, have you?"

"Nope." She raised an eyebrow. "But I imagine you have."

"True." Making the decision to quit football hadn't been easy.

"No regrets?"

Jason shook his head. Eight good seasons were something to be proud of. "Other than having to find a job that doesn't involve Uncle Jimmy."

Kate regarded her hands for a moment before looking back up at him. "If you ever want to talk or anything, I'm here."

"Talk about what?" Jason asked cautiously.

"You're my brother. Football was your dream career since you were seven or eight. Your life. And now it's done. There's got to be some adjustments to be made."

There were definite adjustments, such as not having a goal front and center on every waking day. "Maybe a few," he admitted.

"I can't help but think about Pat."

Jason stared at his sister. "I'm not going to drive my car into a tree."

She let out an exasperated breath. "What I'm getting at is that the transition from professional ball to regular life will take some getting used to—especially if you don't have a job to slide into."

"I'll get a job." He gave Kate a sidelong look. "You aren't joining forces with Dad to get me to go to work for Jimmy?"

Kate smiled, but her heart wasn't in it. She was honestly worried. "No. But I remember how confident Pat was. And how high he set the bar for his postprofessional career."

Pat Madison, Jason's friend and football mentor, had indeed set the bar high for himself upon retiring from football three years before Jason. He'd fully expected to become a sports broadcaster. It hadn't happened. After that he'd set his sights on landing a job coaching for a major college or university and from there work his way into coaching in the pros. After a year with no offers and an increasing reliance on alcohol, he'd dropped his bar another notch and applied for an assistant athletic director job at the university where he and Jason had played football together. He'd assumed the job was his—he was an alumni and he'd had a successful football career. It wasn't. After the first round of interviews, he'd been dropped. A day later, on the second anniversary of his retirement, he'd driven his car into a tree.

"Are you still on this planet?" Kate asked softly.

Jason raised his gaze and decided his sister should know the truth. "Here's the thing. I haven't told Dad yet, but I'm trying to start where Pat gave up. I've been in contact with people at Brandt."

"Really?" Kate sounded surprised and pleased. She was also a Brandt University graduate and loved the place as much as Jason did.

"Really." And even being an alumni and an ex-pro, it would be a long shot, since he had no experience. Brandt was one of the top football colleges on the west coast and hired accordingly.

"Is it the same job that Pat—" Kate gave a small grimace "—applied for?"

"One notch lower. I figure it'll give me toe-hold and then I can work my way up."

Jason didn't mind the idea of growing his career slowly. His plans and dreams were different than Pat's. He'd enjoyed his status as a football player—a little too much at times—but he didn't need the limelight. He was an athlete, not a performer. Pat was both—or he had been until alcohol and the so-called accident had irrevocably altered his life.

"Well," Kate said, "I see some waves ahead

where Pat's concerned, so my offer stands. If you need to talk, I'm here."

"Dad wants me to move in around the corner. Want to talk about that?"

Kate laughed. "He tried to get me to do that, too."

"That makes me feel better about saying no. But I did go talk to Ray Largent. He told me about a place that'd been for sale a while ago, but taken off the market. I took a trip out there this evening."

"Rather than staying home and taking a few hits for me?"

He shot his sister an amused look. "It was your turn and I didn't think it would take long. It didn't. I practically got frog-marched out the door."

Kate gave him an amused look. "Where?"

"The Lightning Creek Ranch."

Kate's eyebrows went up. "I didn't know that was ever for sale. Allie Brody just moved back so she could go to work for the elementary school. She's taking over for Tricia Kettle while she's on maternity leave." Kate wrinkled her forehead. "She frog-marched you off the place?"

"Pretty much and I don't know why."

"You didn't mention Ray's name, did you?"

Jason shrugged. "He's the guy that put me on to the place."

Kate rolled her eyes. "He's also her ex-father-in-law. And it was not an easy divorce from what I hear. Kyle tried to get a chunk of the ranch in the settlement and didn't."

"Well, shit." Jason rubbed a hand over the back of his neck, which was still a little stiff from his discussion with Max. "Maybe he could have told me that."

"Maybe he thought you knew."

"I don't know how." It'd been a while since he'd been home for more than a couple of days, and certainly not long enough to catch up on all the local goings-on. And, honestly, Allie Brody probably wouldn't have been a subject of conversation, even if Ray and his father had been business associates for years and Ray had been her father-in-law. In fact, when he thought about Allie all he could remember was a hot body, a lot of blond hair and an attitude that had smacked of smoldering resentment toward him after he'd bested her for valedictorian.

And it appeared that not much had changed there.

CHAPTER TWO

ALLIE WENT TO bed early after her confrontation with Jason Hudson, but she did not sleep. A wind blew in close to midnight, beating on the house and making the trees creak until the early hours of the morning. Allie finally fell asleep, only to have her alarm ring minutes after she'd dozed off. First day of work. No hitting the snooze.

Yawning, she left the house in her pajamas and coat to do her early morning chores, only to find a few random shingles scattered across the front porch. There were more shingles in the yard. And in the driveway.

Allie had a very bad feeling as she followed the shingles toward the small barn, hidden by the arena—the only building on the property that still had a shingled roof, as opposed to metal. She rounded the corner of the arena then stopped dead. The entire structure lay in a heap of boards, beams and trusses. So much for refurbishing the small barn when they could afford it.

Allie approached the destruction slowly, circling it as if it were a carcass, which in essence it was. It appeared that the roof had been totally lifted off and tossed to the side, twisting the building enough to bring it down. Then she saw the damage to Dani's arena, the canvas covering impaled by debris.

Allie pressed a hand to her forehead. Her first day of work and...*this*.

The ranch hated her.

The feeling was mutual.

As soon as she got into the house, she called the insurance agent and left a message, then showered and dressed for work, debating about whether she should move to the Staley house, with its stainless steel appliances and vaulted ceilings. No bad memories. No curses. Dani wouldn't care.

The ranch would win, but she'd probably be a lot happier.

OKAY, SO HIS dad didn't want a sitter and he had made that abundantly clear again this morning when Jason had asked him again about meds. Cool. Jason didn't want to be a sitter and that hadn't been his intention when he'd come home. But he also didn't want to fight with his dad about how he needed to take care of himself.

He glanced at his watch and continued jogging up the mountain, ignoring the sweat rolling down his back and the dull ache in his knee as he tried to shake off the early morning pissing match he'd just had with his father. Sweat helped. It always did. He might be done with football, but he couldn't imagine life without training. Or a schedule, which he currently lacked.

At least he had a goal. In fact, his entire life had been goal-oriented, as Kate had pointed out the night before. Becoming a professional football player had consumed him since he'd been six and a half, when his dad had first started taking him to games. He'd known then that he wanted to be one of those titans out on the field and even though he'd kept the goal to himself, he'd strived for it. Made smaller goals to achieve; goals that built on one another. Moving to Montana, where his dad had bought a construction company, hadn't helped, but he'd taken the small school to the state championship two years in a row. That had gotten him a scholarship to a powerhouse football school, and the rest had pretty much been history.

Truly history now.

Enter phase two of his life plan.

Jason slowed his steps as he reached the boundary fence to the Forest Service land, then turned to look out over the Eagle Valley. It was a beautiful little valley, stretching between two mountain ranges with a lake dead-center—a lake with a house on it that his father still wanted him to buy. There was a new resort on the far side of the valley—Timberline—where he'd promised his sister dinner. On the opposite side was the Lightning Creek Ranch, cozied up against the mountains with its broad pastures and fields insulating it from encroaching housing developments.

It would have been the perfect sanctuary, but as Ray had told him the day before, there were other places with acreage for sale. Just none as nicely situated as the Lightning Creek or as close.

Jason stretched for a minute, working through the kinks that were part of the territory after eight years of getting slammed to the ground, then slowly started jogging back down the mountain. What was he going to do with his future other than steer clear of Uncle Jimmy's dealership and keep an eye on his dad? Even while jogging the thought of a nebulous future made his stomach start to knot. Pretty soon he was going to have to either come up with some kind of plan or invest in antacid stock.

"I HOPE WE see you tomorrow," Mrs. Lynn, the school secretary, said with a speculative raise of her eyebrows when Allie turned in her key before going home after the first day of her long-term substitute-teaching contract. "I know things get a little wild in the library on kindergarten day."

"Couldn't keep me away," Allie assured her with a quick smile. It was, after all, a job, with a paycheck, and in truth, the lively kindergarten classes had barely fazed her—possibly because she'd been mulling over the call she'd received from the insurance agent just before lunch. The collapsed barn had been underinsured, and while they would issue a check, it wouldn't come close to replacing the barn. The only good news was that the damage to the indoor arena was covered and they'd start to work on that claim immediately.

But despite the rough start and the insurance issues, Allie had a surprisingly stress-free day manning the school library. Classes came and went. Teachers, many of whom she already knew, stopped by to say hello and welcome her. She'd eaten lunch with her friend Liz Belfort, who taught second grade at the school, and caught up on the local news. It wasn't until it was time to head home that she started to feel the familiar stirrings of anxiety, and she knew it was because she fully expected to find a new disaster waiting for her on the Lightning Creek.

She gave a small snort as she drove out of the parking lot. She'd been conditioned to expect the worst there, just as her sister Mel had told her when she'd grudgingly volunteered to hold down the fort while Dani and Jolie were away. It was true. She drove into the driveway and instantly started scouting for fallen trees, escaped livestock, lightning strikes and floods.

Nothing, but she wasn't totally convinced that the ranch was done with her.

That evening, after finishing her evening chores and checking the pregnant cows, all of whom stubbornly refused to show any sign of calving, Allie poked around the remains of the small barn. It had been built in the 1960s and the wood wasn't weathered enough to be salvaged for reuse in offices and houses, which was a disappointment. At school she'd managed to convince herself that there might be some salvage potential to help pay the demolition costs, but no. Now, if the big barn blew down, that wood would be worth something—

Allie abruptly stopped the thought. The way her luck was going, the big barn *would* blow down. Best to focus on getting what was left of the small barn out of there and not wish for trouble in the form of salvageable boards.

EVEN THOUGH JASON had come home to be near his father, and even though he was immensely grateful that his dad was still alive, they'd already begun to slip into their old roles. Jason managed to keep his mouth shut in situations that would have triggered him in his teens, but he felt his patience beginning to wear thin. He and Max made a daily walk around the neighborhood, with his dad's two monster Dobermans leading the way. On every walk Max directed the conversation to

Jason's future and the possibility of him working for Jim, no matter how many times he tried to steer it away. Finally, on a blustery Wednesday morning jaunt, Jason stopped walking, turned to his dad and bluntly asked him what the deal was. Why was he so hell-bent on Jason going to work for family?

"Because business is flagging and you could help. And I don't think it would kill you to do that."

For a moment Jason stared at Max. "I thought you were concerned about my future."

"I am. And my brother's, too."

Jason propped his hands on his hips and stared up at the sky. Then he looked back at his dad. "You want me to do a job I don't want to do in order to draw in business?"

Max gave him an openhanded *duh* gesture. "For the family."

Jason just shook his head and started walking. "I need to think on this."

Max started after him and Jason slowed his steps until his dad caught up, so that he wouldn't tax his father's heart.

"JD." Jason turned and stopped, hoping his dad was going to say something sane. Instead he said, "Jimmy's already got an ad campaign planned."

"Without asking me?"

Max shrugged a shoulder. "You do the pizza ads, so we figured he could tie into that."

"How?"

"We have this Jaromek look-alike—" Jason rolled his eyes at his former quarterback's name "—and he's going to throw car keys and—"

"I'm going to catch them?" As if that wasn't a lawsuit waiting to happen. Maybe if someone else parodied the commercials, they'd get away with it, but he'd starred in the damned things. "No, Dad."

"Look. You might have been the big man on campus for a lot of years, but you're home now and you need to start looking out for your own."

Again Jason stared at his father, unable to find words. Finally he said, "Let's talk about this later." Because if he didn't wait until his rising temper cooled, he'd say something he regretted. "Let's head home."

The Dobermans understood the word *home* and immediately reversed course. Max didn't say a word on the way back, and Jason didn't try to make conversation. It was a tense half-mile walk and once they arrived, Jason went upstairs to take a shower. When he finished, his dad was watching television, the big dogs curled up on either side of his chair.

"Hey," Max said as he walked down the hall.

"Yeah?" Jason asked, fully expecting phase two of the battle.

"Kate forgot to buy dog food. Could you pick some up while you're out? Wildland brand."

"Will do," Jason said, glad to have a chance to make an escape. He still needed some time to work through this owing-the-family stuff. Jimmy was well able to take care of himself and if the business was flagging, it was because of him. People were still buying cars, but his uncle, quite frankly, was a manipulator. He scattered pennies in the parking lot so that people shopping for cars would think it was their lucky day. He wasn't above pretending there were bogus problems with the cars people brought to trade in. In short, his uncle was shady in his business practices and he was not going to help the guy out. It was bad enough he was related to him. And honestly? He was pissed that his father expected him to do just that, in the name of family.

With his jaw muscles aching, he got into his truck and drove to the grocery store, only to discover that they didn't carry Wildland food. He had to go to Culver Ranch and Feed. Fine. He started back to his truck, stopping abruptly to let a car pass in front of him. He recognized the driver in an instant, even raised a hand, but Allie Brody looked through him as if he didn't exist.

And for some reason, that pissed him off even further.

He marched to his truck and took off for the feed store, wondering if he could fit in another run that day to take off some of the stress. At the light, he caught up with Allie's car. He saw her glance up at him in her rearview mirror before fixing her gaze forward again. She turned the corner, drove another mile, then turned into Culver Ranch and Feed.

Good. He had a word or two for Allie.

The lot was almost empty, but he purposely parked right beside her. She got out of the car and walked into the store. He followed, stopping just inside the door to get his bearings.

"Can I help you?" the lady behind the counter called as he caught sight of Allie to his left, tacking something to the bulletin board.

"No thanks," he said. Allie's head came up at the sound of his voice, but she didn't move away from the board. He closed the distance between them, stopping a few feet in front of her. "Have I done something to offend you?"

Allie met his gaze dead-on, her expression cool as she said, "Why do you ask?"

"I don't know…maybe the way you practically ran over my feet at the Food Mart parking lot and the way you're looking at me now."

"I didn't practically run over your feet and I don't think there's anything wrong with the way I'm looking at you."

"Right," he said flatly.

She gave an impatient snort. "Maybe you need to understand that not everyone is a fan."

"Hey," he said, taking a step closer and feeling a touch of satisfaction when her blue eyes widened an iota—not as if she were threatened, but instead as if she were suddenly aware that he was going to continue the conversation instead of accepting the brush-off. "I don't deserve that. I never asked you to be a fan. I asked if I'd offended you."

She folded her arms and seemed to consider his question for a moment. "Let me put it this way. You're the second rich guy who's tried to buy my ranch. I resent people traipsing to my front door, offering cash and assuming we're going to fall all over ourselves to sell our family heritage."

"Who was the other guy?"

Allie's gaze shifted and then she said, "None of your business."

"Is this because of Ray Largent? Because for the record, I had no idea that Ray was your ex-father-in-law. I came because I heard the ranch had once been for sale. End of story."

"It wasn't entirely your connection to Ray that put me off."

"Then what?"

She sucked in a breath, her expression bordering on stubborn as she obviously fought to find a reason for her animosity. "Maybe it's because things are easy for you. So easy that you can simply point to what you want and pull out your wallet."

"What?"

She was starting to get warmed up. She pointed a finger at him. "Even in high school, whatever you wanted, you pretty much got."

He looked at her incredulously. "This isn't about that freaking scholarship, is it?"

"No," she muttered. "Although I could have used that money. You had money."

"Sounds like it's about the scholarship."

She rolled her eyes as if he were dense. "No. It's about privilege and general principles. About paying dues." She unfolded her arms and took a few steps closer so that they were now only inches apart, so close that he could smell her light floral perfume. "What hasn't come easily to you, Jason?"

"My career. I worked my ass off for that."

"How about off field, where most people live their lives?" She nodded at his tricked-out truck, clearly visible through the front windows of the store. "Did you have to save for a down payment?"

"You resent that I make money?"

"Playing a game. A lot of us have to scramble to get by and you got paid a huge amount of money to play a game."

"You're pretty damned judgmental."

"I know, but it doesn't change facts. Some of

us have to work for what we get—at a *real* job—
and others get things because of who they are.
Or *were*. Well, guess what? You aren't getting
my ranch."

"Guess what? I don't want your ranch."

"Good." She smiled tightly at him and when
he gave no response, she pushed by him and
headed for the door.

Jason let out a breath and ran a hand over the
side of his head. The lady behind the counter sent
him an odd look and he turned to face the bulletin board. There in front of him was the notice
Allie had tacked up.

Wanted: handyman to tear down building,
remove debris.

Without a second thought Jason pulled the advertisement off the board, crumpled it up and
jammed it into his pocket.

CHAPTER THREE

ALLIE COULDN'T PUSH the feed-store face-off with Jason Hudson out of her brain, even though she gave it a mighty try. She was not normally confrontational. She left that for Dani and Jolie. She was more of the peacemaker, a retreat-into-the-background kind of person. But today she'd been part of a spectacle in the ranch store. Like it or not, Jason triggered her temper. And she had to face that sad fact that she did harbor resentment against the guy. Why? Because his family was wealthy? Because he'd gotten what she wanted? Because he'd tried to buy the ranch by nonchalantly walking up to her door with more cash at his disposal than she'd ever seen?

The phone rang as she finished washing her few dishes and she practically pounced on it when she saw Mel's number on the display. Her second sister and her husband lived on a remote New Mexico ranch and rarely called unless they were in town, where they got decent phone reception.

"Hey," she said without waiting for a hello. "Back in civilization?"

"Hi, Allie."

She sat up straighter at the sound of her brother-in-law KC's voice. "What's wrong?"

"Mel. She's okay, but she had a bad run-in with a mama cow. Put her over the fence and she broke an ankle, bruised her ribs when she fell on the other side."

"Oh, my gosh." Allie pressed a hand to her chest.

"Damned Charolais," KC muttered. "I told my boss we needed to let a few of these meaner cows go. Maybe he'll listen to me now."

"When can I talk to Mel?"

"I'll have her call you later. She's a little loopy on the pain meds right now and worried about not doing her part during calving."

"But she's okay?" Allie asked, needing to hear it one more time.

"She's fine." But she could hear the stress in KC's voice. "But that's the last time she's checking the cows alone."

"I'll add my voice to yours," Allie said. Even though she was going to do exactly the same thing tonight and every other night for the next several weeks until all of the Lightning Creek calves hit the ground. Their cows were Angus, and all pretty mellow, but a cow with a calf was unpredictable.

"What about you?" he asked, keying into her thoughts. "Do you have any help?"

"I'll call the vet if there's any problems." Even though it was expensive. Living alone, she couldn't risk being hurt. "Promise," she said when nothing but silence met her statement.

"All right then," KC said gruffly.

She hung up the phone after a few more minutes of conversation and then rubbed her forehead. Mel was good with cattle, but things like this happened on ranches and considering her luck on the Lightning Creek...no, she wasn't going to consider that.

Mel called a few hours later, explained to Allie how the accident had been a fluke. She'd expected the cow to charge her, had actually planned to go over the fence, but had caught her boot on the way over and fell end-over-teakettle, landing on a pile of irrigation pipe.

"I need to get less cumbersome boots," Mel explained.

"Right." But Allie smiled, glad that her sister sounded as if she were in good spirits.

"And KC said you promised to call the vet if any calves need to be pulled."

"I will."

"There's a reason there's a ranch fund, you know."

And she and Kyle were the reason that the ranch fund was so low. "Speaking of which, we had a windstorm..." Allie went on about the storm, wondering why it was that when her sis-

Brother XL

2600

Pressure foot /3/7 3°2

ters were there, the fund grew slowly but surely, and when she was there, it shrank. It was starting to give her a complex.

"Keep me posted," Mel said, sounding as if she were glad to have something to think about other than her ankle, which was going to keep her in the house for a lot longer than she wanted. "How's the job?"

Not what she expected. "Let's just say teaching high school art and managing an elementary library are worlds apart," she said dryly. She was a little surprised by the fact that she didn't feel more satisfaction at the end of the day. She enjoyed the kids and the staff, but when she walked out the door, she felt as if she needed…more.

"Hang in there," Mel said.

"Will do. Get some rest," Allie said. "And let me know when you leave for the ranch."

JASON SPENT THREE days driving around with Ray Largent, looking at properties with acreage, before finding eighty acres butted up against Forest Service land on one side and a giant ranch on the other. It was close to what he'd been looking for, only a fifteen-minute drive from his dad's house, yet it gave him privacy. Granted, it was smaller than he wanted, and overpriced, but at least it was one option to consider. Ray encouraged him to make an offer soon, but Jason had done his homework and knew that the property had been on the market for close to a year. Odds were that he didn't need to make a snap decision.

He headed home to what was supposed to be an empty house, since Kate had agreed to take their father to his weekly checkup, only to find an unfamiliar Lexus parked in the front yard. A moment later Jimmy got out and Jason swallowed a groan. Jimmy's name had not come up for a couple of days and Jason was beginning to hope the matter was closed.

"Hey, JD!" His uncle clapped him on the shoulder.

"Jim." Jason clapped him back, then put up his hands in a defensive stance when his uncle threw a couple of fake jabs at him. "It's been a while," he said when his uncle finally quit punching.

"Sure has. Wish we could have seen you here at home more often, but I know how it is."

"Want to come in for a beer?" Jason asked. He'd always liked his uncle, but he also saw him exactly for what he was. An opportunist. Jimmy had made a lot of money being an opportunist, on top of what he'd inherited, but according to Kate he had invested poorly and lately had seen diminishing returns. But he hadn't yet stopped living the high life.

"A beer sounds great."

Jason led the way into the house through the garage door, waved Jimmy to a seat in the great room and got a couple of beers out of the fridge and opened them.

"So how did Jaromek take your retirement?" Jimmy asked as he took his beer. "You guys were a team for a long time."

"He understood and Littleton was ready to step in and take my place, so I think it'll all work out. Plus they have O'Donnell."

"He's over that foot injury?"

"Should be a hundred percent by minicamp."

They continued to talk football, segueing from the pros to the local team and Jason started to relax, wondering if this whole work-for-Jimmy plan was something his father had cooked up for reasons of his own…reasons Jason couldn't begin to guess at. They debated the merits of veteran coaches entrenched in their ways versus new coaches with little experience but lots of ideas, then Jason offered his uncle another beer. Jimmy waved it off.

"Actually, I came by to talk to you about going to work at the dealership."

Jason's stomach lurched. "I—"

Jimmy held up a hand, stopping him. "I heard you had reservations because you have no experience in sales."

"I have reservations because sales aren't my thing."

"Your thing." His uncle blinked at him. "Is money your thing? Because looking at statistics, a lot of retired pro players are broke after a couple of years."

Jason's expression went stony. "I don't plan on being one of those guys."

"So what are you going to do?" There was a touch of belligerence in his uncle's voice. "I can give you a damned good job and you wouldn't have to work that hard."

"Why is it so important that I work for you?" Jason asked, thinking he may as well hear the reason spoken out loud.

"Because we can help one another," Jimmy said earnestly. "A symbiotic relationship. Your name, my expertise in sales."

"I can't."

"Can't?"

"Won't," Jason said coldly.

"I need your help. How can you turn down family?"

"I can loan you money."

Jimmy's lip curled. "I don't want a frigging loan."

"That's all I can offer."

"You won't help me?"

Jason gave his head a slow shake. "Not in the way you want."

"Look. Kid. Your career was already on the skids when you quit. If you think you're going to get any major endorsements or anything, you're wrong."

"I don't."

"So, what? You're going to live here with your father?" He sneered a little as he spoke.

"Until he feels better." Jason got up out of his chair, towering over his uncle. "And I don't want him to get upset." He gestured toward the door with his head. "Finding the two of us here, going at it, won't be good for his heart."

"Neither will your being a selfish prick."

The sound of the garage door going up caught both their attentions. Jimmy sent Jason a look he couldn't read, then a moment later, Max came into the house.

"So did you talk?" his father asked.

And that was when Jason knew he'd been set up. "We talked. The answer is no."

"It's no, no, a thousand times no," Jimmy said sarcastically. "He can crawl to me and I wouldn't hire him now."

Max looked from his son to his brother and back at his son again. "Maybe if the three of us sit down—"

"That's it," Jason said. "Is Kate here?"

"Feeding the dogs."

"Cool. Dad, I'll see you later. Jim…" His mouth tightened and then he walked through the garage door to where his sister was feeding the Dobermans. She took one look at him and shook her head grimly.

"Get out of here for a while," she said. "I'll call if anything happens."

He started to say no, then thought better of it. "Thanks."

THREE DAYS HAD passed since posting her advertisements in all the usual places, and Allie hadn't received one phone call. If she had to hire a salvage company instead of a local guy, it was going to cost more than she was ready to pay, but short of tearing down the barn herself, she didn't know what her other options might be. She'd give it another week, then call Dani and Jolie and explain that they were going to have to dip into the ranch fund to get rid of the thing.

Allie finished her coffee and headed outside to check the pregnant cows. They'd had only five cows when she and Kyle had left the ranch, down from almost a hundred. It seemed as if every few months they'd had to sell off animals to make ends meet or to fund one of Kyle's harebrained projects that she'd been so supportive of...until she finally figured out that her husband was all show and no go. Her sisters had started building the herd again and they were now up to twenty registered Angus cows—eighteen of which were pregnant. If she had a one-hundred-percent calving rate, then they would have even more of a hedge against disaster. She felt bad that she was the reason the ranch had been in such poor shape to begin with…which was why she really hated making that call.

After checking the cows, she turned the goats loose to eat weeds, then started back to the house, only to stop when she spotted the cloud of dust coming down the driveway.

And a second later she recognized the fancy pickup making the cloud.

Jason Hudson.

Allie glanced down at her clothing, glad that she hadn't succumbed to the urge to feed in her pajamas. Her oldest jeans, a ratty T-shirt and her hair pulled back in a rough ponytail weren't much better, but at least she could maintain a semblance of dignity that flannel pants with polar bears on them didn't allow.

The truck rolled to a stop a few feet away from where Allie stood near the barn. She shifted her weight, her arms hanging loosely by her sides as Jason got out of the truck.

"You're back," she said before he could speak.

"I am." In the late-afternoon sunlight, his eyes were the most amazing clear aqua blue. Caribbean Sea–blue. He gave a slight shrug and said, "I'm here about the job."

"Why?" The word burst out of her mouth.

"Maybe I need to pay my dues," he said without one hint of irony.

"You aren't paying your dues here." She gave

a soft snort. "Why would you *want* to pay your dues here?"

"It seems as good a place as any." A few seconds of charged silence ticked by as Allie waited for Jason to either expand on his answer or leave. He did neither. Finally she gave up and shook her head. "I don't see this happening."

"Because you have so many applicants to choose from?"

"Yes. Exactly." Allie felt color start to rise in her face. She was an awful liar.

"I stole your advertisement off the feed-store bulletin board." Her jaw literally dropped. "Heat of the moment," he continued. "And now I'm here to either tear down your barn or put up another advertisement."

She studied him, wondering if he'd been hit in the head too many times, although there was nothing foggy in the way he was studying her back. He looked like a guy on a mission. Why would he want to tear down a barn when he probably had a whole lot of money sitting in the bank, drawing interest?

"You can't tear down my barn, so I guess I'd better print out another advertisement."

"I think you should at least give me a shot."

Allie blinked at him. "At the risk of repeating myself, why?"

"I need gainful employment."

"Jason, no offense, but can't you catch pizzas or something more in line with your talents?"

"I could catch pizzas if I were still playing ball," he said. "But not many companies want an ex-player as a spokesperson unless they were truly great. I wasn't."

There was something in the unflinching way he assessed his career that touched her. She quickly brushed the feeling aside. "Have you ever torn down a barn?" Or swung a hammer? His father had owned a construction company, but as far as she knew, Jason had never been involved in anything except for sports.

"No. I figure it's all a matter of logic. Start from the top and work down and from the outside in. One piece at a time."

Again there was something in his honesty that tugged at her. He didn't know how to tear down a barn, and he didn't pretend he did.

"Do you have the equipment necessary to do that job? And to haul away the debris?"

"I have contacts."

She bet he did.

"Here's the deal," he said, tilting his head as he held her gaze. "My dad had a heart attack and almost died. I came home, but if we continue to live in close quarters, he's very liable to have another because I won't let him take over my life. I need to be close for the next couple of months in case of emergency, but I also need something

to fill my time. Something where I can just..."
He shrugged.

Be alone with his thoughts, work through stress. Allie could have finished that sentence for him because she knew the feeling well.

"...do something physical."

For a moment common sense battled with empathy. She needed the barn hauled away and Jason honestly looked like he needed the job, for reasons other than the money, but this was Jason Hudson. Did she want him on the property, putting her on edge? Because that was what the guy did. He put her fully on edge. On the other hand, the feed-store advertisement he'd taken was one of many, and not one of the ads had produced results.

"One-day trial," she finally said. "And you have to sign an agreement releasing me from indemnity if you happen to hurt yourself. And I only pay minimum wage."

His expression didn't change. "I don't know how much I can get done in a day."

"If I'm not unhappy, we'll talk about another." He raised an eyebrow and she said, "I don't like commitment. Take it or leave it."

She expected him to leave it, but the half smile, which in turn triggered a slow warming sensation in her, told her he wasn't going to leave it. "Don't try to charm me," she warned.

"Into what?"

Bed was the first word that popped into her head. He'd probably charmed a number of women into bed. "Anything," she said with a snap.

"You got it. No charm. When do I start?"

"Tomorrow," she said matter-of-factly.

"Sure thing. I'll go find some tools."

"And I'll find those agreements."

CHAPTER FOUR

JASON PULLED INTO the family driveway hoping Kate didn't walk out in a frustrated huff as he walked in. He wanted a little backup when he told the old man about his new "job." Max was getting stronger every day and had made it clear that he no longer required a sitter. As long as someone was with him when he took his walks—which Jason intended to keep doing—Max didn't mind some time alone. But that didn't mean he didn't want Jason on call.

After he broke the news to his dad, he needed to buy some work clothes and gloves. Boots. And a hard hat. It would be ironic to have spent years in a physical occupation and then get taken out by a falling board or beam.

Except he was pretty certain Allie would laugh her ass off.

Let her. Safety first and all that.

Jason pocketed his keys as he walked into the house. "Hey, Dad. Ready for the walk?"

The dogs jumped to their feet. "Yeah." Max

pushed himself out of his chair. "You've been gone awhile."

"I, uh, took a temporary job."

"Doing what?"

"I'm tearing down a barn for Allie Brody."

"I'm not even going to ask how this came about," he said, grabbing his Vandals cap off the sideboard. He sounded so disgusted that Jason had to fight the urge to laugh. Yes, he was turning out to be quite a disappointment now that he was no longer ripping up the gridiron "Have you ever torn down a barn?"

"No."

Max simply shook his head and headed for the door, the dogs on his heels. He stopped with his hand on the doorknob. "Are you still living here?"

"Until I buy a place…if that's okay with you."

Max nodded and pulled the door open, but Jason had the distinct feeling that the wheels were turning in his head.

THE NEXT MORNING when Jason showed up at the ranch wearing his new boots, with his new gloves stuffed in his back pocket and the tools he'd borrowed from his dad riding in the back of the truck, Allie was sitting on the porch with a mug of coffee cupped in both hands. As he walked up the path, her gaze traveled over his squeaky clean new work clothes, making him glad he'd left his hard hat in the truck. "You look well outfitted," she commented.

"I'm hoping to be here for more than one day."

"We'll see," she said, picking up a folder of papers sitting beside her. "I just need some signatures."

Jason signed and then she gestured at the collapsed barn. "Have at it. I'll be back from work by four. Do you need anything?"

"I don't think so."

Allie drove away not long after, leaving Jason to analyze the structure he was about to disassemble. It'd fallen into a heap after the roof had blown off, and the easiest thing to do would be to dismantle the roof, which lay several yards away in a crumpled mound. His dad had offered to send equipment and operators to dispose of the barn in a day or two, but Jason thanked him and said no. The purpose of his temporary job was to have something to do with his hands as he thought. Watching a guy bash the building with a front-end loader wasn't going to be the same.

Jason went back to the truck, put on the hard hat, grabbed a crowbar and hammer and set off across the field to where the roof had landed. After circling the thing, he chose a place to start prying wood away from wood and began the dismantling process. Within a few hours, his shirt was soaked from the unseasonably hot May weather and he was getting hungry. He had a nice pile of salvageable two-by-fours, a pile of scrap, a bucket full of old nails…and a whole lot of work ahead of him. He ate while sitting on the tailgate of his truck, studying the ranch. All the buildings had been reroofed recently and most of the buildings had been freshly painted, with the exception of the big barn. There was a large building next to the big barn, canvas stretched over ribs, which had been damaged by debris from the building he was working on. Curious about what was inside, he opened the man door on his way back to the demolition site. There was sand inside. A lot of it. And judging from the barrels stowed in one corner and the tack hanging from the wall, the thing was some kind of a horse arena.

Did Allie ride?

He sorted through what he knew about her and came up with very little other than tying for valedictorian and both belonging to chess club. Not that she ever spoke to him there—not even when they played. They'd pretty much coexisted at Eagle Valley High without a lot of interaction. But he'd known who she was. Thought she was attractive in a cool and distant sort of way. She still was attractive, but he saw now that cool and distant hid a rather prickly personality.

What made Allie Brody so prickly?

Did he care to find out?

Better question—did he dare to find out? Allie was kind of scary.

Jason went back to work, putting in his hours without a break until Allie's little white car turned into the ranch driveway. Then he grabbed the only tools he'd used that day—the crowbar and hammer—and headed back to his truck as Allie got out of the car. She shaded her eyes as he approached, a smile tugging at her lips. An amused smile. And then he realized he was wearing the hard hat.

"Once you get used to wearing a helmet, it's hard to go without," he said as he approached.

"I think legally you're supposed to wear a hard hat."

"There's that, too."

She started walking toward the rubble and he fell into step beside her as she passed the collapsed main building and walked to the roof, where she stopped to silently study his progress.

"This will take a while." She nudged a truss with the toe of her shoe.

"I can haul in the big equipment. Just say the word." Inwardly he was fairly certain she wouldn't say that word. She was doing this to save money.

"No. It looks like you got a good start." She brushed her hand over her cheek as if to push her hair back from her face, even though there'd been no hair in her face, and tilted her chin up to look him in the eye. "We'll give it another day."

He let out a soft snort. "Another day."

She nodded as if working day-to-day on approval was a normal business practice.

"I assume then that you'll be paying me daily?"

Her eyebrows lifted as if she hadn't considered that. "That does make sense," she said slowly. "Will you take a check?"

He exhaled. "Yes...you can pay me for two days tomorrow. Unless, of course, you wanted to go wild and hire me for an entire week."

"Do you think it will take that long?"

He was about to explain to her exactly how long he thought it would take when he realized that she was kidding. "Why the day-to-day bit, Allie?"

"So I don't overspend."

"You're just going to shut down demolition when you hit the end of your budget?"

"Something like that. I can't afford to go into debt. Not when I have student loans."

"You're paying for this yourself?"

Her expression started to frost over. He was edging too close to personal. "Never mind. If you want to work day-to-day, fine by me. You can pay me at the end of the time."

"I made up a time sheet."

"Of course you did."

She shot him a look, which he met with an innocent look of his own.

This was kind of fun.

ALLIE WAITED UNTIL Jason had driven away before checking on her stubborn calfless cows and found to her surprise that calf number one had been born. The adorable little black heifer peeked at Allie from the safe side of her mother, who was placidly grazing near the edge of the herd, so Allie assumed that all was well.

"See that?" she called to the other cows. "That's what I want to see—healthy calves on the ground when I get home from work."

Talking to the cows. No sign of insanity there.

Allie grimaced as she headed back to the car to get her purse. After the wild day in the library, staying home and talking to cows didn't seem like a bad idea.

Be grateful that you have a job.

Allie was grateful, which made it all the more difficult to deal with the growing doubts she had about whether she'd trained for the right career. One week in and, while she enjoyed parts of her temporary job, she was becoming painfully aware of her shortcomings as a future elementary-level teacher. She liked little kids, found them entertaining and charming, but she had no experience managing them and no natural talent in that arena. High school kids…

they were different. After completing a double major in elementary education and secondary art, she'd done her practicum teaching in high school, where she'd had no problem with discipline. Smaller children... Dani and Jolie would laugh their asses off if they knew that she was being taken advantage of by six-year-olds. Oh, they'd started off sweet and shy, like new puppies, then, the next thing she knew, they were practically chewing on her shoes.

Allie pulled her purse out of the car and shut the door again. She'd get better at managing the kids as time went on. If her friend Liz could do it, so could she. She just needed practice holding the hard line and ignoring the cuteness factor. Or pray that the impossible happened and the high school art teacher quit, something Liz assured her wasn't going to happen anytime soon.

The next morning Jason showed up early, just as she'd stepped out of the shower. Jolie had taken her dog with her, so Allie had no warning system, and she might have to rectify that. She'd only known that Jason had arrived because she'd happened to glance out the window and noticed his truck was parked near the arena, at least an hour earlier than he'd arrived the day before.

He was at the back, unloading a bucket of tools, and Allie leaned forward to get a better view. The guy was something, she'd give him that. She wondered how long he'd continue on her job before he'd had enough thinking time and moved on to pizza catching.

Allie's mouth quirked as she turned away from the window. That hadn't been a nice thing to say, but he hadn't taken offense. In fact, Jason Hudson seemed like a patient guy in general. She'd never sensed that about him before.

Yeah, in all the many minutes they spent together.

Even their chess games had been relatively quick. And, if she recalled correctly, they'd tied there, too. Not the games themselves, but the number of wins.

Allie put on a summery dress and cardigan, pulled her damp hair into a loose knot, slipped into flats and headed out to feed her cows.

"Remember," she said to the ladies, "healthy calves on the ground when I get home."

Then she looked over her shoulder to make certain that Jason was indeed where he was supposed to be and not witnessing her cow conversation. Another reason she needed to get a dog. Talking to dogs was socially acceptable.

ALLIE LEFT A little earlier than she had the day before, stopping just long enough to say a cool hello before heading off to her job at the school. Jason watched her car until it turned onto the road, then tossed a two-by-four in a pile a little harder than necessary. If he hadn't been working today he would have been running—straight up the mountain. His dad was driving him crazy and his former teammate Pat wasn't helping matters.

Jason had gotten home yesterday to find his sister one step away from throttling their old man. Jason had stepped in to referee and the fight had shifted to him. It was so hard to hold his tongue as Max outlined all of his usual gripes, but he managed. Barely.

Once Max had stomped off to his bedroom, Jason and Kate had had a summit. They decided that Max was still working on facing his own mortality and that they should give him a little more time to come to terms with his current life situation. In other words, they gave him a pass. But the passes weren't going to last long if he continued the controlling, demanding behavior.

In the morning his father was back at it, trying to pick a fight about Jason not being available for his walks. Jason hadn't reacted, but his jaw had been clenched tightly by the time he got to his truck. Then to top things off, he'd received a text from Pat, whom he hadn't heard from in weeks. It'd been short and to the point—was Jason applying to Brandt?

The "for the job I didn't get" went unsaid.

Jason texted back, saying that if he had an opportunity to apply, he would, but that the job hadn't officially opened yet.

Pat never responded, which concerned Jason

on one level and irritated him on another. Not once had Pat confided in him during his downward spiral. He'd never reached out for any kind of help and when Jason had tried to express his concern, offer support, Pat had turned away. Now he resented Jason for having legs.

Another two-by-four hit the pile with a clatter and Jason realized that he had the perfect job in which to take out his frustrations. Easier than running up a mountain, and almost as satisfying.

ALLIE HAD JUST unlocked the library and snapped on the lights when the door behind her opened.

"Sorry to be here so early," Liz said without fully meeting Allie's eyes. "I need to find a couple of books on butterflies for my science lesson today."

"What's wrong?" Allie asked before her friend could brush by her. Something was definitely wrong. Liz's usually perfect hair wasn't so perfect and there were dark circles under her eyes.

Liz hesitated, then let out a shaky sigh. "It's Zach." She sank down into one of the tiny chairs next to the kindergarten table as if no longer able to support herself. "He rolled in at four o'clock this morning. I was worried sick about him, so now that he's home safely, I'm furious."

"Of course you are."

"And I blame Derek as much as I blame Zach." Allie sat in the small chair on the other side of the table. She reached out and touched Liz's hand. Liz and her husband had broken up less than a year ago and their high-school-age son, Zach, had been coping fairly well until his dad moved his new girlfriend onto the family ranch a few weeks ago and told Liz that he didn't think that Zach should work for him as planned that spring.

"Now I wish I hadn't encouraged him to graduate early so that he could work for his dad...and now I know why Derek kept putting off having Zach move to the ranch."

It was not a good situation and there wasn't one thing Allie, the problem solver, could do about it, except listen.

"At least I have the day to cool off before I deal with him." Liz looked up at the ceiling briefly as if blinking back tears.

"I'm so sorry," Allie said. "If I can do anything to help...let me know." Although she couldn't think of anything she could do, except to listen, and she was happy to do that.

"Will do." Liz got to her feet and headed for the lower elementary science section while Allie booted up her computer. A few minutes later, her friend left the library with the butterfly books and Allie let out a sigh before focusing back on her keyboard.

She knew how rough it was to get divorced,

but she could only imagine what it felt like to have a failed marriage affect your child.

BY THE TIME Allie returned from work, Jason was feeling more in control—almost to the point of being ready to go home and take a few hits. Kate had texted him earlier to say that she was leaving Max in Uncle Jimmy's capable hands and all Jason could think was that it served Jimmy right for being in cahoots with his father. Let him get a taste of the wrath of Max.

Allie went straight into the house after parking, but he figured she'd be out to inspect soon. It took her longer than he'd expected, but eventually she came out of the house dressed in jeans and a V-neck T-shirt that looked pretty damned good on her. Her long blond hair was caught in a messy knot that gave her a disheveled, just-tumbled-out-of-bed look that could spark a fantasy or two if he allowed himself. And then she spoke.

"This is taking longer than I thought it would."

"It'd go faster if I didn't take those naps in the afternoon."

Her head snapped around and then color rose from the neckline of her shirt as she realized he was playing her.

"If you mess with the boss, she'll dock your pay," she said. She propped a hand on her hip, looking him up and down. "But you're here more for the workout than the paycheck, right?"

"Allie?"

"Yes?"

"Why are you being so snarky toward me?"

She frowned as her lips parted. But she didn't say anything. He held her gaze, refusing to let her off the hook. She moistened her lips. "I, uh, am perhaps taking my day out on you?"

A question. As in "Would you accept this as an explanation?" No, he would not.

"I know you explained it all in detail in Culver Ranch and Feed, but I admit, I still don't get where all the animosity is coming from. Do you hate all football players?"

"I…"

"Or all people with money?"

"Just those that try to buy my ranch when it isn't for sale." She'd gotten an unexpected toehold.

"I don't want your ranch anymore. So maybe you can quit sniping at me."

Another pause, then she said slowly, "All right," sounding as if she hadn't been aware she had been sniping at him. Or maybe that was how she treated the men in her life. Maybe that was why she was divorced…but he didn't think so.

This had something to do with him personally and he wanted to know what and why, but now was not the time. "Thanks," he said easily.

"No problem," she replied stiffly.

Yeah, he decided as he loaded his tools a few minutes later, patience was a good thing and he was going to be patient with Ms. Allie Brody. Because as odd as it seemed, this job was one of the few bright spots in his life right now.

ALLIE STRODE OFF to the house after Jason started loading his man toys in the truck. Once inside, she pulled out the band that had held the knot in her hair and shook her head. Better.

Why *was* she being so snarky toward him?

Easy answer. Because he put her on edge. He'd been tall, good-looking and well-muscled in high school, but ten years later he'd acquired an aura of casual sensuality that was flat-out doing things to her every time they came into contract. Things she didn't want done to her. What choice did she have but to defend herself with snark?

She could keep her distance. Check his work after he left.

Yeah. That would be the safest way to handle things. Just stay away. Then she wouldn't be catching herself ogling him when she should be discussing the job.

She turned on her computer and checked to see if Dani had sent any new photos of her little niece, Clarice. Nothing. Damn. She could have used a good niece fix. She fired off touch-base emails to her mother and all three of her sisters, then shut down her computer and sat listening to the silence.

This was not what life after Kyle was supposed to be like. Living in the house where she'd been so unhappy, distracted by a man whom she had nothing in common with. A pro football player? Really?

Former pro.

All the same. When she'd finally hit her breaking point five years after being wed—four of which had been spent with her eyes wide shut as she supported her husband in endeavor after endeavor while the ranch fell down around them— her life was supposed to move forward. Yet here she was living in a house from her past, employing a man from her past. Working at the job she'd trained for, yet coming home feeling empty and unsatisfied.

She needed to give her life strategy some serious thought. And in the meantime, she was going to check for new calves. She'd just headed out the door when a car pulled into the driveway and once again she became aware of just how alone she was on the Lightning Creek. If trouble came, what means did she have available to deal with it?

And as the car pulled to a stop she realized that trouble had indeed just showed up in the form of her former father-in-law, Ray Largent.

She was definitely getting a dog. A big one. With lots of big teeth.

"Hi, honey," Ray said as he got out of his car.

Honey, her ass. Ray had been the one pushing Kyle to get a part of the Lightning Creek in the divorce settlement. And when he didn't get the real estate, he settled for everything he could get on the place, even going so far as to haul off an antique tractor that had belonged to her grandfather. The tractor was back and Kyle was gone, working in another part of the state.

But Ray was here.

Allie didn't say hello. She wasn't one for playing games. She and Ray knew where they stood with one another and he could waste energy playing nice, if he wanted, but she wasn't going to.

"The ranch isn't for sale, Ray."

"Kyle's been hurt. Earlier today."

Allie felt the blood drain out of her face. "How?"

"Car accident while he was coming home from a job interview." Kyle had been a deputy sheriff while they'd been married, but he'd quit over a year ago to seek out the big bucks in the oil boom on the other side of the state. Rumor had it he'd recently been fired, and now Ray had all but confirmed it.

"I'm so sorry," she said.

"He wanted me to tell you in person."

"How bad…?" From Ray's tone she was starting to fear permanent injury.

"Neck damage. Broken ribs and some sprains. He's in a lot of pain."

"But he'll recover?" Allie asked, needing to hear that he would. She had issues with Kyle, but she didn't want anything to happen to him. Once upon a time she'd thought she loved him.

"With time."

Allie swallowed and raised her chin. "Thank you for coming by, Ray. I appreciate not hearing this secondhand."

"He'd, uh, like it if you stopped by to see him. The boy has had a lot of time to think."

Allie felt as if she were a split second away from hyperventilation. She was sorry Kyle was hurt, but they were done. How could it possibly help him if she visited?

"I know he's been wrong in the past, but it would make him feel better."

"I'll think about it," Allie finally said.

"Thank you." Ray spoke so sincerely that Allie felt like a jerk for not instantly saying she'd see him. But she needed to think. "He's at Our Lady of the Mountains Hospital. He'll be there for some time."

Allie pressed her lips together and nodded. "Our Lady of the Mountains. Thank you."

Ray got into his car and with a lift of his hand, drove away, leaving Allie standing in her driveway, feeling like hell.

CHAPTER FIVE

MAX HAD LOST a little of his fight after his day with Jimmy. Jason didn't know whether to be suspicious or relieved. He decided to go with relieved, although he couldn't come up with any good reason for his father's change of attitude. Maybe Jimmy had explained reality to him...

Naw.

Jimmy was more likely to come up with a new scheme. Whatever the cause, Jason enjoyed his evening, which he spent watching a Giants game with the old man.

"How's your job?" Max asked during the seventh inning.

"Slow, but it'll get done."

"Don't know why you don't bring in the equipment."

"She can't afford it."

"Yet she can afford to pay you an hourly wage."

Minimum wage, but he wasn't going to tell his dad that. Max already thought his job was beyond stupid. "When she runs out of money, I'm done until she gets more."

Max stared at him as if he'd lost his mind. "Do you have the hots for her or something? Because there's easier ways to get women."

Jason debated. "She's attractive…but she's not real fond of professional athletes." And she had a chip on her shoulder the size of Kansas. He'd love to know why.

Max shook his head and focused on the game. Nothing more was said about Allie Brody or the barn. Jason sent Pat another text while watching the game, but again received no response. Finally he called and was put straight through to voice mail. He was contemplating his next move when the text came in.

I'm fine.

Good to know.

Jason's mouth tightened as he set down the phone, wishing he had his old friend back. This new Pat, he wasn't sure what to do with him, but the one thing he wouldn't do was abandon him. Too bad Pat made it so difficult to stick with him.

JASON DIDN'T KNOW if Allie expected him to show up on Saturday, but he much preferred pulling nails and sorting boards to hanging around the house, so he headed off to work at the usual time. When he got to the ranch, he parked near the rubble pile and pulled the bucket of tools out of the back.

"Jason?"

Allie appeared from around the corner of the canvas building. She looked both out of breath and relieved to see him. "I need help." She looked as if she half expected him to turn her down.

"With what?"

"A calf."

"Sure." He could chase a calf or hold a calf or whatever she needed doing. She gestured for him to follow her to the pasture where the cattle grazed, stopping at the gate to pick up a bucket she'd left there. She opened the gate and held it while he passed through, a quizzical frown on his face. The stuff in the bucket looked medical—medieval medical, because there were chains in there.

"I appreciate you doing this. This way I won't have to get the jack."

He didn't have to pretend to understand what she was talking about because she was already on her way across the field to where a cow lay on her side. As they got closer, he could see that she was straining, in the process of giving birth.

Allie set the bucket near the business end of the cow and pulled on a pair of surgical gloves.

She didn't hand him a pair, so he figured he was good. He was also a touch apprehensive about his role. He'd seen puppies born once and that movie in sex ed, but birthing wasn't a common occurrence in his world. Judging from the cool way in which Allie was pouring disinfectant over the rear end of the cow and what he could only think of as the feet, it was a common occurrence in hers. She looked up at him, her blond ponytail sliding over her shoulder.

"Hand me the chains, okay?"

Jason reached in the bucket and pulled out what looked like a long choke chain for a dog.

"Have you done this before?" she asked, taking the chains from him.

He shook his head, but she wasn't looking at him as she expertly looped the ends around one small ankle, so he said, "Uh, no."

"It's easy. I just hope we're in time. This is one big baby and I don't know how long she's been down. She was pretty exhausted when I found her this morning."

"I see."

She attached the chain to the other ankle, having to reach inside the cow a little to get the job done. Jason realized that he was grimacing as he watched and forced his face to relax. No worse than a compound fracture and he'd seen a couple of those.

"Now you take hold of the middle, right

here—" she handed him the chain "—and when I say to pull, you apply a steady pressure. We are not jerking the calf out of the cow, we're just helping her along. Understand?"

"Yeah." A wave of sweat broke over his forehead.

"When I say release, just keep the baby from sliding back in."

Allie started massaging the area where the feet were sticking out, then she said, "Pull. Gently."

Jason pulled and a bit more leg showed, and then a nose, maybe.

"Let up."

He let up, but kept enough pressure to keep the baby where it was. It truly did want to slide back inside.

"Pull," Allie said, reaching in the cow a little to put her hand over the calf's head. "Let up." She tore open the slimy bag that covered the calf's nose and a long bluish tongue lolled out. Jason was grimacing again and he didn't try to stop. "Pull."

Jason pulled. Once the head had emerged, the rest of the body slipped out in a rush of fluid and flopped onto the grass.

Allie's shoulders sank in relief. "It's alive." She unhooked the chains, then stood up as the mom looked over her shoulder at her new baby.

"Best stand back." Allie shot a look at him and then the corners of her mouth twitched. "First birth?" she asked dryly.

Jason shrugged, feeling distinctly out of his element. "I saw puppies born once. I was six."

She laughed as she dropped the chains in the bucket. It wasn't a full-on share-the-mirth laugh, but it was a start.

"Were all of these—" he gestured at the two older calves lying side by side in the grass near their grazing mothers "—born like this?"

"No. They came out the usual way. This mom's a heifer—first birth. They have trouble sometimes."

Well, the cow seemed to be getting into motherhood now, licking her calf all over as the little guy started squirming. "What would have happened if I wasn't here?" he asked.

"I would have gotten the jack."

"I don't want to know."

She laughed again as she peeled off the gloves and dropped them into the bucket on top of the chains, but when she raised her gaze back up to his, her expression grew serious. "Thank you for the help."

"Not a problem."

"After our discussion yesterday, I kind of thought—"

"Let's straighten a few things out, Allie."

"What things?" She looked both wary and curious.

"I don't hold grudges. It's a waste of energy." He held her gaze to make his point, noting that

Allie's lips were pressed together, as if she were afraid of something slipping out. "I'm not the enemy, Allie. Never have been. Never will be."

"I never thought of you as an enemy."

"Or treated me like a friend."

She gave a slow nod, pressing her lips even more tightly together as she glanced down at the gravel between them. When she looked back up at him he was struck by the shift in her expression, as if she'd just made a momentous decision. She drew in a breath and said, "Would you like to come to the house for a cup of coffee?"

A half smile lifted one corner of his mouth. "Thank you, Allie. I'd like that."

JASON FOLLOWED ALLIE into the house and sat down at the table after washing up. She poured him a cup of coffee from the stainless steel carafe she'd filled before going out to check on the cows that morning, her mind racing as she tried to get a handle on this situation. The one she'd taken pains not to think too much about, despite their previous conversation on the matter. As in how much her less-than-friendly attitude had to do with her preconceived notions about Jason, and how much it had to do with the fact that she found him ridiculously attractive.

Definitely a mash-up of the two, but she was still trying to put her life back on track and it wasn't fair that he should suddenly appear and introduce unwelcome thoughts and sensations.

It also wasn't fair for her to take her frustrations out on him…even if he did cause them.

Jason took the cup she handed him and then waited until she'd sat down before taking a slow sip. Allie did the same, acutely aware that she was horrible at making small talk because she had no patience for small talk. But something needed to be said. The elephant in the room was growing larger.

"Kind of reminds me of our chess matches," he finally said.

Allie choked a little and set her cup down. "You intimidated me."

"Right back at you."

"Bull."

He shrugged his big shoulders and settled back in his chair. "I'm not going to lie to you, Allie. Birthing that calf was gross."

"Birth is not gross." And wasn't she thankful for the sudden shift in topic?

"Did you somehow miss that blue tongue? Or all the gunk that came out?" He spoke seriously, frowning a little for emphasis, but warmth lit his eyes and Allie found herself wanting to smile.

Do not be charmed. Stop now. "All I saw was an addition to my herd instead of a loss."

"Do you have many losses?"

"We used to have more until we started calving later in the season."

"It seems to me that you'd want to have them later. When it's warm."

Allie smiled a little. "Not if you're selling them. You want them to have as much growing time as possible before they go to market, which is why most ranchers calve in February. March at the latest. We're missing out in some ways by calving in April and May, but making up for it in others."

Jason frowned at her. "It's got to be nerve-racking, going to work and wondering if your cows might need a midwife."

"That's just how it is for a part-time rancher."

"Do you think you'll ever become a full-time rancher?"

"No. As soon as one of my sisters comes home, I'll move elsewhere."

"Out of the Eagle Valley?"

"Maybe. But definitely off the ranch."

"You don't like it here?"

"I didn't say that."

"No," he agreed. "You didn't."

But her tone and her body language had. After reminding herself that she didn't need to protect herself from Jason, that he wasn't the enemy, she said, "The ranch and I... We have our differences."

Jason took another slow sip of coffee and when

Allie didn't expand on her answer, he said, "My dad and I have our differences. I guess it happens to everyone."

Allie smiled in acknowledgment, glad for the shift of subject. She was the only Brody sister who had issues with the ranch, but she was also the only sister to suffer tragedy there twice. One quick and devastating and the other slow and torturous.

"That's life. So…how has the Eagle Valley changed since you left?"

"I have been back a time or two." He smiled ruefully. "But not that many. Mostly I was training or playing." He stopped, as if analyzing his past, then his clear aqua gaze met hers. "A lot has changed. For one thing I miss the old movie theater. That new thing at the edge of town is ugly."

"Yes. I guess it was going to take too much money to bring the old theater up to code, so they shut it down." Allie had also loved the historic brick theater with the balcony and classic early-twentieth-century woodwork. "You're right. The new one isn't the same."

They finished their coffee while discussing the safe topic of local changes, and Allie told herself more than once that since she wasn't all that fascinated by hands, she could stop studying Jason's—but it was better than looking at his face as they spoke and finding herself thinking that he was simply too damned good-looking for words.

Finally Allie pushed back her chair and started tidying up the table, carrying the coffee cups to the counter. "I need to get going," she said on an apologetic note. "I have to visit someone in the hospital."

"And I need to get to work." He started for the door, then stopped. "Do you have many more pregnant cows?"

"Fourteen."

"You know that you can call me anytime you need help."

"Thank you." She smiled politely at him. What else could she do?

After Jason had gone, Allie finished wiping the table, then rinsed the cups. She did everything she could to keep from slowing down long enough to acknowledge that being around him shook her. She wasn't supposed to be thinking about guys. She was recovering from a guy. She needed to be thinking about making a future and not letting the ranch disintegrate while she was in command, as it tended to do.

After the kitchen was back in order, she grabbed her purse and went out to her car. She was going to see Kyle—and not because she felt guilty not doing it.

As she drove to the hospital, she told herself that this was a good thing to do. A way to prove to herself that she was done with that chapter of her life. Because she really had to move on past this bitterness. It was going on two years and she still felt anger toward the man—both for the promises he hadn't kept and for the crappy things he'd done after the divorce.

Kyle, as it turned out, looked terrible. Two black eyes, a swollen lip, but no stitches that she could see. His other injuries, whatever they might be—bruised and broken ribs and sprains, according to Ray—were hidden by the sheet covering him.

Allie took a few steps into the room, hating the smell, hating the circumstances that had her there. Hating that she'd come. And what did she say now that he'd focused on her? "How're you feeling?" wasn't appropriate.

"I'm glad you're okay. I mean, other than…" She gestured weakly.

"Yeah." He spoke softly, his words slightly slurred.

Allie moved forward, but still kept her distance from the bed. She wished him no harm, but he had been so adversarial toward her and her sisters after he'd failed to get part of the Lightning Creek, that she was also having a hard time feeling anything other than regret that he'd been hurt. Seeing him like this did not stir any feelings of warmth or desire for a reunion. Was that why he'd wanted to see her? To rekindle something?

If so, injured or not, he was in for a rude awakening. Allie wasn't about to complicate her life now that she was on the road to straightening it out.

"I just wanted to stop by, let you know I was thinking about you."

"Appreciate that."

And then there wasn't a whole lot to say. "Well, I don't want to wear you out. I wish you a speedy recovery."

"Allie?"

"Yes?"

"I'm going to have trouble covering my part of the medical bills because I'm between jobs."

Allie's heart dropped. He'd wanted to see her to shake her down?

"I'm sorry to hear that, Kyle." She made a backward step toward the door. "I'm sure you know that I don't have any money with all of my student loans. Maybe your dad could help you out."

"Yeah. Uh, he's not in a position to do that."

And she was? Honest to Pete.

"Sorry. I'm sure the hospital will take payments."

"I'll need therapy afterward."

Allie's patience was about to snap. "What do you want, Kyle?"

"It's what I don't want. I don't want to file medical bankruptcy." His gaze held hers and she searched, trying to find a hint of the guy she'd fallen in love with. Had time changed him so much? Or had she fallen in love with an illusion?

"And…"

"Would you co-sign a loan for me?"

"I'm up to my neck in student loans!"

"If you used that eighty-acre parcel on the far side of the creek as collateral… Not that you'd need collateral. I have some savings to use to make payments until I land a job."

"Oooh, no…" Allie shook her head. "Uh-uh. I'm not attaching the ranch to a loan." She'd taken great pains not to do that while funding her education.

"Only part of—"

"No." At any minute she expected Kyle's heart-rate monitor to top out. If she'd been attached to a monitor, it would already be there. "I'm sorry about your predicament." But it was not her predicament, no matter how guilty she felt saying no. "The ranch belongs to all of us. I couldn't make a decision like that alone if I wanted to."

"Will you talk to your sisters?"

"I have to go, Kyle."

Allie turned and left the room, walking to her car in a haze of anger. She hated not helping people, but Kyle was asking too much.

Yet, she still felt jabbing guilt beneath her anger. Why? What was wrong with her? She'd spent five years of her life supporting this guy, believing in him, and she'd been let down every single time. Wasn't that enough?

AFTER ALLIE HAD driven away, Jason finished dismantling the roof and then took a break before starting on the main structure, which was going to take some time. A couple weeks, maybe, working by hand. He was glad. As Max got healthier, he got more cantankerous and controlling, reminding Jason of a little kid pushing boundaries.

He sat on the tailgate of his truck, drinking from his water bottle and studying the barn wreckage, debating where to start. He honestly did need a hard hat for this part of the job. Part of the structure was still intact and several beams were attached to the top of a standing wall, although their opposite ends rested on the ground. Potential for trouble there. He had no idea how well the upper ends of the beams were attached, or what it would take to bring the standing wall down. He'd find out soon enough.

After stowing his water bottle back in the cooler, he approached his project. In the rubble, he could see old hand tools and gardening implements that had been stored in the building. A beat-up saddle lay in the jumble between two wooden barrels, one of which was now smashed. Dismantling this part of the building was going to feel like a treasure hunt. He wondered how much of the stuff was useful and how much had been stored instead of being thrown away. That was how a lot of valuable antiques had survived until present day, but none of the stuff he could see looked particularly valuable...except for the old bit-and-brace drill sitting just under a fallen beam. He loved bit-and-brace drills—had spent a lot of time as a kid drilling holes in boards his grandfather had given him to keep him busy. Rather than wait the day or two until he'd got to that area by knocking things down, he carefully started picking his way across fallen boards.

Oh, yeah. He bent and picked up the drill. He'd never worked in the construction trade, but his dad collected old tools and he knew a good one when he saw it. The knob at the top was black walnut if he wasn't mistaken. He started back toward safety, the drill in one hand. He'd ask Allie if she wanted to sell it and he'd also let her know that it was worth something before she made the decision.

He was just about to step off the two-by-six he'd been using as a balance beam onto a sturdier-looking fallen beam when he heard an ominous crack. Before he could save himself, the board snapped and his leg plunged down into the jumble of debris, shoving up his pant leg as his shin skidded down the rough surface of a broken board. Shit.

He grimaced as he pulled his leg out of the hole. It stung. Gingerly he made his way to his truck, trying to remember the last time he'd skinned himself up good. When he was a kid on his bike maybe?

Blood had seeped through his jeans by the time he got there. He'd had a lot of injuries over the years, but few of them bled much, if you didn't count getting cleated, or that one time his nose had gotten broken. He was just working his pant leg up over the scrape when he heard the car coming down the road.

Allie. He pushed the pant leg back into place and stood next to his truck, hoping she'd keep going past him. No such luck. She pulled up beside him and rolled down her window.

"Done with the roof I see."

"Just finished." He picked up the drill, noticed the blood on his fingers and hoped she didn't. "I found this in the main part of the building."

"How?"

"Wasn't easy." Not only that, it'd hurt. He nodded at the tool. "It's got some value to it and I was wondering, if you don't have a sentimental attachment because it was your dad's or something, if I could buy it for my old man."

"I don't see why not."

He started to smile, but it stalled out as her gaze dropped and then fixed on his lower leg, where the blood was gluing his pants to his skin.

When she brought her gaze back up to his, there was a question in it, and he could see that she didn't expect to have to ask that question out loud.

"I had a mishap while getting the drill."

"You're the second beat-up guy I've dealt with today."

"Who was the other?" *And were you responsible?*

"My ex. He got into a car wreck."

"Nothing too serious, I hope."

"Broken ribs, black eyes. He's hurting, but nothing life-threatening. He was lucky." She said the words in a way that did not invite further comment. "Do you want to go to the house and clean up your leg, or what?"

Well, yeah, he did. "I don't want to bleed all over your place."

"Won't be the first time," she said. She jerked her head toward the passenger side of her car, but he shook his head.

"I can walk a hundred yards."

"Suit yourself."

"Walking is easier than getting into your car."

"Oh." Her eyebrows lifted as she considered his size compared to the space available in her tiny passenger seat. "I guess so. And here I thought that you were going all macho on me."

"I know," he said with a half smile. She did

tend to think the worst of him and he might have to do something about that.

She waited for him at the gate and then he followed her into the house. She gestured for him to wait in the living room and then walked through the kitchen into the adjoining mudroom. She came back with a plastic bucket of neatly folded terry-cloth towels with gauze pads and athletic tape resting on top. She held out the pail with a small shrug. "Vet bucket. All the towels are clean and bleached. You can get them as bloody as you want."

"Thanks."

"I hope you don't mind using the same towels used for animal emergencies, but like I said, they're clean."

He raised his hand. "No. Honest. I'm good with it. Glad I don't have to make do with wet paper towels."

'That was kind of what I was thinking. I usually use duct tape with the animals, but I thought you might be more comfortable with athletic tape."

A joke. Cool.

She pointed the way to the bathroom and Jason headed down the hall, bucket in hand. He casually glanced back before he opened the door. Allie hadn't moved, but her chin jerked up as he met her gaze. He lifted an eyebrow and then walked into the bathroom, closing the door behind him.

Allie Brody had been staring at his ass.

CHAPTER SIX

WELL, THAT WAS the very first time ever she'd been caught ogling a guy's ass and it had happened in her living room.

Allie scrubbed her hands over her cheeks. That's what she got for giving in to temptation. What was it with this guy? Why was he her Kryptonite?

Okay. No big deal. Surely she wasn't the only woman he'd ever caught staring at him, but…this was different. She was his employer. He was her employee. Temporarily, but all the same.

But what it really came down to was that it was Jason Hudson, whom she'd thought of as an arrogant jock and who was turning out to be much more together and pleasant than she'd ever expected.

And attractive. Don't forget attractive.

How could she? He was right there. Being attractive.

She wasn't comfortable being attracted to him because that wasn't part of her go-it-alone-and-be-secure plan. She'd had enough heartache over the past several years. Being alone equaled no more heartache.

Being attracted meant being tempted to not be alone, which in turn tempted heartache.

Allie lifted her chin and headed off for the kitchen, where she went to the sink and poured herself a glass of water. Maybe if she hydrated, she could gain control of her hormones. She took a long drink.

Yes. Better.

Or maybe it was the fact that there were now a couple of walls and a healthy distance between herself and the guy with the great ass.

Allie emptied the glass, then opened the dishwasher and started putting the dishes into the cupboard, resolutely pulling her thoughts away from Jason until she heard the bathroom door open and her nerves jumped. Jason's tread was heavy on her old wood floors and each step made her heart rate speed up just a tiny bit more.

Then the steps stopped.

Allie froze, wondering what he was doing, until he started moving again and she busied herself arranging glasses in the cupboard. Unaware. Unaffected. Yes. That was her.

"I didn't know you painted," Jason said as he came into the kitchen, carrying the bucket in one hand and the soiled towels in the other. His pant leg was soaked from the knee down, where he'd washed the blood out of it. Just looking at it made Allie feel a little clammy. Wet jeans were never comfortable.

Nor was facing the guy who'd caught her checking him out.

"I don't paint," she said matter-of-factly. "Not anymore. It was just a...phase."

He cocked an eyebrow at her in an expression that said he'd like to know more, but wasn't going to ask—probably because of her forbidding expression. "I only used one towel, but I did a number on it. Where should I put it?"

She gestured toward the mudroom and he followed her to the washing machine. She lifted the lid and he dropped the wet, bloody towel inside.

"I'm sure there'll be more to follow," she said as she closed the lid again.

"Do you have a lot of injuries here?"

"No, but when you have this many animals, stuff happens. If not blood, then mud. Trust me—that washer will have a load in no time."

"Huh." He flexed his knee as if testing whether or not his administrations would hold. "Well. I'm good as I'll be. I guess I'll head on back and try not to get hurt." He pointed to the back door. "Can I go out this way?"

"Of course."

He paused, his hand on the door handle. "Are you going to dock my pay for this?"

"Not if you don't sue me for having an attractive nuisance on my property."

"I recall signing a paper releasing you from indemnity if I got hurt."

"Good call on my part."

"Looks like it." He held her gaze and when she didn't say anything more, he turned and headed out the door. After he was safely out of the house, Allie moved to the window to watch him walk to his truck, free to watch his ass all she'd like. She let out a breath as she let the curtain drop.

The house felt empty and as she started toward the kitchen, it seemed to echo *alone, alone, alone* in time with her footsteps.

Alone had been her natural state for the past year, but not one that she particularly welcomed, even though she wasn't certain how to change that without jeopardizing the fragile sense of control she had over her life right now. It was crazy, but even when she was with people she felt alone—probably a holdover from all those years that she pretended everything was okay with her and Kyle when they were not. She'd been the great pretender, with her sisters and her mother. With herself. She'd protected her deep secret, the fact that she was barely holding herself together in the face of the disintegration of both her marriage and the ranch, by erecting barriers. Not letting conversations get too deep, or herself get too close to others. Her sisters had been off in distant places, living their own lives. And she'd been here on the ranch, lying about hers.

Lying hadn't turned out well in any respect, so she was determined to be honest with herself this time around.

Truth number one—she wasn't certain that she was well-suited to work in an elementary school, but she was going to give it more time. Truth number two—she was attracted to Jason.

Truth number three…

That was enough truth to deal with right now. Allie paused briefly at the painting Jason had commented on, squinted at it, trying to see it through someone else's eyes. She couldn't do it. She had too much time and emotion tied up in the work to see it as anything except for a piece of herself that she wished wasn't on display.

The phone rang a half hour later as she pulled dinner out of the microwave. She kind of hoped it was a sister, so that she could talk, kind of hoped it wasn't, because her sisters were more watchful of her now. Not a sister. Liz.

"Hey. How are you?" Allie asked, keeping her voice light.

"I'm good. I have a question for you, though." Liz was making an effort to sound casual, but Allie caught the edge of anxiety in her friend's voice.

"What is it?"

"Do you still need help demolishing that wind-damaged barn?"

There could be only one reason Liz was

asking—her son, who'd been causing her a lot of worry of late. "I hired a guy."

"Oh."

There was a note in Liz's voice that made Allie cautiously say, "Why do you ask?"

"It's Zach. I, uh, we're having more issues and I'm trying to find something for him to do to keep him focused on something other than not going to the ranch to help his dad." Liz sighed. "Full disclosure—he tried to get a job in town, but he can't find one. He's angry at his dad and... Allie, I don't know what to do."

Allie pushed the hair back from her forehead, her heart breaking a little at the pain in her friend's voice. "I, uh, might be able to come up with a few days work," she said.

"Really?"

The hope in her friend's voice was almost as gut-wrenching as the anxiety. She was committed now. "Yeah. There are some things he can do. There's still a lot to be done with the demolition and if I have Zach on the job it'll go that much faster."

Then Jason would be gone that much sooner and she'd have fewer opportunities to get caught staring at him. Not that she should be blamed for that. She'd like to find a red-blooded woman who wouldn't stare at him as he was walking away.

"That would be so great."

"I do need to talk to the guy that's working

for me and make sure that he's okay supervising Zach. He didn't sign on for that and, well, you can see—"

"Certainly," Liz said in a strained voice. "I totally get that. Who is he?"

"Jason Hudson."

"The football player?"

"Yes."

It took Liz a moment to digest that. "Maybe that would be good for Zach, working with a guy like Jason. A role model and all that." She hesitated for a moment, then said, "He was at a party that got raided this weekend. He got away, but a deputy recognized him and called me. When Zach finally got home, he was so out of it—" Her voice broke, and then she said, "It's not the first time, but it's the first time law enforcement was involved...or almost involved."

"I'm so sorry."

"I blame Derek. If he'd just act like a freaking father—" Liz broke off abruptly. "I'm sorry. Zach hasn't been the same since his dad left and now that working on the home ranch is no longer an option, his behavior is escalating."

Allie pressed her fingers to her forehead, wondering what she'd gotten herself into. *It'll only be a week or two.* No need to feel as if she'd swallowed a rock. Zach may not even last more than a couple of days. She hoped he did, for Liz's sake, but there were no guarantees. Of course,

Zach may be impressed by the idea of working with Jason and that might keep him coming back to work.

In the end, that was what both Liz and Allie had hung their hopes on.

"But if he's disrespectful to you or Jason, just send him on his way," Liz said. "This is my problem, not yours. I was just hoping that being able to do something with his hands, to accomplish something, might jar him back to reality...before I lose him for good."

And how did one say no to that?

One didn't.

ALLIE HAD ALREADY left for work by the time Jason arrived at the Lightning Creek on Tuesday morning—probably because he arrived almost forty-five minutes later than usual. It couldn't be helped. He'd had another go-round with his dad about his diet and exercise regimen, which his father followed only when one of his kids was there. He loved his dad, admired many things about the man, but was it too much to ask for a relationship that was more...normal? They had good times, but only when Max felt as if he were in control.

While driving to the Lightning Creek Jason made himself a solemn promise that he would not try to control his children's lives. If he had kids. Right now, he'd settle for simply getting a job. A real one, not a sanity saver such as demolishing a barn, although he had to admit to getting a certain amount of satisfaction from slowly cleaning up the wreckage.

The spring day turned stormy late in the morning, but Jason didn't use the weather as an excuse to head home. Kate had texted to say that Jimmy had stopped by to take Max to the dealership for coffee and man talk, so no worries there—for a while anyway—and Jason didn't feel like kicking around the empty house any more than he felt like having another bout with his dad over health issues. So when the showers came, he hung out in his truck, listening to music and watching the dramatic sky until the rain stopped and he could go back to work.

After spending the majority of his life being part of a team, flying solo day after day was a new experience, and he liked his days alone on the ranch, the wind in his face, rain on his back and all that. But he also enjoyed contact with people and he didn't know how Allie did it, living on the Lightning Creek, without even a dog for companionship. There were some friendly goats, but for the most part, she was alone.

Shut off.

Yeah—that was it. Shut off. In many ways. That, he realized, was his concern for her, if he had a right to be concerned. She seemed to be fighting private battles on many fronts. All by herself, despite having three sisters.

But he was only seeing part of the picture, he reminded himself as he got out of the truck yet again and waded through the wet grass to pick up the bar he'd been using to pry boards off a broken beam. The nail squealed as it came loose from the wet wood and Jason bent down to pick it up and set it in the nail can, now half-full of water. He strained the water out of the can, set it back upright and stared out over the fields. This really was a good life, but it wasn't his life.

His life—or rather his future—was making him antsy, even though it was still early days. After hearing that Brandt had been inundated with applications for the two open offensive coaching jobs, he'd peppered the country with college coaching applications and made calls, but his lack of experience in actual coaching, rather than playing, hurt him. No, it paralyzed him. No one knew if he could coach. No one was beating down his door. Several suggested starting on the high-school level. Jason preferred to skip that step if possible.

Finally, during a particularly heavy downpour that hammered the roof of the truck, Jason pulled out his phone and punched in the number for his contact, and his chief reference at Brandt, his former Offensive Coach.

"Jason. How's your dad?"

"Better. He should have a full recovery." If he would follow the regimen.

"Good to hear." Coach cleared his throat. "No word yet. The wheels move slowly, but there are a ton of applicants."

"Great."

"A lot of them have decent experience at the college level."

"Don't tell me to coach high school for a decade or so, okay?" Jason said, doing his best to inject a smile into his voice.

"Heard that, have you? Not bad advice, but no guarantees, either. You might consider moving back down here. Volunteering your time."

"I've thought about that." If push came to shove, he'd do it, although he'd have to get some kind of job. San Diego was an expensive city and he wasn't going to chip away at his retirement nest egg. He wasn't going to end up like Pat.

Speaking of which… "The same thing must have happened to Pat."

"Yeah, but he didn't do himself any favors, either, coming to the interview and acting like a rock star."

"Yeah?"

Coach snorted. "He was an arrogant jerk."

"I didn't know."

"I think he was scared and desperate. I even took a shot at explaining that to the committee, but the damage was done." He made another disgusted noise, but this one had an edge of emotion to it. "Hard to watch a guy self-destruct like that."

"Yeah." Jason swallowed.

"Sorry I don't have better news. Since I retired, I'm out of the loop, but Finley keeps me updated when we golf."

"I appreciate your help, Coach."

"I'd love to have you in the area, Jason. If I have any insights, I'll let you know."

Jason thanked the man again and then hung up, leaning his back against the cushioned headrest. Yes, he had money. No, he was not desperate in that regard. But he was a guy who needed a purpose and a goal. He was a guy who needed to put his talents to work and he knew for a fact that he could offer something of value to Brandt. Now the question was how to convince a hiring committee of that fact, short of eating up his nest egg by volunteering for a season or two.

ALLIE WAS GLAD to catch sight of Jason's truck parked next to the barn when she rounded the last corner before turning off the main road to the Lightning Creek. She wanted to hire Zach, but there was no way she could have him tearing down a building on the ranch if Jason wasn't on board. Too much liability there.

She stopped next to Jason's truck, leaving her car running as she walked around the big Ford to where he was stacking the last of a small pile of broken boards.

"Just finishing up," he said as he stepped over a pile. His jeans were torn near the knee and caked with mud, but Allie didn't ask what had happened. Apparently it hadn't required first aid.

"I have a favor to ask."

"Yeah?" He pulled off his gloves, which were no longer anywhere near new-looking.

"I want to hire a kid to help you."

He shot her a confused look. "You think I need help?"

"I think this kid needs help." And more than that, his mother needed help. "He needs something to keep him busy this summer."

Jason's eyes narrowed. "Is he in trouble?"

"He's not a bad kid." Jason didn't say anything and Allie added, "His parents broke up. He's having some issues and I want to hire him to keep him busy."

"I've got to be honest here. I'm not good with kids."

"How do you know?"

"I've never been around kids."

"I thought you wanted to coach."

"Coaching football is different from babysitting a troubled teen."

Allie knew she couldn't force him to oversee Zach, because he didn't need this job. He was there because... She still didn't know why he was there, except to escape his family during the day.

"His mom is a friend of mine. She's worried and I want to help." She crossed her arms. "I'd like to try him for a day or two and then assess."

Jason looked down at his damp boots, his jaw tightening before he met her eyes again, and said, "Fine."

Allie held his bluish-green gaze and when she realized that he was done speaking, she gave a small nod. "Thank you. I'll go call his mom."

"Why don't you call him?"

Good point, but she'd been dealing with Liz and would continue to do so until Zach actually went to work for her.

"He'll probably start the day after tomorrow," Allie said without answering his question.

"Great. I'm sure we'll do well together." Jason spoke with apparent sincerity and Allie decided to take him at face value.

"Thank you. I hope so. I'll keep you posted as to what's going on." And with that she turned and headed back to her car.

JASON SHUT THE door a little too hard as he got into the truck. The thing he liked best about tearing down the barn, besides the actual physical labor, was the time he had to think things through. Or just be. There was no way he'd be able to do that with someone else around. Even if the kid didn't talk, he'd be there and Jason wouldn't be able to lose himself in his thoughts.

And he didn't like hero worship, which had been his experience with the few kids he'd met over the course of his career. Coaching at Brandt...no hero worship there. The kids already considered themselves elite, and a coach was a coach, regardless of his background.

He knew because he'd once been one of the Brandt elite. And then he'd made the pros. There'd been a time when he'd eaten up praise over his abilities, enjoyed that fact that he'd done what a lot of his college buddies hadn't been able to do. Those days were gone. After Pat had retired from the game and found that he couldn't live without the applause, Jason had taken a long hard look at his life and discovered that he didn't like what he saw, didn't like the persona he'd developed. A ball player had to be confident, but Jason had been edging toward arrogance and self-absorption, to the point that he'd been one step away from being a total asshole.

Jason snorted as he swung the truck into a tight circle on the wide driveway. Ironic that he'd worked so hard to improve himself and Allie had still viewed him as an asshole.

Hopefully those days were gone. Strange, but he honestly cared what Allie thought about him. Maybe because she was one of the few who wasn't bowled over by who he'd once been. She didn't care. If anything, it was a strike against him.

Kate's car was still parked next to his dad's truck when he got home. A positive sign, he hoped. Maybe a day hanging with sales associates and drinking decaf had done his dad some good. Hell, maybe his dad should go to work for Uncle Jim.

He was smiling when he walked through the back door and hung his keys on the hook. The smile faded as Kate, who was reading at the kitchen table, grimly met his eyes.

"What?"

In answer she shoved the printout she'd been reading across the table. *Why Patients Refuse to Comply.*

"I thought if I understood the psychology, I could counter," she explained.

"And…?" Jason sat down opposite her, stretching out his legs. His pants were damp and uncomfortable.

She let her head flop to one side. "It's going to take more than an internet article to delve into the depths of Dad's psyche."

"I don't think so. He's stubborn, controlling and manipulative."

"And those are his good points?" Kate asked with a weary smile.

"Mine, too," Jason said, rubbing his hand over his face. "But I don't know if I can outstubborn and outmanipulate the master."

"Jimmy is taking him on a road trip tomorrow."

"I hope they're not cooking up another scheme."

Kate just shrugged.

"Ms. Brody!"

Allie carefully stepped between two groups of fourth-graders sitting on the reading rug and crouched down next to the girl and boy who were supposed to be team reading, but were instead facing off.

"What's up?" Again. And why did Madeline, the fourth-grade teacher, keep pairing these two who never worked well together?

"Mason took my pencil."

"It's my pencil," Mason asserted, jutting out his chin at Briana.

"Those are my teeth marks in it!" Briana was approaching screeching level.

"Indoor voices," Allie said, but she may as well not have spoken.

"You took my pencil and chewed it up," Mason growled.

The kids behind Allie started getting louder and the words she heard were not words from the stories they were reading together. She heard movement and glanced around to see who'd gotten to their feet. Then the sound of a resounding slap, followed by a yelp of pain, had her head snapping back around.

Mason's eyes were wide and his cheek was red. Allie instantly put herself between them. She couldn't touch them, but she could separate them with her body.

"Briana, go to the hall," she said, since Briana was the child she was facing. The girl looked as if she were taking Allie's measure, so Allie gave her the same look she gave her sisters whenever they defied her. Several seconds ticked by and then Briana jerked her chin in the air and marched out of the library. On her way out, she stumbled on the edge of the rug and the rest of the students started laughing.

"Quiet down," Allie commanded.

These sweet kids could be heartless at times and you had to have six sets of eyes to watch them all...yet, they seemed perfectly behaved when she walked by their class. It was her, not them. They sensed weakness and took advantage. She should have started out tougher.

"Stay here," she said to Mason before crossing the room to call for backup. Two conferences and several written forms later, the incident was documented, parents contacted and discipline doled out.

"Heard you had a tussle in here," Liz said on

an amused note when she came into the library at the end of the day.

"One of many." Allie rubbed the side of her face, wishing she could vent to her friend about her growing doubts as to how unsuited she was for elementary education, but Liz was so dedicated to teaching that Allie really didn't think she'd understand. Besides, Liz had problems of her own. Despite her smile, her features were taut and the smile faded as soon as she sat on one of the small chairs at the reading table.

"I talked to Zach. He'll be at the ranch at seven o'clock tomorrow so that you can go over your expectations and have him fill out his W-2."

"How does he feel about working for me?"

Liz's expression shifted ever so slightly, giving Allie her answer. "He'll do a good job," Liz said tightly.

Allie hoped so. It was enough that Jason agreed to let the kid work with him...or allowed her to strong-arm him into letting the kid work with him. He didn't need to have trouble with Zach on top of that. If he did... Allie hoped it didn't come to that.

After Allie got home, she stopped at the demolition site on her way by, as she usually did. She liked to keep track of the progress and take advantage of having another human being around to talk to. After Jason was gone for the day, the ranch would feel empty, and the ghosts of traumas past would start to appear, reminding her of all she'd gone through. She was getting tired of spending her nights like that and she wanted to talk to an actual person.

"Hey," Allie said as she walked over to where Jason was loading his tools in his truck. "Just so you know, Zach will show up at seven o'clock tomorrow."

Jason pulled off the hard hat and tossed it onto the seat of the truck. "Then I'll set a good example and be here on time."

"It seems to me that you are usually early, except today when I wanted to talk to you before work."

"I wonder why I'm usually early when things are so excellent at home," he said dryly. He cocked his head at her as if a thought just occurred to him. "You want to grab a pizza with me?"

"I, uh…" She narrowed her eyes at him. "Are you asking me out?"

"I'm asking you to have a pizza with me. I don't have a lot of people to hang with and I don't feel like going home."

It all made perfect sense.

"A friendly pizza, Allie. Not a romantic moonlit dinner."

She felt her color start to rise. "I didn't think…"

"No. You reacted. And I'm explaining what my intentions are, so that you can adjust your reaction."

"What do you mean I reacted?"

He made an exaggerated expression of horror, holding his hands up as if to protect himself, and Allie couldn't help but laugh. And that made it almost impossible to say no. She even made an attempt to sound gracious as she said, "You're right. I am hungry. A pizza sounds…nice."

He smiled at her, a smile that told her that he wasn't for one minute fooled.

"Let me drive and I'll bring you back home."

It was on the tip of her tongue to say no, but instead she said, "All right."

"Hope you don't mind that I'm not going home to shower first."

"It's just pizza, remember? Not a date?"

He gave her a look that she couldn't quite interpret.

The pizza place was wonderfully empty and they sat in a booth at the back, Jason with his back to the door.

"I don't usually eat here," he said after they'd ordered.

"Mobbed by fans?"

"On occasion, but it's not happening as often. No, usually I eat at home watching TV with my dad while he gives me advice on life."

"What kind of advice?"

"Go to work for Uncle Jimmy."

She gave a surprised laugh. "The car guy?" Hudson Motors was the go-to dealership in the area, although she'd never personally gone there. Allie bought her vehicles used from friends and acquaintances.

Jason leaned back in the booth, his long legs bumping the underside of the table. "You can't believe what they have planned."

She leaned on one elbow. "Tell me."

"Well, there's going to be a Jaromek—" She frowned at the name and he said, "My former quarterback. A Jaromek look-alike throwing car keys—"

"He's the guy who throws the pizzas at you."

"Exactly."

The waitress showed up with their drinks and smiled at both of them, but her gaze lingered on Jason. Allie put the straw in her drink, then settled her forearms on the table and asked, "Just how hard is it to catch a steaming-hot pizza?"

"Would you believe that ability is the product of CGI?"

"No." She took another sip, but didn't register the taste. It could have been Coke. It could have been root beer. "So what did your uncle and your dad cook up?"

"The beginnings of a lawsuit. They were going

to mimic the commercial, only I'd catch car keys instead of pizzas."

"Like…wearing your uniform and everything?" She had to admit to a certain fondness for football pants.

A small smile played on his lips. "Have you ever seen me in my uniform?"

"I've seen photos," she said with an overly casual shrug. Google Images had given her a lot of photos. Some of them were pretty spectacular.

"But you never watched me play."

"I *think* I've seen you play, but you have to understand that I haven't seen many football games in my life."

"Your sisters were cheerleaders."

"And I was studying."

"And not dating."

"How do you know that?"

"Because I racked my memory about what I did know about you and I can remember now that you didn't date. A couple of my teammates called you Ice Princess."

Again she felt heat rise in her cheeks. "I wasn't cold."

"No, you were probably shy and the average horny teenage boy isn't too good at discerning shyness from aloofness." He reached out and covered her hand with his and Allie felt the urge to turn her hand over and press her palm to his, which was crazy. Totally crazy. She somehow maintained her senses, noting that his fingers were long and elegantly shaped as a way of distracting herself. And strong. She could sense the strength in his hands.

"I'm making my apology now," he said, startling her out of her finger analysis. "I'm sorry for thinking you were cold and distant."

"I probably was." Her mouth quirked wryly. "Still might be."

The waitress approached the table with the pizza and they both leaned back as she placed it on the table in between them. Allie settled her hands safely in her lap, but she still felt the warmth of Jason's touch. He was simply a warm guy—his expressions and his touch. She felt herself being drawn in and had no idea how she was going to handle it. One day at a time, one encounter at a time, she imagined.

"It's huge," Allie said, nodding at the pizza.

"No."

The single word made her laugh again. Jason placed a piece of pizza on her plate and two on his. "We'll factor this by weight," he said. "I figure you're roughly half my size."

He was right. She probably was. And there was something about his size that made her feel safe. How long had it been since she'd felt safe? For the past decade and a half she'd been expecting the worst to happen at every turn and she expected to have to handle it alone. She'd hated to lean on her mother, since her mom had so much on her plate caring for the ranch and her three little sisters. She didn't have a father, and when she'd married, her husband had turned out to be a guy she couldn't depend on.

They ate the pizza slowly, neither seeming to be in any hurry. Allie had a lonely ranch to go back to and Jason had his dad. After they finished the last piece by splitting it, Jason paid the bill and then they walked to his truck.

"Did you enjoy 'just a pizza'?"

"I did." She met his eyes briefly as they walked. "You're more down-to-earth than I gave you credit for."

"I don't think you gave me credit for anything. You formed an opinion of me a long time ago and that's the opinion that you're sticking with," he said as they came to a stop on her side of the truck.

True. Very true.

"Now that you've helped me birth a calf and agreed to help me help a friend, I've revised my opinion." Allie glanced down at her shoes and gathered her strength before looking back up into his eyes. "I apologize for my close-mindedness." And she was starting to feel a little too warm, a little too aware of how close they were standing.

"Accepted." Jason clicked his keys and unlocked the door. "Do you want to go out for real some time?"

Allie felt herself step back at the unexpected question. She hadn't meant to—she'd moved instinctively. "I, uh…"

"That's okay," Jason said easily. "I got my answer."

And heaven help her, even though she liked him, that was the answer she was leaving him with.

Because she was afraid of any other answer.

CHAPTER SEVEN

ANGRY KID.

Jason glanced over at the boy silently jerking nails out of boards with a cat's-paw. He wouldn't have been surprised to see steam rolling off the kid's back. He'd shown up late that morning, driving a tricked-out '81 Chevy, and had totally ignored Jason as he stomped up the front walk to the house. About ten minutes later Allie had come out with him and introduced him as Zach. Jason had smiled and the kid had given a cold nod. And things had just gotten better from there. Allie went to work and Jason decided that if the kid was going to act like a butt, then he could pull nails from old boards while Jason pried lumber loose from the standing frame of the barn—after he forced him to wear the extra hard hat he'd brought.

Zach smirked as he put it on, and after that he barely looked up when Jason set new boards in the pile. So Jason worked faster than usual, giving the kid a good supply of boards to work out his frustrations on. He didn't know anything about the kid except that he'd gotten himself into minor trouble and Allie was friends with his mother.

Frankly, he didn't want to know more.

Finally, about midmorning, Jason stopped for a water break, but Zach kept sullenly pulling nails. One of them flew through the air and landed several yards away. The kid ignored it, so Jason said, "You need to get that in the bucket so it doesn't end up in the tire of one of Allie's vehicles."

Zach met his eyes coldly, then got to his feet and walked over to the nail, picked it up and then walked back to the bucket, where he made a big show of dropping it straight in. It landed with a metallic ping and then the kid went back to work.

"How old did you say you were?" Jason asked.

Another cold look, but this time color crept up from the kid's collar. He looked back down without answering. So it went until lunchtime. Apparently teenage hunger trumped teenage point-making—although Jason really wanted to tell the kid that he was wasting his time trying to make any points to him—because when Jason said it was time for a break, he went to his truck and pulled out a small cooler. Jason wasn't surprised when Zach dropped the tailgate of his own truck and sat on it to eat.

After Zach had devoured two sandwiches and chugged most of a bottle of water, he wiped his mouth with the back of his hand and again met Jason's gaze. "You're that football player."

"I am."

"What are you doing tearing down a barn? Are things that bad?"

"What if they are?"

The kid shrugged and pulled out a third sandwich. "Nothing." He opened the sandwich bag. "My dad was a fan of yours. I think you know him. Derek Belfort."

"Yeah. I remember him. He was older than me. Played cornerback."

Zach nodded and said nothing else. If anything he seemed even colder. *Fine, kid. Play it your way.* The only issue Jason had with the situation was that he'd enjoyed his time ripping apart the barn up until now. It'd been like a puzzle, figuring what to take down next. He'd made mistakes, but since he'd been alone, who cared?

Now he had a sullen kid watching his every move even though he was pretending not to.

The afternoon passed slowly. Allie pulled in a little after four o'clock and the kid immediately dropped the cat's-paw he'd been prying nails with and headed for his rig.

"You're not done."

Glacial eyes turned his way. "What?"

"You're not done. We work until five o'clock."

"My mom told me four."

"Your mom was wrong."

They faced off for a tense moment, then the kid muttered a curse under his breath and went back to where he'd been working.

"Another thing. When you get done, you put the tool away." He almost added, "Didn't anyone teach you that?" but this was about the kid's behavior, not what anyone had or had not taught him.

Zach grunted at him and yanked out a nail. It flew through the air and landed at Jason's feet. Again their gazes connected, then Jason bent and picked up the nail and dropped it into the can.

"Thanks." Jason didn't know if Zach was being snotty or not, so he gave him the benefit of the doubt. It never hurt to assume the best.

One hour later Zach stood and made a show of taking the cat's-paw to Jason's truck and storing it in the box it had come out of that morning. He took off the hat and Jason said, "Take it with you. Bring it back tomorrow or you don't work."

"Fine."

"Thanks," Jason said. "See you tomorrow."

He got a curt nod and then Zach strode over to his truck, got inside and fired it up. Loud truck. Jason stood where he was as the kid swung it in a wide circle and then tore out of the driveway. Tomorrow he and Zach would discuss driveway etiquette, but right now he wanted a few answers from Allie.

He stowed all of his gear, took off the hard

hat and ruffled his hair, enjoying the feel of air over his bare head. Allie came out of the house and headed across the drive to the barn. She saw him heading toward her and stopped, pushing her loose blond hair over her shoulders, but the breeze blew it forward again. She had great hair. The kind a guy thought about spilling over him at she took advantage of the top position.

Not that he was thinking about sex and Allie. Not a lot anyway. Just the normal amount for a guy who hadn't been laid in a while...and who thought his boss was hot.

"Hey," he said as he approached.

"How'd it go?" There was a healthy measure of concern in her voice.

"Like working with an angry badger."

"That good, huh?"

"What's the deal, Allie?"

Allie glanced to the side, obviously debating about how much to say. Jason waited. He wasn't going to push her, but surely she could see that the more he knew, the easier it would be for him to deal with the situation.

"Whatever it is, could I find it out in a local bar?"

Her gaze flashed to his. "Probably," she admitted.

"I'm not looking for gossip. I'm looking for insight. It'd help to know, in general, why he's so angry. Has he always been like this?"

"No. He used to be a sweet kid. When he was twelve anyway." Allie gestured with her head for him to walk with her "Zach's mom is a friend of mine. She thought she had a great marriage until her husband left her. Zach was supposed to go to work on the family ranch with his dad during the summer. He was really looking forward to it, then his dad moved his girlfriend onto the place and decided it'd be too uncomfortable having his son on the ranch with his live-in."

"Okay," Jason said as he automatically opened the barn door before Allie could reach for it. "Now I get the anger. Which makes it easier to deal with."

Allie gave a small sigh as she opened the barn door. "Sometimes I wonder if there is such a thing as a great marriage."

"It's a tricky business," Jason agreed.

She gave him a sidelong look. "Have you been married?"

"Too focused on my career to get that involved with anyone." The sad truth. He'd had a lot of girlfriends, but never found anyone that he'd felt like sharing the rest of his life with.

Allie gave a small snort. "I thought I was building a life with someone, only to find out that I was the only one swinging the hammer. Not to sound bitter…sorry. I probably shouldn't talk about Kyle right now."

"What happened?"

"Nothing. He's out of the hospital, but…" She shrugged. "Nothing."

Nothing, his ass. There was something about the ex that was eating at her or irritating her. Maybe both.

"Do you think you can continue to work with Zach?" she asked.

He smiled down at her. "Do I have a choice?"

"You could walk."

"Then who would oversee the kid?"

"He probably doesn't need overseeing once the beams are laid down," Allie said. "He worked beside his dad on the ranch since he was eleven or twelve."

"So you're saying that I'm the superfluous member of the demolition team?"

Allie's smile touched her eyes and lit her face, and made him want to kiss her…just to see what she tasted like. "Maybe," she admitted.

"I'll have to up my game."

"By the way, Zach's mom is glad that you're making him wear a hard hat."

"I had that drilled into me since I could walk. If you're carrying a tool, you need to have a hard hat and boots." He took the bucket of grain she'd just filled. She didn't relinquish hold of it easily. Jason was about to give up to circumvent a tug-of-war when she let go.

"You know I can do this?" she asked with a

cool who-the-hell-are-you-to-do-things-for-me? lift of her eyebrows.

"I'd be pretty thick if I didn't."

"Then—"

"It's a courtesy, Allie. It's something that I do. If it makes you uncomfortable, I can stop."

"It makes me uncomfortable."

"Why?"

"Because I feel like I owe you."

He gave her an incredulous look. "This isn't tit for tat. No one's keeping score."

"I am. I kept score for years and now it's a habit I'm having a hard time breaking."

"What do you mean you kept score?"

She walked out of the barn and over to the fence, where she motioned for him to dump the grain into the trough. For a few seconds he thought she wasn't going to answer.

"With Kyle. I kept score with Kyle. I didn't start out doing that, but after several years of making excuses, I started to realize there wasn't an excuse. Not one I could live with anyway. I did all of the day-to-day stuff and he started things. If I didn't finish them, they didn't get done." Her mouth flattened for a moment. "You know how I said I wasn't bitter? I lied. I'm totally bitter."

His hands settled on her shoulders before he even realized he'd moved. He felt her muscles go tense, but he didn't take his hands away. "Recognizing it is the first step to letting go." She pulled back ever so slightly and he let his hands drop away. It wasn't what he wanted to do. He wanted to pull her up against him and hold her. Try to soothe the tension out of her stiff body.

"Thank you, Yoda."

"Anytime."

She took the grain bucket from him and started back toward the barn. "I don't talk about Kyle with my sisters anymore. For a long time it was all I could talk about and, even though they're patient, I could see that it was hard for them to keep listening to my bitching."

"You can't let this guy continue to control you."

"He doesn't—" She broke off, then her mouth twisted a little at one corner. "Maybe he does." She gave a small sigh, then looked out over the pasture. "I need to finish chores." She held out the bucket. "Would you refill this while I throw hay to the cows?"

"You bet."

ALLIE SAT ON the porch step and watched as the dust from Jason's truck settled. He was gone for the night and that feeling of lonely isolation once again settled over the ranch. But tonight she was glad he was gone.

Way to pour out your guts, Allie.

There was something about Jason that allowed

her to pour her guts out and she couldn't figure out whether or not that was dangerous.

And if so, what was the danger?

All of her instincts said *keep your issues to yourself* and then she'd gone against instinct.

Probably because there was something steady about Jason, but despite that steadiness, she had a feeling that he was just as leery of strong feelings and commitments as she was. Or maybe it was just that he was fighting demons of his own, so that when the conversation turned to his issues, he became cagier.

Jason with issues. She'd always assumed his life was perfect, but apparently even golden boys had their difficulties... Although, despite her past prejudices, maybe she needed to stop thinking of him as a golden boy. Privilege had rendered him clueless in some regards, but he was also a good guy. Intuitive, empathetic, easy to talk to and he called her on her bullshit. Definitely not the person she'd judged him to be, but that said, she didn't need further complications in her life, such as those that might arise from being attracted to an ex-football player. Not when she wasn't fully recovered from her last failed relationship.

And not when she didn't know what she wanted to do with her life.

The thought was absolutely depressing and

Allie pushed it aside as often as possible...but sometimes she couldn't. Like now.

Allie pulled off the top of a wilted bachelor button and played with the feathery blue flower, twisting it between her fingers as she watched the cows happily toss hay in the air as they looked for the good bits.

She enjoyed the library, but couldn't see working in a school for the rest of her life, and that was a scary thought considering how much time and money she'd put into training. She liked kids, but didn't feel comfortable taking command of them. She felt almost trapped at the school...but she hadn't minded working in the accounting office while she'd been supporting herself and her husband. She'd been glad for the income, glad to be around other people. So what was the deal here? She'd put all of this time into an education degree and she didn't feel any kind of excitement to go to work.

It'll be different when you're full-time and not just subbing.

But what if it wasn't?

Then you'll suck it up and figure something else out.

What else could she do? Start over? Ha.

But she hated the feeling that she was spinning her wheels yet again and that she'd wasted time and money training for a career that didn't satisfy her. Allie tossed aside the flower and pushed herself to her feet. The interior of the house echoed as she walked inside and closed the door behind her. Lonely, lonely house.

She headed toward the kitchen, pausing at the sideboard and studying the painting that hung above it. The painting Jason had commented on after cleaning up his scrape in her bathroom. Even though she'd created it during a dark time in her life, the painting of her garden was bright—brighter than the garden had actually been. The colors popped and seemed to convey a feeling of hope and happiness.

Where had that hope and happiness come from? Allie hugged her arms around herself as she studied the painting, trying to recall how—or even why—she'd produced such a positive statement when her world had been so damned dark. Dark enough that Kyle had seemed like a knight in shining armor.

Kyle, who'd resented the time she spent painting and had laughed when she'd said that maybe she could sell a few pieces and bring in some extra income. "You're good," he'd said, looping an arm around her and pulling her close, "but be realistic. If you want to bring in extra income you need a real job."

He'd been right.

She'd quit painting less than a year after they'd married and focused her energy elsewhere, feeling as if that phase of her life were over. She no longer needed to pour her feelings into her art-work as she dealt with grief—or create lies about what her world was like.

They weren't lies, per se.

All right. Wishes. She was depicting the way she wanted her world to be. Again. The way it had been before she'd lost her dad.

Allie pulled her gaze away from the painting and headed into the kitchen, where she took a container of day-old pasta out of the fridge and set it in the microwave. While it heated, she went back to the painting, then studied its companion, another garden scene, done in the late summer.

How many more paintings were stored in the attic? Probably five or six. Maybe more.

And what if Jolie hung the rest of them when she came back? It was uncomfortable enough having these two on display.

She needed to get rid of the others while she had the chance.

MAX WAS STRETCHED out on the sofa instead of in the recliner when Jason got home. He didn't budge, and neither did Duke or Barney, when Jason went upstairs to his bedroom. And his dad was snoring softly when Jason came back down.

A day with Jimmy had worn him out. A day with Jimmy would wear anyone out.

He'd just settled at the table with a turkey sandwich and club soda when his phone buzzed.

Coach's number came up and Jason's pulse jumped. Good news would be a nice change of pace.

"You aren't in the running for either coaching job," Coach said immediately after his hello.

The coach never had been one to sugarcoat. Jason let his head drop back in defeat before he said, "Thanks for letting me know." The form email would no doubt follow.

"There's an opening in the athletic department," Coach blurted out in his gruff way. "An assistant to the assistant athletic director."

"Assistant to the assistant?"

"You're not qualified for this job, either, but it would be a toe in the door and I put in a good word for you. Actually...I talked to them for half an hour, pulled in a favor, and I think I got you an interview."

It had come to this? His former mentor having to pull in favors? It was strange to go from being on top of the world a few months ago, a starter in a playoff game, to this—unqualified for anything.

Humbling, to say the least.

"Lots of people want to coach for Brandt, Jason. You're an unknown entity off the field."

"I know. And I appreciate what you did. Are doing. Thank you."

"You have to go to the website and apply. Do it tonight, because the posting closes tomorrow."

"I appreciate this, Coach." He had a rock in his gut, but he did appreciate it.

"Yeah, yeah. Just don't screw it up."

"I won't. Thanks."

"No problem. I'll be in touch."

Jason ended the call, then jerked guiltily as his father said, "Who was that?"

He put the phone down and turned to see his dad and the Dobes standing in the kitchen doorway. He hadn't realized that Max had gotten up from his nap—in fact, he'd considered himself lucky that the call had come while he was alone.

"Coach Whitmore. From Brandt."

Max's expression clouded. "Brandt?"

Jason nodded then went to the fridge, where he reached for a beer, then, remembering Kate's comment about Pop turning them into alcoholics, grabbed another club soda instead. He twisted off the cap before turning back to his father.

"Yes. I wanted to apply for a coaching job there."

"Wanted? Past tense."

"They don't have anything that they would consider me for right now, but there's an opening in the athletic department itself. Kind of an assistant to the assistant athletic director."

Max grimaced. "Sounds like a secretarial job."

"It might be, but it's hell getting a toehold at Brandt and that's the place where I want to work."

"It's seven hundred miles away."

"It's no different than when I went to college there."

"It's different."

"How?"

"I wasn't on death's door then."

Jason cocked an eyebrow. It was serious when his dad went for sympathy points on top of guilt points. "I can always find a place for you down there."

An expression of horror crossed his father's face. He'd left California because he'd had enough of the state, with its high taxes and overcrowded cities, and on top of that, he truly loved the Eagle Valley. So, of course, he wanted his kids there. Where he could help them manage their lives.

"You'd do that to me? I really would conk out."

"If I got the job, and that's still a big if—" which had been made very clear to him in the phone call "—I could come home fairly often." That was what airplanes were for, after all—to visit family…and to escape from them when necessary.

"Why Brandt?"

"Top-notch football program. Progressive coaching. A way to stay in football. The place did me a lot of good, and I think I can return the favor." Jason ticked the reasons off on one hand.

Max held up his hand and did some ticking

of his own. "You don't have to work. You have family that wants you close. You could coach locally. Jimmy will be crushed."

He would have been better off if he hadn't mentioned Jimmy, and Max seemed to realize that. His eyes narrowed and he asked, "What about Pat?"

"What about him?"

"Wasn't Brandt the school that did him in?"

"Pat did himself in." Jason rubbed the back of his tight neck with his free hand. "Look, Dad. We'll work something out so that I see a lot of you, but I plan to have a career in athletics. It's what I always planned, and if I'm able to start at a primo school like Brandt—even if I have to work my way onto the coaching field—I'd consider myself blessed."

"Good for you," Max said sourly. He abruptly turned and stalked into the living room. Jason closed his eyes as he heard the distinctive sound of dead weight falling into the recliner and then the squeak of the footrest rising. A second later the television started blaring and Jason took a long drink of club soda. Not the same as beer, but Kate was right. If he drank every time he had a flare-up with his dad, his liver would be shot within a year.

WHEN ALLIE GOT up the next morning, one of the cows was down, looking like she was ready to calve, but as soon as she saw Allie, she got back to her feet and ambled off toward the rest of the herd. Because of the cow, she was reluctant to head to work early as she'd planned and instead waited until Jason showed up.

"Would you keep an eye on that cow there? Number fifty-three?" The cows were identified by numbered tags in their ears. Even though Allie knew this particular cow as Lou, many of the cows were known simply by their numbers.

Jason squinted at the herd as Allie pointed. "The black one. Yeah." Which made Allie smile because all of the cows were black. He sent her a cautious look. "This is one of the easy calvers, right?"

"She should just pop it out, but if there are any problems, call the vet." She handed him a card. "Or call me first and then call the vet."

"Will do."

She pushed her hair back as she studied the herd. She really hated to leave. So many things could happen even with an easy calver.

"It'll be fine," Jason said beside her.

There was something about his tone that was ridiculously reassuring. The guy had almost puked while helping her pull a calf, yet she felt like believing him when he said everything was going to be okay.

"I'll call if things start happening." He pulled out his phone and handed it to her. "Put your number in, would you? Then I won't have to worry about finding the card."

Allie took the phone and put in both her number and the vet's number. "The vet is under Vet."

"Clever," Jason said as he took the phone back. Their fingers touched and she was struck by how nice it felt to simply touch and be touched. When he'd settled his hands on her shoulders the night before, it had been the same. She liked being near another person...another person who wasn't Kyle.

"I'm going to be late," she said.

'Yes," he said with that gentle smile.

Her face felt warm, as if she were blushing. Was she blushing?

She hoped not. Being fair-skinned, it was always a possibility.

She forced a smile and headed for her car, trying to focus on her workday instead of the guy she'd left standing near the pasture. She was going to do her best to find some positives in the day. Education was a good occupation. She'd trained for it, and paid a bundle for that training, and damn it, she was going to use her degree.

ZACH SHOWED UP almost forty minutes after seven. He slapped his hard hat on his head as he swaggered toward what remained of the barn.

"Do you want to pry boards off today?" Jason asked, deciding to pick his battles. If the kid was late tomorrow, he'd address the issue. Right now he wanted the kid to work and not argue.

"Whatever," Zach replied.

"Pull nails."

The kid shot him a dark look, but headed to the stack of boards that Jason had already piled. They worked in silence, just as they had the day before. Jason spoke to the kid every now and again, testing the waters, expecting nothing in return. Yes, the boy was angry. He was also seventeen and needed to find a different way to deal with anger than punishing the world around him.

During lunch, Zach ate sitting on his tailgate while Jason ate sitting on his. He was determined not to let the kid's attitude get to him, but truth to tell, his patience was wearing thin. After lunch, he tried one more time to make some kind of peace.

"Why don't you tackle that frame over there," he said, nodding at a section of the wall that was lying flat on the ground.

Zach practically sneered at him as he got off the tailgate and slammed it shut.

"And while you're at it, pull your head out of your ass."

Zach stopped in his tracks, his color rising as he turned to face Jason. "What did you say?"

"I said you need to pull your head out of your ass." Jason gave the kid a dead-eyed look. Zach knew exactly what he was talking about—he'd have to be pretty dense not to—so he didn't feel the need to explain. After a nice long stare-down, Zach shouldered past him, grabbed the cat's-paw up from where he'd been pulling nails and headed off to the section of wall that needed to be dismantled.

Jason watched him go, glad that the kid hadn't decided to chuck the cat's-paw at his head or something. The way the kid started ripping and prying boards, he figured that the thought had probably crossed his mind.

Jason went to work on his section of the building, far enough away from Zach that he was out of harm's way should something go flying. Finally, after thirty silent minutes, he set down his hammer and walked around the barn to where Zach was working.

"Look," he said. "I might have been abrupt a while ago, but your attitude would get you fired from a normal job."

"I have my reasons."

"You're also almost an adult and you can't take them out on the world. There are other ways to deal."

"Oh, yeah? How do you suggest I deal?"

"No easy answer there. But what you can't do is be rude and combative to other people. That solves nothing."

"It makes me feel better."

"Does it?"

Zach started to answer, then abruptly closed his mouth. He turned back to the frame and jammed the crowbar into a crack and started reefing. Jason also went back to work. He didn't know if he'd made things better or worse, but he firmly believed in what he said—rudeness didn't solve problems. It just made other people miserable, too.

"You know," he finally ventured, "we're going to be together for a few weeks, so maybe we could talk. Like people do when they work together."

"What do you want to talk about?"

"General stuff. I don't know. The weather, women...whatever."

"The three Ws," Zach said with a smirk.

Jason shot him a quick look, but the kid wasn't smiling. He also wasn't flinging nails quite as far. Breakthrough?

Probably not quite.

"Why don't you tell me about women?" Zach said a few seconds later, his tone polite, yet with a hint of sarcasm.

Jason gave him a look that the kid met blandly. Too blandly.

Fine. He'd tell him about women. "Treat them with respect," he said.

"That's it?"

"Treat everyone with respect. Life will be better."

Zach shook his head and went back to work. Jason did the same while the air between them vibrated with sullen resentment.

ALLIE HAD WAITED all day for Jason's call but it never came, and when she got home, Lou was still as big as a house, standing next to the windbreak, idly switching her tail. But one of the other cows had a brand-new baby frolicking around it.

"Sorry about no call," Jason said, pointing at the calf. "The thing was born before either of us noticed the cow was on the ground."

"That's the way I wish all the calves would come." Allie studied the demolition sight because it was easier than looking at Jason and feeling her breath go all wonky. "So how'd it go with Zach today? It looks like you made some headway on the heap."

"Better."

"You got him talking?"

"Not really. I told him to pull his head out of his ass and he complied as best he could."

Allie's jaw dropped. "Was that the best strategy?" She didn't want Zach to quit and thus cause Liz more anxiety.

"It worked."

"Seems harsh to me."

"There's harsh and then there's harsh. I told the kid that he wasn't going to solve his problems by being rude and combative. I don't think that's too harsh."

"But pulling his head out of his ass?"

Jason gave a small snort. "That was to get his attention."

"Did it work?" Allie asked.

"The situation had to be addressed. Zach was setting it up so that I had to address it."

"You think so?"

"Yeah. I do. So I gave him attention that he could handle. I honestly think had I gone all touchy-feely on him and offered to listen while he poured his guts out, he would have really crawled inside of himself."

"I can see why your dad wants you to sell cars."

His expression went flat. "Meaning?"

"You seem to understand human nature."

"I'm used to reading opponents."

"It seems like a little more than that."

One corner of his mouth lifted. "Careful, Allie...you're edging close to a compliment."

She smirked at him.

"Guess I'll see you tomorrow," he said in that low voice she was starting to really love to listen to.

"Guess so," she said. Damn it, she didn't want him to leave.

"Are you okay?"

She narrowed her gaze at him, as if it were his fault that she found him attractive. "I'm think I'm as good as I'm going to get for now."

"Want to talk?"

She shook her head. "I don't need anyone telling me to pull my head out."

Jason laughed and Allie fought her answering smile. She lost.

"I'll see you tomorrow, Jason." She turned and started toward the house, wondering if she looked back suddenly if she would catch Jason Hudson watching her leave.

Was it wrong that a small part of her hoped that he was?

CHAPTER EIGHT

ZACH SHOWED UP at exactly seven o'clock the next morning and he seemed to think he deserved a medal or something. Jason merely directed him back to the wall he'd been dismantling and started pulling nails out of the used board. He actually liked pulling nails. There was something satisfying about the feel of the metal pulling free of the wood.

Simple pleasures…like running a pattern, dodging his coverage, looking over his shoulder and seeing the ball coming in right on target. Yeah. A simple pleasure that he'd been paid lots of money to partake in, which in turn prepared him for absolutely nothing once his career had ended.

He was lucky, though, that he'd taken care with his money instead of blowing it all. Financially, he was going to be fine, as long as he didn't do anything extravagant—like try to live without an income. He needed a job and he needed a reason to get out of bed in the morning. A plan.

Zach didn't glower at him today, but he wasn't exactly a ray of sunshine, either. As long as he wasn't blatantly rude, Jason planned to ignore him. It worked out well. Zach ignored him, he ignored Zach. Finally the kid couldn't take it anymore.

"So you're all rich and shit, right?"

"I planned for my future, if that's what you're asking," Jason said.

"So why are you doing this?" Zach stood upright, holding the crowbar loosely in one hand.

"I like it."

Zach stared at him. "How can you like this?"

Jason shrugged. "I like being outdoors." More than he ever thought he would when he wasn't practicing or playing. He wedged his crowbar in between two boards and pried. "What's not to like?"

"Pay's crap, it's temporary and like you said, it's outdoors."

"I would have thought you'd like the outdoors," Jason said.

"Why?"

"You're a ranch kid."

Zach's gaze narrowed dangerously. "*Was* a ranch kid."

"So you never liked the outdoors?"

"Let's just say that I've come to realize that I won't be working on a ranch."

"There are other ranches."

"You know my situation, don't you?" Zach spoke flatly, in a voice that indicated that he didn't want sympathy. That he would find it embarrassing.

"I know that you were supposed to work on your family ranch and it fell through."

Zach snorted. "That's an interesting way to put it. Fell through. Yeah."

Jason didn't reply. There was nothing to say and talking would only make Zach feel more self-conscious.

"My dad hooked up with this woman and he doesn't want me on the ranch." His expression was openly challenging, although Jason didn't know what he was being challenged to do. Or not do. "My dad sucks."

"My dad wants me to sell cars for my uncle."

"How the hell is that the same?" Zach demanded.

"It's not, and you know what? You can drop the *hells* and *shits* around me."

"Do they offend you?" The kid sneered as he spoke.

"Yeah. They do." He didn't have the cleanest mouth in the world, but he was conscious of what he said and when.

"Bullshi—" Zach's voice trailed as Jason gave him a hard look. "Fine. I'll watch my language. I'd hate to burn your ears."

"Thank you." Jason went back to the woodpile.

"Is this for real?" Zach asked from behind him.

"When we know each other better, we can hang out and drop the f-bomb and have all kinds of fun. But one thing you need to know—people judge you by your language. If you're not with friends, watch what you say."

Zach's forehead wrinkled and Jason thought the kid was on the edge of telling him to go to hell. Just because. He didn't. Instead he gave his head a shake, as if trying to make sense of a world gone mad, and went back to stripping boards off the frame.

Once again they ate on their respective tailgates and Jason wondered if he'd made a mistake by telling the kid to watch his mouth, because now he was totally silent. He didn't know if he was being taught a lesson, or if Zach didn't trust himself not to curse. Jason assumed it was the former, so once again he ignored the boy.

His phone rang in his pocket and he was tempted to ignore it, but couldn't because it might be Kate calling about their father. He pulled out the phone and was glad he hadn't given in to the temptation to reach into his pocket and silence it. A San Diego area code showed on the screen.

His heart gave a hard thump as he answered.

"Mr. Hudson? This is Amanda Morehouse from Brandt University athletics department. How are you today?"

"Doing well," Jason said. Except for a sudden and unexpected clenching of his gut.

"Excellent. I see where you applied for the position of assistant to the associate director of athletics and I would like to set up a time for a preliminary interview if you're interested in pursuing the position."

"I'm interested."

"Excellent. We can schedule you for Wednesday at eight or Thursday at nine."

"Wednesday."

"Excellent. You'll need a phone and a laptop…" She continued with the instructions while Zach, who'd been watching him closely, balled up the paper bag his sandwiches had come in and eased himself off the tailgate. Three "excellents" later, Amanda finished, wished him good luck and Jason hung up.

"Hot date?" Zach asked.

"Job interview."

"Huh." Zach reached for his hard hat and plopped it onto his head. "If I was rich, I wouldn't work."

"Guess we're different, then." Because Jason would be bored out of his skull.

JASON AND ZACH had been getting ready to leave when Allie drove onto the ranch, late due to grocery shopping. After she'd unloaded her car and put away her purchases, she set a frozen dinner in the microwave and then paced the kitchen a few times. She felt antsy, unsettled. In need of something that didn't have a name.

Jason?

Okay, maybe part of what she needed did have a name. But this edgy, unsettled feeling had to do with something more than Jason's overall hotness and her reaction to it. It was tied in with her job and her future and her general frustration about having no clear direction. And there were other things she needed to face.

The microwave dinged, but Allie ignored it. She wasn't hungry.

Do it. Now.

Squaring her shoulders for battle, Allie headed upstairs to the attic entrance at the end of the hall. Once there, she folded the rug back so that the door could swing out. A wave of cold musty air hit her as she opened the door, and she wrinkled her nose as she reached up to pull the light cord.

She hadn't been up these dusty stairs since Kyle left. She hadn't wanted to go up them. Hadn't wanted to disturb the memories she'd stored away. Her sisters had had no such qualms. They'd raided the attic, brought down her garden paintings and hung them, thus shocking the hell out of her when she'd come home on a school break.

The rest of her paintings were leaning against

the far wall of the attic, each covered with an old bath towel or cloth in a weak attempt to protect them from the dust. It had worked...kind of.

Allie didn't look at the paintings as she stacked them, covers still in place. There were eight in all. Her "major" works. She took them downstairs, leaving the attic door open behind her, and then slowly uncovered each painting and laid it out on the living room floor.

She remembered them, yet she didn't. There were landscapes, garden scenes and two still lifes of different arrangements of Jolie's rodeo gear. They were all colorful, all done with loose brushstrokes that her art teacher had once told her he envied. He'd liked her work a lot, had encouraged her to go to art school, but now that she'd had a good half decade away from painting, she could see things she would change.

A knock on the door made her jump. Jason. She got to her feet, crossed the room and opened the door. He shifted his weight, just as he had that night he'd first shown up. If anyone had told her then, after she'd sent him packing when he'd asked to buy her ranch, that not only would he be on the ranch on a daily basis, but that her body would also go on high alert every time she was close to him, she would have laughed. But right now she didn't feel like laughing. She felt self-conscious about her life laid out on the floor behind her.

"You're still here?"

His mouth tilted. "It appears I am. What's up, Allie?"

And just like that the focus shifted from the reason why he was standing at her door to what was eating at her. She was going to have to work on her game face.

She gave a slight shrug. "Just facing my past."

"Sounds heavy."

She forced a smile. "It's not really." She gestured at the canvases on the floor behind her. "I hauled paintings down from the attic." She hesitated ever so briefly before saying, "I need to do something with them."

It was the honest truth. The need to see the paintings in decent light, to gauge her personal reaction to them, had been weighing on her for the past several days. It was as if her artwork were yet another chapter in her life that needed to be closed.

"You said this was a phase."

Allie made a noncommittal noise as Jason edged by her to get a better look at her work. After a few seconds, he glanced up at her, his gaze clear and questioning. "Why did you stop painting?"

"I had other things filling my time."

"These are good."

"Know a lot about art?"

The comment came out sounding snottier than

she'd intended, but before she could take it back he surprised her by saying, "Yeah. I do. I dated a gallery owner for a while. Learned some stuff. Took a few classes." He shrugged.

Her lips parted a little as she held his gaze. "Okay." She swallowed, then allowed herself a frown. "Why *are* you still here?"

"I'll be late on Wednesday. I have a Skype interview at eight o'clock."

Skype meant not local. It was on the tip of her tongue to ask what job he was interviewing for, and where it was located, but it really wasn't any of her business. Right? And she shouldn't have this hollow feeling growing inside of her at the thought of him leaving. Of course he was eventually going to leave. "Good luck."

"Thanks. It's with my alma mater. Assistant to an associate athletic director."

"Oh."

"What?"

"Assistant. I, uh—" she shrugged before plowing ahead with the truth "—thought that you'd be applying for a major-league coaching job of some kind. College, the pros…"

"You have to work your way into those. It takes time."

"I see." But she didn't. She'd assumed that Jason, with his career and connections, would slide into some top-level job after his dad convalesced. *Assistant* to an associate?

"There are a lot of guys leaving the pros every year. It's not as easy as you would think to remain in the sport."

"That makes sense."

"I'll get here as soon as I can and I'll tell Zach he doesn't need to show up until after nine. He shouldn't tackle things alone."

"True. And you know, you could interview here if you wanted. The house will be empty and you could have privacy. Not that you wouldn't have privacy at your home."

"I wouldn't," Jason said flatly. "Not unless I pay my sister to entertain my father."

Allie smiled a little. She'd met Jason's dad a time or two and he did seem like a strong character. "I don't lock the door when I leave, so if you want to use this place, do."

"You don't lock up?"

She raised her eyebrows. "You're here and I assume you'd notice if anyone was robbing me. And there's always the off chance you'll need to clean a wound or something."

"Or something." He hooked his thumb in his belt loop, fighting a smile. "I might take you up on the offer."

"Feel free," she said again.

"Thanks. Well, I'd better be going." He nodded at the paintings. "I like your work, Allie."

"Thank you." Once he'd gone, she turned her back to the door and leaned against it, trying to see her paintings through his eyes—the eyes of an uninvolved bystander. He was the first person other than her sisters and Kyle to see her work. And he liked it.

Allie didn't want to feel validated by his assessment, but she did. When she'd started painting, it'd been for her and her alone. A way to push reality aside as she disappeared into her own realm. And then, when Kyle had pointed out that the time she spent painting could be better spent on other things, she'd had to agree. Stuff needed to be done. Money needed to be earned. Even when she'd painted in short sessions, Kyle had tried to pull her away. At the time she'd felt gratified that her husband had wanted to spend so much time with her. Looking back, it seemed more likely that he'd simply been jealous of anything that didn't involve him.

Allie stacked the canvases and headed back up the stairs. When she'd brought them downstairs she'd hoped she'd be able to throw them away. Cart them out to the trash and be done with them.

Didn't happen. For whatever reason, she wasn't yet ready to let go.

Nudging open the partially open attic door with the toe of her shoe, Allie headed up the narrow attic stairs and then deposited the artwork against the far wall. Maybe all she needed was a little more time—or to forget the canvases were there and move on with her life.

JASON CLOSED HIS laptop and rubbed a hand over the top of his head. It was nine o'clock in the morning and he felt wiped out. *So this was an interview.*

Nothing in Jason's career or schooling had prepared him to field forty-five minutes of questions from a panel of four—none of whom seemed that thrilled with him or his accomplishments.

Over the years he'd done the occasional sports show interview and had met with various company representatives to discuss possible endorsements, but those people had wanted something from him. They weren't trying to weed him out of the pack so that they had fewer candidates to choose from. And, according to the rather dour lady in charge of compliance, they had a large field of qualified applicants. By the end of the interview, Jason was very much aware that he'd been interviewed as a courtesy, because he was an alumni. Because Coach had called in a favor.

Not a good feeling.

In fact, it was depressing.

Jason packed up his laptop and headed for his truck. He'd appreciated Allie's offer to interview in the privacy of her home, but ultimately had asked Kate if he could use her place while she played gin with Max. Now he was glad he'd done that so that he had some time to come to grips with his new reality—the reality in which he wasn't all that important to the world at large—

before going to work with Zach, who was a rather observant kid and not shy about sharing his observations.

Damn it, he'd thought he'd had a pretty good handle on things—the reality of what was possible and what wasn't—but now he had a small taste of how Pat must have felt after rejection after rejection. A very small taste. Pat was a performer who thrived on being the center of attention. Jason didn't need that, but he was fairly used to being valued for his abilities. Now that the interview was over, he was wondering if he possessed any marketable skills at all. The Brandt panel had not been encouraging.

He stowed the laptop and started the truck, waiting for a car to pass before backing out onto the street. So what now?

More résumés. More interviews. There was something out there for him.

He didn't want to work just anywhere. He wanted the job at Brandt.

WELL, IT HAD certainly been a day.

Allie headed up the walk to her front door feeling totally wrung out. After story hour had gotten out of hand, Allie scheduled a sit-down with the principal, who assured her that, oh, it was always difficult to control twenty-five kindergarteners when their teacher wasn't present. Allie wasn't lacking—she simply needed practice in classroom management. And she was getting better!

"It's a knack," Mrs. Wilson-Jones had reiterated.

A knack that Allie didn't come by naturally. Nor one that she necessarily wanted to develop... and it was killing her. Then to add more joy to her day, she'd thought she'd seen Kyle's truck parked on the street near the school as she and Liz and Margaret, the kindergarten teacher, had walked to their cars. The truck pulled into the street as they reached Allie's car, leaving her to wonder if there were two light-blue F-350s with cab lights in town, or if Kyle had not wanted to approach her while she was with friends. Whatever the case, Allie found herself checking her rearview mirror every few blocks until she left town and, by the time she got home, she was irritated and tired and drove past the barn site without stopping to check on Jason and Zach's progress, although she did note that the two of them looked a lot more satisfied with life than she felt at that moment.

What did Kyle want? She'd been clear about having no money and not cosigning a loan, so what? Maybe he thought he could wear her down.

That was probably it. Kyle could be tenacious, as long it didn't involve following through on ranch repairs and improvements.

Feeling restless, Allie changed her clothes and

left the house, following the path to her sad little garden spot. Oh, the hope she'd poured into this patch of ground. She'd had some good harvests when she and Kyle were first married, but as her day job and ranch chores ate into her time, her garden had suffered. Her marriage had suffered.

As did she.

But that part of her life was over and her garden spot was still here, overgrown with weeds. Stepping over the low fence, she bent down and pulled a handful of dry grass and weeds and tossed it over the fence. Another handful followed and then another. By the time Jason showed up, she had a good quarter of the space cleared and she was so focused on what she was doing that she didn't hear him until he was almost at the fence.

"Oh. Hi." She pushed the hood back from her head. "How'd the interview go?"

Jason shrugged, his expression unreadable. "Time will tell."

"I see." And she did. The interview hadn't gone as he'd expected. He might be putting on his inscrutable man-face, but Allie could sense his tension.

"Gardening?"

"For the first time in about five years. I have some work ahead of me."

"Want some help?"

She almost said no. She always said no. It was a habit she wanted to break. "Sure."

Jason stepped over the fence much more easily than she had, bent down and started pulling weeds out of the damp ground. "Couldn't you till the weeds in?"

"We could, but I'm working out a few frustrations."

"Huh. I may put in a garden."

"Your dad?" *Or the interview?*

He hesitated just long enough before saying "Yes," to make Allie certain that the interview hadn't been a slam dunk...or maybe he just didn't know if he wanted the job. Yes. That seemed more likely.

"You?"

My ex-husband is driving me crazy.

"I'm seriously wondering about what I want to be when I grow up."

From the look he gave her, she knew that he was reading her as easily as she was reading him. And what did that say about them? That they were closely tuned into one another?

She was certainly tuned into him. How could she not be when he was so close that she was aware of every move he made?

"The teaching thing isn't working out?"

"I have serious doubts about teaching little kids and the only jobs listed are for elementary." She tugged on the thick stalk of a volunteer sunflower, slowly easing the roots out of the soil. "I also have a secondary credential, but it's in art. It's where I did my student teaching and I loved teaching art, but it's practically impossible to get a high school art job with budget cuts. I need another secondary endorsement. Social studies. Math. English. Something of 'value.'"

"Do you like little kids?"

Allie pushed the hair from her cheek with the back of her wrist. "That's the problem. I do...so much so that I let them get away with murder." She reached down and yanked a weed. "They're cute, you know. The lower grade teachers use library time to prepare for their classes, and when they leave the library...well, the word *mayhem* comes to mind."

Jason gave a soft snort, but Allie couldn't tell if he was laughing or commiserating. He stood up and tossed two handfuls of weeds onto the pile on the other side of the fence. "Can you make a living here on the ranch?"

"I don't see that happening." She spoke too quickly, sounded too defensive, so she made an effort to scale back her adamant response. "My sisters will be coming back."

"Only one will live on the ranch, right?"

"Yes. Dani and Gabe will live in the Staley house."

There was a long stretch of silence and then

Jason said, "It's not just your sister coming back to live here, is it?"

"No." And that was as far as she was willing to go with that line of questioning.

"Personally, I think it's a mistake to do something you don't feel any passion for."

"Easy enough to say when you haven't worked in the real world before." Allie looked up at Jason. "I'm sorry to sound harsh, but it's true."

The expression that chased across his face made her wish she hadn't said anything. It appeared that Jason *was* getting a taste of the real world—the world where actual professional credentials counted.

"Maybe so." He yanked up a handful of weeds. "But I stand by what I say."

"I have a passion," she said lowly, pushing back the prickles of guilt as she went back to work. "A passion for survival, a secure future and money in the bank. I have never found that ranching could give me that."

"Yet you wouldn't even consider selling me the ranch."

Allie nearly tumbled over backward pulling a particularly stubborn plant, and Jason put his hand on the small of her back, steadying her until she regained her balance. She felt the warmth of his palm through her shirt. "It isn't mine to sell."

"What if it were?"

She stopped pulling weeds, but stayed crouched

where she was for a moment. What if? "Yes, you could have it."

"Even though it's been in your family since it was homesteaded?"

"I have no tender feelings for this place." She tossed another handful of weeds over the fence, then wiped her muddy hands on her pants. "So, what about you?"

"What about me?"

"What's eating at you?"

"I told you."

"I don't think so." Bold move, but it would get him onto a different track.

His expression cooled and Allie realized that she'd just hit a brick wall. There would be no secrets shared tonight.

Fine with her. It made going into her house alone that much easier.

She stepped over the fence and had just made it to the other side when Jason took hold of her upper arm, keeping her from moving any farther. "I'm sorry."

"For what?"

"For telling you what to do with your future, when I'm still figuring out mine."

Excellent point, but she barely registered the logic as heat flared inside of her. There was something about the way he was looking at her—or rather her mouth—that made alarm bells go off in her head. But she did not step back and less than a second later, his mouth was on hers and his hands were in her hair, holding her face as he kissed her. Stunned her. Made her knees go wobbly. When he raised his head, Allie had assumed some witty remark would spring to her lips.

Nothing.

All she could think was that she really wanted him to apologize again. She pushed her hands up over his very hard chest, the picket fence separating them pressing into her thighs.

"Do you want to talk about that future?" she asked.

He shook his head. "Not yet."

"Why?"

"Because it involves someone else."

Allie's heart hit her ribs. "Do you have a girlfriend, Jason?"

"No."

"I shouldn't feel so relieved by that," she muttered as she dropped her hands and stepped back.

"Why not?"

She gave a small scoffing laugh. "Because I'm working extremely hard to be self-sufficient and someone like you could throw a monkey wrench into that." And judging by the deep urge she had to step over the fence and kiss him again, that was a true danger.

"Someone like me?"

She simply gave a shrug. How was she sup-

posed to explain things when she was still figuring them out?

"Have you dated since your divorce?"

"No."

"Maybe you should."

She lifted her chin, her eyes narrowing slightly
as she did her best to hide the fact that her stomach had just somersaulted. "I'll take that under
advisement."

"Let me know when you do."

She worked up a smirk. "You'll be the first."

CHAPTER NINE

YOU'LL BE THE FIRST.

Allie's reply had been dry, loaded with snark, but he'd seen the uncertain look on her face after they'd kissed. The whoa-something-else-to-screw-up-my-life look.

He wasn't going to screw up her life. They'd only kissed and it'd been a long time coming.

He wanted to kiss her again.

His mouth quirked wryly as he covered the distance to his truck, which was parked near the demolition site. She might have thought he was yet another complication in her life, but she'd also responded to the kiss...and given him something to think about besides his next move.

What was he going to do?

Pursue other colleges. Maybe go back and get his master's—although he'd probably forgotten more than he remembered about his bachelor's degree in physical therapy. And he didn't even want to work in that field.

He and Allie had more in common than she

knew. Neither of them knew what their next step would be if the current one didn't work out.

Jason got into the truck and turned the key. He wasn't going to stagnate. New horizons. If Brandt didn't pan out he'd apply elsewhere, volunteer, whatever it took to get the experience he was so clearly lacking.

ALLIE PACED THROUGH the house. The problem with living alone was that it gave a person too much time to think—about good things, bad things.

Hot things.

She'd kissed Jason Hudson yesterday—or he'd kissed her. One of the two. It felt pretty damned mutual, actually. She touched her fingers to lips. The guy could kiss—and that had been just a small kiss. What would it be like if he put his heart into it?

Allie felt like fanning herself, and that was a bad sign. Could she really afford to let things like this happen when she was still trying to get her life back on track?

Hell. No.

She pushed her hands through her hair as she stopped at her desk and regarded the pile of bills there. Her student loan was due tomorrow and she'd just received the news today at work that because of a computer error—which she suspected was actually human error—her information hadn't been loaded into the system in time for her to receive a check this pay period. The accounting department was very sorry for the inconvenience.

Allie took a couple more paces around the room. Inconvenience.

Now she'd have to rob the ranch fund to survive, which always made her feel anxious. She and Kyle had tapped the ranch fund so many times in the name of survival that there'd been nothing left for a major emergency. She'd paid back as much as she could afford to after divorcing Kyle, but it'd be a long time until she'd be able to pay back what she truly owed and now she had to use the fund again, when it was already taking a hit from barn demolition.

Her head was throbbing by the time she went to bed. There was no way around using the fund, but she truly hated being in financial straits. Again.

JASON WAS PRETTY sure that Allie was avoiding him. She didn't check the progress on the barn for two days and he'd found his weekly paycheck on the seat of his truck, where Allie had left it when she'd briefly stopped on her way to work that morning. Before she was due to write him another check a week from today, the barn would be gone and he'd have nowhere to spend his days.

Of course, he'd also no longer have to put up with a sullen teen.

So what was he going to do after the last bit of scrap had been loaded on the truck he'd borrowed from his father's construction business?

Brandt hadn't called and while he told himself that no news was good news, a small voice in his head countered with the fact that no news meant they were not done interviewing candidates.

All he wanted to do was to make the first cut—and then get the job. That was it. First cut. Second cut. Job.

Future. Nailed down.

He was looking forward to that, especially after the past few challenging evenings with his dad, who'd come to the conclusion that the doctors were being overly cautious. Translation—he was starting to feel well enough to be bulletproof again, as he'd been before the heart attack, when his doctor had told him his lifestyle had to change, or else.

The "or else" had happened.

"Hey, Jason."

Zach rarely called him by name, so this had to be a moment of import.

"Yeah?"

"A cow's gone down. I'm going to check her." Zach was always watching the herd, and Jason had found himself doing the same, but he hadn't noticed the cow that had wandered off on her own.

"I'll come, too." It'd been a while since he'd been grossed out by a birth and if things went south, Zach might need help—help that he was fairly certain the kid wouldn't ask for.

Zach gave him a quick frown, then shrugged. "Sure." His surliness quotient had dropped maybe half a point over the past day or two, and Jason considered that to be significant progress. By the time the barn was demolished, they might even have a conversation that consisted of more than three or four words each.

"Do we need to have anything at the ready?" Jason asked.

"I don't think so." In his preoccupation with the cow, Zach had forgotten to snap out his reply and Jason felt a twinge of satisfaction. Yes. Progress.

The cow went on alert and struggled to her feet as the gate banged shut, but Zach ignored her as he walked purposefully to the small holding pen behind the barn. Jason closed the gate and followed.

"We won't bother her as much here."

Sure enough, a few minutes later, she went back down to her knees, then flopped over onto her side.

"And now we wait."

Jason leaned his forearms on the pleasantly

warm metal rails and settled his chin on his hands, keeping his gaze trained on the black cow, who was not number 53, the cow that Allie had expected to birth next. Number 53 ambled past them to the water tank, still hugely pregnant.

"Here we go," Zach said softly as the cow started straining.

Once it started, the birth progressed rapidly. In less than ten minutes, the new calf was on the ground and the mother was enthusiastically licking her new baby.

Jason shot Zach a sidelong look and caught the satisfied expression on the kid's face before it once again went stony. Then he turned to meet Jason's gaze.

"You really don't like this life?" Jason asked.

"It's not an easy life," Zach said in a way that made Jason think that he was echoing words he'd heard.

"Where is it written that easy is good?"

Zach frowned at him, looking as if he wanted to argue, but couldn't come up with anything. "Easy is…easier."

"Profound," Jason said, pushing off from the fence and starting back toward the demolition. From behind him he heard a faint snort that sounded like the beginning of a laugh, but he didn't look back.

"You know, there's more to this life than calving." Zach caught up with him as he spoke.

"Yeah? What?"

"Well, there's pasture management. Herd management. Maintenance. Mechanics. Vet emergencies. Weather problems. Snow. A lot of snow. Rain. Muck. Crap."

"And you don't like that stuff."

"All I'm saying is that ranching looks kinda, I don't know…different to people who aren't part of it. But when you're doing it every day, it can be hard."

"The same can be said for football."

"Except you won't get rich ranching."

"Touché." Jason started loading his tools in the truck. "But there's something about being outside, working with your hands… I like it." It reminded him of being on the field in some ways. You practiced and played regardless of weather. You had a goal and you worked toward it. Shit happened and you dealt with it.

Zach cocked an eyebrow at him in a way that made him feel like a rookie who'd just demonstrated how much he didn't know. Well, in a way he was.

Jason had originally wanted to buy a ranch in order to isolate himself with land. That was before he'd gone to work on the Lightning Creek and discovered that there was a great deal of satisfaction to be found in working outdoors every day, demolishing a barn, overseeing the small cattle herd. Not to mention the satisfaction found in pulling weeds in an overgrown garden and kissing the boss.

He'd give Ray a call tonight, see if that parcel they'd looked at earlier was still on the market. He'd like to have cows, chickens. Pasture and hay fields. He'd also want a manager, of course— someone to run the place right, but that could wait until he nailed down his new profession. The ranch didn't need to be a working property right off the bat.

The important thing was to buy the right piece of land. Something he could use as both a retreat and an investment. A place close to his dad's, but not so close that they'd kill one another.

THE BELLA RIDGE RANCH was a beautiful property, edged up against Forest Service ground, which allowed for a healthy measure of privacy. It was a smaller property than Jason wanted, but as Ray pointed out, large enough to graze cattle—as long as his herd was small—and the federal land would isolate him from close neighbors. The house was two-story log, with large windows and a deck overlooking the Eagle Valley, larger than one person needed, which suited him fine. Jason liked to spread out. The kitchen was modern, the rooms had been professionally decorated and all in all, it would make an excellent getaway.

"You can bring in a manufactured home if you

decide to have a caretaker on site when you're not here," Ray said. "If you set it up over there—" he pointed to an area opposite the barn "—you'd have all the privacy you need while in residence."

"Let me talk to my finance guy and get back to you."

Ray said, "You'd better hurry..." but the words trailed off as Jason met his eyes. They both knew he didn't need to hurry. It was probably the ridiculously high price tag, which Jason fully intended to negotiate, but the Bella Ridge was not a hot property.

"Give me a couple of days and I'll get back to you. In the meantime, if anything else suitable comes onto the market, let me know."

"Sure thing." Ray clapped Jason on the upper arm, as if he were an old buddy.

"Is it all right if I stay here for a bit and just get the feel of the place?"

Alone?

"Sure. Sure." Ray smiled in an understanding way before heading to the shiny black Chevy truck with the Largent Realty sign on the side. Jason leaned back against the side of his truck, crossing his arms over his chest as he studied the property. Ray let his engine idle, and Jason ignored him, wishing the guy would drive away already. The house was empty. There was nothing on the property and the gate had no lock, so Jason saw no reason why he shouldn't be able to get the feel of the place without having a real estate agent breathing down his neck—or rather, wanting to breathe down his neck, but taking pains not to look pushy.

Ray wanted to make this sale badly and he finally came to the realization that Jason wanted to be alone. He put his truck in gear and backed into an arc, waving at Jason before driving by. Jason waved back and then let out a breath. Once the sound of the engine had died down, he took in a deep breath. Yeah. It was quiet here. Picturesque. Secluded. And there was a lot of pasture. He could have his own herd of cattle, his own new calves this time next year. He had friends who'd get a kick out of visiting a ranch and Kate would love this place.

But again, that ridiculous price tag. He was willing to pay a lot for a spectacular view—just not as much as the owner wanted.

One thing that struck him was that the Bella Ridge lacked the character of the Lightning Creek—the sense of having survived bad times and rejoiced in good times. This place was too new to have that kind of a feel, but he could live here. Jason took one last look around, and nodded to himself. Yes. He could make something of this place. He pushed off from the front of the truck just as his phone rang, and he dug it out of his pocket.

Brandt.

He hadn't expected to hear back so soon, but he was glad he was alone when the call had come. He sucked in a breath and said hello. Surely a call meant that he was still in the running…

"Mr. Hudson, this is Amanda Morehouse from Brandt University. How are you today?"

"Doing okay." He hoped.

"I'm sorry to say that I'm not calling with good news."

Jason's stomach dropped. "I didn't make the cut?"

"Not at this time." There was a note of apology in her voice.

"I see." Which was a lie.

"The top three candidates progress to the next interview tier."

"And I'm number…"

"Five."

"Of how many?"

"Ten."

Middling. When in his life had he ever been middling?

"While we applaud your accomplishments," Amanda continued, "your lack of administrative and management experience deeply concern members of the committee. We've made exceptions before and it has never worked out."

Well, great.

"I'm a quick study," he said before he could stop himself. "Highly motivated. I have a deep understanding of athletics of all sorts. I'm more than willing to do whatever is necessary to bring myself up to speed. At this point in my life, my only commitment is to my career."

"Good to know." There was a brief pause, and then Amanda said, "If any of the candidates decline the interview, you will move up in the rankings."

But he was still number five. Close didn't count. The final score counted.

"What can I do to improve my chances, should another position open up?"

"If another position opens up at this level, you need administrative experience to be a viable candidate—even to be an assistant. You should consider starting classes, working toward an MBA." Amanda cleared her throat. "There might be lower-level positions opening up in a few weeks, once the budget it settled. Internships. Would you be interested in applying?"

Jason pushed a hand through his hair. "I wouldn't say no to anything until I knew more about it." Honest enough.

"Then I suggest you keep an eye on our website. Look for future announcements and stay in contact with Coach Whitmore."

"I'll do that," Jason said as the hollow feeling continued to grow inside of him.

"Thank you so much for your time and considering Brandt," she said gently. "Goodbye, Mr. Hudson."

"Goodbye."

Not one *excellent* during the entire conversation. How things had changed.

Jason hung up the phone and leaned back against his truck, staring out across the fields. Middle of the pack. Not even close to the goal.

How was that for a reality check?

Allie was right. He'd worked hard during his athletic career, but he hadn't lived in the real world.

ALLIE CARTED HER flats of cold-hardy plants out of the house and started down the path to her garden. It was early days yet, but she could put in kale and cabbages. Her sisters would be so proud. Allie pressed her lips together as she undid the garden gate latch.

It wasn't about making her sisters proud. It was about regaining her footing. Not throwing out every aspect of life she enjoyed because it reminded her of anxious and painful times.

It was about getting a grip.

She was trying. Damn it, she was. But she couldn't help but feel she had a better shot somewhere else; that she should put off making her new life until she left the site of her old one. It always came down to finances and her lack of them if she didn't work in her degree field. So what if she didn't love her job? She enjoyed the kids themselves.

Allie had just set down the flat when she heard the sound of an engine and turned to see Jason's truck pull into the driveway. Her heart did a double beat, a reaction she chose to ignore.

It was Sunday and it was early. Jason never worked on Sunday. He watched baseball games with his father, so why was he here? Another blowup with his father?

Jason parked near the remains of the small barn, got out of the truck and headed through the pasture gate to the site without so much as glancing toward the house. He carried no tools, so he wasn't there to work. Allie pulled off her gloves and jammed them into her back pocket before leaving the garden and heading down the driveway. She couldn't help herself. She was curious as to why he was there, and a touch concerned.

Jason hadn't seemed to notice her approach, so she purposely kicked gravel, making noise, and his head snapped up. The intensity of his blue-green gaze stopped her in her tracks. His expression shifted almost immediately, and he worked up a smile that didn't reach his eyes.

Oh, yeah. Something was going on.

"How's your dad?" she asked.

"He's pissy, but good."

Okay, the problem was not his dad and it didn't appear that Jason was going to hand out answers.

Not until Allie came through the gate to join him anyway.

"You're probably wondering why I'm here," he said.

"A little," she admitted.

"I thought I'd take a load of these better boards to the house and see if I can get my dad interested in some kind of project."

"Instead of watching the games with him?"

He must have seen the speculative look on her face because he gave his head a weary shake. "Not totally true, although I'd love to get Dad interested in something. I'm here because I didn't know where else to go. I thought maybe I'd just... work."

"If you do too much, Zach will be out of a job soon."

"Yeah about that." He shifted his weight. "I think we should take out the foundation, too. It's kind of a hazard, and if you ever put in another building here, you'll need it gone." Allie opened her mouth, but before she could respond, he said, "You don't have to keep paying me."

"Keep paying you? You haven't cashed one check."

"Zach needs the work," he said as if she hadn't mentioned the checks. "You can use what you would have paid me to pay him."

"First of all, you're screwing up my accounting, and second, I don't feel right having you do it for nothing."

"Allie…let me worry about that."

How many times had Kyle said the exact same thing to her? "Next you'll be explaining things to me."

Jason had no problem following her train of thought. "I'm not going all manly on you. I want to help you out. Help Zach out. And I hope we've moved beyond thinking this means you owe me."

"I do owe you. You refuse to cash your checks."

"And I owe you. You gave me the gift of sanity by allowing me to take out my frustrations on the barn."

So they were even. She could accept that—for the most part. She put her foot on the foundation, keeping a distance between herself and Jason, mainly because she didn't want to. Being near Jason made her want to reach out and touch him. Feel his solidity. Gain strength from him. And it wasn't right to gain strength from someone else, because the strength, the comfort, could be yanked away at any time. "Why are you really here?"

He dug the toe of his steel-toed boot into the soft soil. The breath he drew in expanded his broad chest and again Allie felt that urge to reach out and touch him. "Because this place makes me feel, I don't know…at peace, maybe?"

Allie frowned at him, at the sincerity in his voice. "It does?"

"I can't explain it, but I like being here. Like being outside, working. I like being in my head."

"You can probably do that in a lot of places." Because she didn't want to hear from yet another person that the Lightning Creek was special. Her sisters all thought so—even Mel—and now there was another convert?

"Maybe, but I like it here." He sat down on the old stone foundation and stretched out his long legs, giving Allie the height advantage. Although she would bet that Jason was never at a true point of disadvantage. He might have trouble with his dad, but really, his life was charmed. He'd had money even before he became famous, because his family was wealthy. He made more money after he became famous. He was athletic, intelligent, he'd even gotten her scholarship…not that it would have mattered, because she'd quit school to marry Kyle.

"I'm buying a ranch."

"Must be nice." The bitter words were out of her mouth before she realized it.

Jason sighed. He just…sighed. Then he got to his feet. "I'd better go. The game starts soon."

The game he hadn't planned to watch.

Apologize.

Allie swallowed, trying to jar the stubborn

words loose. "Sorry. I didn't mean it the way it sounded."

Jason stopped and turned back toward her. "You didn't mean to sound rude and acerbic? To lash out?" Allie pulled in a breath but before she could speak, he said, "Or you didn't mean to let your true feelings show?"

"I can't help but be jealous of you," she blurted. "You know what you want and you have the resources to get it."

She was answered with a long, hard look. "You have no idea of what you're talking about, Allie."

"Then explain it to me." The irony of her words hit her hard. She'd just snarked about having things explained to her.

"Why? Because you want to hear that the golden boy has problems?" Her mouth opened and he added, "Yeah. I know you call me that."

Heat flared in Allie's cheeks. And yes, she did want to hear that he had problems, just as she did, and what kind of person did that make her? He started for his truck again while Allie stood rooted next to the old foundation. Did she call him back? Apologize again?

Had she actually apologized the first time?

Jason got into his truck without looking at her. Would he be back?

Would she be back if their positions were reversed? Allie sank down onto the foundation as he drove away. She'd said just three small words, but they had represented an ocean of repressed resentment—even though she liked Jason, she couldn't get around the fact that she resented the ease with which he strode through life, throwing money at problems—and Jason had perfectly read the situation. Just as he seemed to perfectly read her so often. Allie closed her eyes, drew a breath.

Something had to change.

She had to change.

CHAPTER TEN

MONDAY WAS TURNING INTO…one of those days. Kate was behind schedule and Jason decided to wait for her because she was taking Max to the therapist—which meant he wouldn't see Allie before work, and, frankly, he was good with that.

"Afraid he'd bolt?" Kate asked when she came in the back door and saw Jason sitting at the table, drinking coffee.

"The thought had crossed my mind."

Honestly, he had no idea what Max would do anymore, but his dad hated seeing the doctor. "Depressing," the old man had grumbled more than once the previous evening. He'd been so focused on his own issues that he didn't notice Jason quietly simmering. Was Allie ever going to get past his perceived circumstances? Could he expect her to, if he didn't explain? Yeah. He at least expected her to recognize that he wasn't in the easiest of situations. Money didn't solve everything.

"I just hope he listens to the doctor."

"Thanks for running the gauntlet today. I know it's a pain."

Kate shrugged. "No big deal. Dad doesn't fight me as much as he fights you." Jason had planned to go, but Kate had told him it would be better if she went alone. "You should get to work before your boss docks your pay."

Jason smirked as he handed Kate a cup of coffee. "Right. Dad's shaving. He promised to be ready on time. Call if you have difficulties."

She waved her hand and Jason headed out the door.

Zach was already on-site, stacking boards, when Jason arrived.

"You're late," Zach said.

"Couldn't be helped. Issues with my dad."

"We should start a club." Jason shot the kid a look, but he was focused on gathering more scrap lumber. "Allie stopped by. She didn't seem to think you'd show up."

Jason shrugged. "Must have been a miscommunication."

Zack tossed a board. "We should be done here by tomorrow."

"We're taking apart the foundation."

"Really?" The kid's face brightened before he forgot himself. His expression sobered, but he sounded sincere when he said, "I could use the money."

"Not a lot of jobs out there right now." As he well knew.

"No kidding," Zach muttered. "I'm supposed to start college this fall, but it's so expensive, I don't know if I will. If I don't go, I have to find steady work. So far this is the best I can do."

There was no way that Jason was going to tell Zach that he was in the same situation, because he was, yet he wasn't. Zach needed a job to support himself. Jason needed a job so he didn't go crazy. His circumstances weren't as dire, but his concerns were legit. Right? A guy couldn't go through life feeling useless. The one thing he never wanted to be was useless.

"I can finish with the boards if you want to start on the foundation."

Zach perked up. "You brought tools?"

"I did."

"Sledgehammers?"

"And mallets and bars." Jason jerked his head toward the truck. A few minutes later the equipment was unloaded and Zach was weighing a sledgehammer in his hands.

"And these." Jason held out a pair of safety glasses. Zach grimaced, but took them and slipped them on.

"How do I look?"

"Like you're ready to break up a foundation."

Zach gave a satisfied grunt and started back toward the barn, hammer in one hand, pry bar in the other. A few seconds later he was hammering away at the most crumbled part of the foundation. It looked…satisfying. Jason abandoned the boards and returned to his truck to get his own hammer, when he happened to notice a cow down in the field. The cow that Allie had been waiting forever to calve.

She didn't look like she was having an easy time of it. He watched the cow strain and then stop. Strain and then stop.

"Hey," he called as soon as he was close enough for Zach to hear. The kid looked up and Jason pointed toward the cow.

A concerned look instantly crossed Zach's face and he put down the crowbar and headed toward the pasture. Jason fell in step and then they stopped simultaneously thirty yards from the cow.

"She's definitely in distress," Zach said. "Do you know where Allie keeps the chains?"

"That shed," Jason said, working over the fact that everyone seemed so nonchalant about hooking chains to a calf and yanking it out of the cow. They walked to the shed together and Zach grabbed the bucket and the antiseptic.

"Any idea if she's friendly?"

"I don't think she's in a position to challenge us."

"You might be surprised," Zach muttered.

"Allie said she's one of her favorites."

"Good."

Zach set about doing almost exactly what Allie had done previously, reaching into the cow, easing things around, attaching the chains.

"Allie said this wasn't all that common."

"Depends on the bull." His tone was clipped, but matter-of-fact. He put tension on the chains as the cow strained. He eased his hand inside again. "Everything's normal, but the calf is really big. This is the point where my grandpa would have said, 'Get the tractor.'"

Jason didn't even want to think how a tractor would be involved in the birthing process. "There's a jack thing."

"Yeah?" Zach looked over his shoulder. "Would you get it? We might need it."

"I, uh, don't know what it looks like."

Zach muttered something that sounded like "It figures," then handed Jason the chains. "Keep them tight when—"

"I've done this before."

"Great. Back in a few." Zach got to his feet and jogged to the shed, coming back a few minutes later with a medieval torture device that he propped against the back end of the cow. He attached the chains, then when the cow strained, he started cranking. When she stopped, he stopped. But it was working. The nose appeared and Zach ripped open the sac. That nasty blue tongue fell out and then Zach was cranking again. After the head appeared, the rest of the calf slipped out onto the grass. Zach quickly removed the apparatus and after peeling the bag back from the calf's head some more, stepped back to stand behind Jason.

"Now we just got to hope that she doesn't have any internal damage." The exhausted cow raised her head and looked over her shoulder at her baby. Jason could have sworn he saw a cartoon heart forming over her head as she laid eyes on the newborn.

"Ain't no love like mama-cow love," Zach said as the cow maneuvered herself around to start licking her baby. Jason smiled and then Zach put his who-cares? mask back on again. "We should check her again in a bit, but I think she's going to be fine."

"I hope so." The calf was pretty damned cute and it needed a mother.

"Every lost cow or calf is lost revenue," Zach said as they started back to the site. He sounded matter-of-fact and businesslike and didn't seem swayed by the cuteness factor.

But he was an old hand at the cattle business. Jason was not, but he liked the idea of getting a small herd. Learning more. Hell, maybe he could employ Zach as his property manager.

ZACH WAS STILL at the ranch when Allie got home after her best day of work since she'd started.

She'd actually anticipated trouble and headed it off before it happened. The library was the calmest it had been in weeks, story time with the kindergarteners had gone well and Mrs. Wilson-Jones had given her kudos at the end of the day. Her sense of accomplishment and well-being faded, however, when she saw that Jason's truck wasn't there—even though she was home earlier than usual. Maybe he was done with her and the Lightning Creek, although she couldn't imagine him abandoning Zach.

She parked and got out of her car as Zach started toward her.

"Hey," Zach called. "We pulled a calf for you today."

We. Jason had shown up. She was glad of that.

"Did Jason turn green?"

Zach smiled. "He didn't."

Allie pushed her windblown hair back from her face. "I'd hoped to speak with him."

"He had to leave early. His dad went to the doctor today and he had to spell his sister."

"Ah." She wanted so much to ask, "Did he seem all right?" But, of course, she couldn't do that.

"You need to think about getting a smaller bull," Zach said. "That calf was ginormous and Jason said you had to pull others."

"Only two." But he was probably right. It was the first year they'd used this bull. She'd discuss it with Jolie the next time her sister called to check on her. Because that was what they were doing—tag-teaming to check on her. She was glad they hadn't involved their mother. Small mercies and all that.

"Thanks for pulling the calf," Allie said. "It's hard not being on the place during calving. I've been lucky so far." Not that she was the only part-time rancher who had to work a day job, but it still didn't make it easy.

"Yeah, I can see that," Zach said. He closed the tailgate of his truck, then leaned against the bumper.

"Between the two of us, someone will be here, so you don't have to worry about the last calves."

"And then my sisters will move home and I won't have to worry at all next spring."

"You're leaving?"

Allie hadn't said anything yet to Liz about her doubts about her teaching career, so she smiled at Zach and said, "I won't stay here at the ranch. It'll be too crowded with two sisters and two brothers-in-law."

"There's always the bunkhouse," Zach teased.

"You haven't seen the inside of that place." Allie rolled her eyes. Talk about chaos. They'd stored grain and old tools and anything that needed protection from mice in there for years. It was one of the few places none of her sisters had tackled—probably due to the intimidation factor.

"If you need someone to muck it out after I'm done with the foundation…"

Zach shifted uncomfortably and Allie gave a considering nod. "Not a bad idea."

"Yeah. Well…" Zach shrugged. "I'd better get going."

"Yeah. Thanks again for the healthy calf."

"Not a problem."

Allie went to check the cow as soon as she got to the house. The old girl seemed no worse for wear and the calf wobbling around her was indeed ginormous, as Zach had said.

Yes. New bull.

She breathed deeply, pulling in the familiar spring scents of damp earth and sun-warmed grass as she headed back to the house. Lilac buds were popping and the daffodils she and her dad had planted around the base of the trees in the front yard were bobbing their golden heads in the breeze.

Her dad had loved this ranch so much. And she'd loved him so much.

What would her dad think of her now? Would he be proud?

She let out a breath and walked around the house to the backyard, where she sat in the swing he'd built when Jolie was a baby. The wooden seat was worn from the weather and just a little damp.

Her dad would be proud that she'd finished

her degree. That was an accomplishment. He'd hammered in the importance of committing to a task until it was completed. She'd done that, after a five-year hiatus.

She turned the swing, twisting the ropes until the seat rose higher, just as she'd done as a child.

Her dad wouldn't be so proud of what the ranch had turned into while she'd been married to Kyle, but he'd also have understood. The ranch had gone to hell before. It was the nature of the business, but her father had poured his heart and soul into the ranch during good times and bad. Believed in the worth of his occupation.

The thought made Allie cringe a little. She believed in the worth of her occupation, but even though she'd had a better day and was beginning to believe she could be successful, she didn't know if she'd ever love education the way her father had loved ranching—or the way Jason had loved football.

Yet another unspoken reason she was jealous of the man. She felt as if he'd experienced everything she hadn't.

Her dad would not be proud.

She twisted the swing again, until her toes barely touched the ground, then pushed off and launched herself, swinging as the ropes unwound, making the world a blur as she spun. She felt a little nauseous by the time the swing slowed, something that hadn't happened when she'd been younger.

Or maybe she'd enjoyed the good part of the ride so much that she hadn't noticed the resulting vertigo. Enjoyed the good instead of dwelling on the bad.

Yes, she'd had traumas here, but the ranch wasn't to blame any more than the Eagle Valley or the state of Montana was to blame. It wasn't the locale…it was what she'd attached to that locale in her mind. The locale was an excuse for not dealing fully with her past.

Instead of being proactive, she'd been avoiding. Pushing aside everything that reminded her of the past as if it would change her past—even pushing aside things she loved.

Tough people adapted and grew.

Allie got out of the swing, picked up her purse off the grass and headed for the back door.

Tough people also picked up the phone and apologized when necessary. A tough woman would call Jason.

"ABOUT TIME," KATE muttered as Jason walked in the back door. "I think we're going to have to hire a professional."

"Hit man?"

"It's crossed my mind." Kate's shoulders slumped. "I'm not worried about Dad physically so much as I'm getting concerned about the way he's trying to manipulate everyone around him."

"What happened?" Jason automatically opened the fridge and pulled out a beer. It was becoming a ritual. Come home, drink a beer, face his father. Not the healthiest lifestyle. He put the beer back.

"We went to the doctor and Dad lambasted him. I'm surprised that he was allowed to make another appointment. It's everyone's fault but his that he's eating a bland diet and can't drink and blah, blah, blah. If I were the doctor, I would have decked him."

Great.

He went into the living room, where his dad was stretched out in his chair. The Dobes barely raised their eyelids. "What's the deal, Dad?"

"What do you mean?"

"You gave the doctor a hard time?"

"I didn't like his attitude."

"Find someone else."

"It might have been different if you'd come along instead of doing that ridiculous bullshit you're spending your days doing. It's just to get out away from me, isn't it?"

"Why would anyone want to get away from you, Dad?"

Max narrowed his eyes at his traitorous son. "Don't get all smart-ass with me. You might have been a big-shot pro, but now you're just a guy without a job."

His dad was angry and Jason was getting there faster by the second. But instead of saying, "Speaking of bullshit, Dad, I didn't come home to take yours," he said, "I think you should see someone about your anger before you have another attack."

The way Max's eyes bulged, Jason was afraid that he'd tipped over then and there. "You mean a shrink?"

"Whatever you want to call it. A counselor, therapist, whatever."

Max's expression went cold. "I'm not angry over anything that I shouldn't be angry over. The doctor is taking away the things I enjoy in life, and I have a right to be angry."

"Replace them. Replace the things you love with new things."

"That's what I told him," Kate said from the doorway.

"I can't believe you guys are double-teaming me. Get out. Both of you." Max waved a hand and Kate instantly turned and walked back into the kitchen.

"See?" she said once Jason had joined her there and the swinging door had gone shut.

"Let's just take a minute. Regroup."

"I'm doing what he said." Kate grabbed her sweater. "You should, too."

"What if—"

"He knows how to operate a cell phone," she

said impatiently. "It's right there next to his chair."

"Good point."

Jason's phone rang, stopping Kate at the door. She looked back over her shoulder as Jason answered.

"Jason, it's Allie… I want to apologize."

Jason let out a breath and directed his gaze downward. "Accepted." The word dropped from his lips like a stone.

He expected her to say goodbye and hang up now that her duty had been done, but instead she said, "Are you all right?"

"Yeah. I'm fine."

"I'd like to talk sometime, if we could." She paused for a split second before adding softly, "Explain some things."

"Sounds good. Look, I'll, uh, see you tomorrow. Thanks." He hung up before she could say anything else. Now he'd be the one apologizing tomorrow. He met his sister's gaze.

"I just need some time away," she said.

"I'll stay."

"Thank you. I'll be back tomorrow, after I get a chance to cool off," she muttered before opening the door and disappearing into the garage. A few seconds later Jason heard her small car start.

Max came into the kitchen then and stopped just inside the door. "I thought you were gone."

"Just Kate. She's the one who needed a break."

"You need to leave, too."

"Careful what you wish for, Dad."

"I'm not kidding. Get out of my house."

"Shall I take my stuff?" Jason asked grimly.

"Just go. Give me some space. After all, I do know how to use a cell phone."

He'd been listening. Fine. "Then you'd better damned well use the thing if you need it," Jason said, feeling like he had a rock in his stomach. "I'll be back in a couple of hours. That'll give you time to decide if you want me to move out or not."

But Jason didn't drive away. Instead he sat in his truck, which was parked next to his Dad's Jeep, and stared through the windshield at the garage doors, wondering if he should go to Kate's house or let her have the time to herself she needed. If they got together, it'd become a bitch-fest about Max, and neither of them needed that. The curtains were closed, but when Jason glanced over at the house, he could see the light from the television change as his father flipped through channels.

He needed to go somewhere—at least until Max went to sleep. Allie had said she wanted to talk. Well, no time like the present. He hit Redial on his phone.

"Are you busy?"

"No." There was an edge of caution in her voice, but when wasn't there?

"Could I come over? I...just got kicked out of my house and I'm waiting for my dad to cool off." No sense pretending things were different than they were. If Max told Jimmy, then the world would know by the end of the day tomorrow.

"Uh, sure. Come on over."

Jason set down the phone and started his truck. Like Kate had said, Max had a cell and he knew how to use it. If he didn't feel like calling his kids, he could call his brother.

Less than fifteen minutes later he pulled into the drive of the Lightning Creek and Allie came outside to meet him, pulling on her denim jacket as she walked. He got out of the truck and met her at the gate.

"You got kicked out of your house?"

"Yeah...can you believe it? I feel like I'm sixteen."

"What are you going to do?"

"Wait until he falls asleep, then go back home."

"Really?"

"If he kicks me out again tomorrow, I'll figure something out, but I don't think he's going to. He's overwhelmed by the fact that he can't control every facet of life—mine, Kate's, his—and is lashing out."

Allie shifted uncomfortably, perhaps seeing a parallel between her behavior and his father's. "He controlled your life?"

"Not since high school, but now that I'm back, I think he's trying to make up for lost time. It irritates him when I don't fall in with his thinking."

"Going to work for your uncle."

"And ignoring it when he doesn't follow doctor's orders."

"How's your sister holding up?"

"Kate has pretty much hit the end of her rope. It's on me now."

"If you need a place to stay, you know you can bunk here."

He smiled a little. "Is that an honest invitation?"

She raised her chin. "Yes. And I'm sorry about the way I acted earlier."

"I already accepted your apology."

"I don't think so," she said softly. "Not that I blame you." She held his gaze, as if daring him to challenge her words.

He couldn't, because she was correct. He hadn't accepted her apology so much as he'd mouthed the expected response and then stewed—not about what she'd said, but about the way she treated him like the enemy. He glanced down at the cracked sidewalk, and when he looked up again, he caught the uncertainty in Allie's expression.

"Okay. Maybe I didn't."

"And you don't have to. I have no excuse."

She put a hand on the picket gate between them, reminding him that during the one kiss they'd shared, they'd had a fence between them. "But I can explain…if you care to listen."

He did. "Let's go for a drive."

"Yes," Allie said quietly. "I'd like that."

OF ALL HER SISTERS, Allie had the least difficulty saying what needed to be said—although Mel was a close second—but now, as she sat a few feet away from Jason and had things to say, words failed her.

Jason didn't seem to care. At the end of the driveway, instead of turning left toward town, he turned right toward the Staley house and then a mile later, he turned onto a seldom-used track that led to the trestle road. He seemed to know this part of the country—her part of the country—which surprised her. He pulled to a stop where the track intersected the road leading to the bridge and put the truck into Park, letting it idle.

Time to talk.

So where did she start? All of the clever openings she'd practiced as they drove through the darkness stalled on her lips.

Finally she took a deep breath. "After my marriage broke up, I had a hard time getting my footing again." Total truth. Still the truth in many ways.

"I can imagine." He sounded like he knew what she was talking about, which again made her wonder about his former relationships.

"My world changed radically in a short period of time, but it had also been changing slowly over a long period of time. I'd stubbornly refused to acknowledge that, so it seemed as if everything hit me at once." She spoke without looking at him. "I've been angry and afraid and..." Her mouth tightened as she glanced his way. "Did I mention that I was angry?"

"And afraid?" His tone was cool, but not cold.

"Yes." She looked at the windshield again. "But mostly angry. At Kyle. At myself. At the world." Her hands twisted in her lap and she made a conscious effort to stop moving. "As for being afraid...anger is so much easier."

"What are you afraid of, Allie?"

"Failure." One corner of her mouth tightened. "More specifically, I'm afraid of not being secure. Money will make me secure, however, the job I trained for—"

"You don't love it."

She shook her head. "No. I do not."

"And you don't see yourself as having the time and money to train for something new."

"Just thinking about it makes me feel like my stomach is twisting into a pretzel. And the ranch fell apart while Kyle and I were there. Dani and Jolie worked hard to build it back up again, and even though I probably don't have the time to ruin it again, I did lose a barn."

"Mother Nature had a hand in that."

Allie pressed her palm to her forehead. "I need the ranch to do well until my sisters come back at the end of the year and I need to get over the fact that my job is just a job. A lot of people work at jobs that are just jobs."

She cast him a sideways look. "I'm sorry that you've been the object of my frustration on more than one occasion. I've been jealous of the fact that you had a job you enjoyed and that you have the security of money."

Silence stretched between them for a couple of long seconds. *And this is where you say you understand.* Because, whether she liked it or not, it was important to her that he understand.

"And," he finally said, "I did get that scholarship."

Allie gave a small snort. "Which you didn't need."

He made a dismissive gesture. "You would have wasted it training for a field you don't enjoy."

A joke. At her expense, and she was good with that. "Are you using *your* degree?"

"I can't remember my degree."

This time she laughed. "Do you need it? Your degree?"

"I need something," he said on a dark note. He

shifted in his seat and put the truck in gear. The truck rolled forward and Jason turned onto the trestle road. A couple miles later, he turned again onto a narrow dirt road that seemed remarkably well traveled, and drove another half mile before pulling to a stop in a large clearing that was nearly devoid of vegetation. He turned off the engine and got out of the truck. After a second's hesitation, Allie followed looking around at the stone fire rings and the old metal oil drums used as trash cans.

"What is this place?"

He shot her an incredulous look. "You're kidding, right?"

"I'm not."

"Kyle never took you here in high school?"

"Kyle and I didn't start dating until after I went to college. But…I think I get it." This was a party spot. A make-out spot.

"In high school, this was the second-best place on earth—the best being the gridiron, of course." He walked toward the rickety wooden bridge crossing the creek.

"I'll have to take your word on both of those," Allie said, catching up to him. She started across the bridge ahead of him. On the other side of the creek, the grass was long and green and springy beneath Allie's feet as she stepped off the bridge.

"I didn't get the job."

The words came out of nowhere. Allie stopped and turned back toward Jason, who stood at the edge of the bridge.

He wouldn't be assistant to the assistant? That had to sting.

"I'm sorry."

"Yeah." He let out a long breath. "Not everything in my life works out."

"I never thought that." Allie had automatically defended herself, although she was guilty of thinking his life was a lot better than hers in many ways. Ways that mattered to her.

"I thought I'd have a decent shot at it, because of, well…"

"Who you are?"

"I worked hard to be who I am. I—" he gave a small shrug "—expected it to continue to pay off. My former coach, who's something of a legend, put in a good word for me. It wasn't enough."

Ouch. They took a few silent steps, walking side by side, and then she said, "So what now?"

"I send out more résumés. Call other people I know to see if they have any leads."

"I bet you'll find something," Allie said as she moved past him. He took hold of her arm, stopping her progress, and her lips parted as she looked up at him.

"Why didn't you date in high school, Allie?"

He barely had hold of her, but she had no intention of pulling away. This was a night of truths for her and she liked the contact. Liked it a lot, but wouldn't let it get to the point that she had to make any big decisions about complicating her life any further.

"I was still recovering from my dad passing away and the ranch was in trouble, so I preferred to hang with my mom and help her as much as I could."

"Were you afraid of losing her, too?"

"I think I was."

Jason let go of her and they fell into step again, following the creek. "My mom left right before we moved here. Dad had the money and the lawyers, so he got custody of Kate and me."

"I never knew that." Their shoulders bumped pleasantly and Allie told herself to relax and enjoy it.

"I did my best to block out their stuff."

"But you understand what Zach is going through."

"To a degree."

"So you told him to pull his head out of his ass."

"It needed to be done."

Allie had clung to home during high school, so it was no wonder that she had no idea that this make-out spot existed. She wondered if her sisters knew.

"I thought the big make-out spot was on Hanley Hill, overlooking the lake."

"Decoy. All the cops went there, so we went here. Those of us in the know anyway."

Allie laughed. "I so wasn't in the know."

"Well, you kind of have to go on a date to do that."

"Excellent point… Would you have dated me then?" Because he was interested in her now.

Jason cocked his head. "You were…intimidating."

"Intimidating?" Allie made a face. "When you looked at me, you thought intimidating?"

Jason thought about it, then said, "Yes. Definitely."

"What do you see now?"

"A woman who's working to regain her footing in life and is still a little intimidating. What do you see when you look at me?"

Allie shook her head. "Any guy who had groupies must know exactly what women see when they look at him."

"I don't have groupies."

"You did at one time. I've Googled the hell out of you, Jason, so don't try to deny it."

"Why did you Google me, Allie?"

"Because despite all of my good intentions to the contrary, you intrigue me." She pushed her hands into the pockets of her denim jacket. "You lived this life that not many people get to live."

"I guess I have."

"I was curious. So I researched you." She started back to the bridge, back toward the truck. Twilight was falling and it felt like a good time to go home. "You look good in those football pants. I won't lie."

When she looked at him, he was smiling, but he was also watching her intently. Figuring her out. She always had the feeling he was trying to figure her out...and that he was pretty close to having success now that she'd given him important data. And now she was going for the entire truth. Night of truths.

"I enjoyed kissing you. I find you attractive and that also frustrated me, because—and, I promise you, I mean this from the bottom of my heart—the last thing I will do to myself right now is to allow attraction to overcome my common sense."

"Being attracted to me defies common sense?" A corner of his mouth twitched. "I should be offended, right?"

"No." Allie crossed the narrow bridge over the creek and waited for him on the other side. "You should understand that I need a friend, not a lover. As crazy as it is, Jason, right now, you're the closest I have to a confidant." He didn't look exactly stunned, but an expression of interest crossed his face. "I refuse to worry my sisters. Liz has her own issues."

"Yeah, she does," he agreed as they started back to the truck. There would be no making out in the make-out spot tonight. Allie had just made certain of that. But they understood a few things about one another that they hadn't understood before.

They walked back to the truck without speaking. Jason started the engine and turned the truck in a wide circle before heading back down the narrow road. Allie replayed her confession in her head. It hadn't been easy telling Jason the truth—that she was attracted to him, but didn't need a lover.

Jason seemed to understand, even though he wore a pensive expression the few times she'd cast a quick glance his way. He waited until he'd pulled up in front of her house to give voice to his thoughts.

"I have a question, and I mean no offense by it."

Allie's spine automatically stiffened. Promising no offense was never a good sign. "What's that?"

"Are you punishing yourself for choosing poorly when you married?"

Allie's chin went up. "I'm not punishing myself. I'm just not ready to dive back into a relationship."

There was something about the way he was looking at her that made her want to shift in her seat.

"What do you do for fun? For personal satisfaction?"

"I don't have time for fun." And didn't that sound totally defensive and, worse than that, lame? *"Yet."* She emphasized the word with a cool lift of her eyebrows, as though she had fun scheduled for some time in the near future. "I'm busy—"

Now his eyebrows lifted and she could almost hear him say, "Punishing yourself?"

Sucking a breath in through her teeth, as if he'd actually spoken, she said, "I'm busy with a new job and a ranch."

"But what about personal satisfaction?"

"I…" Allie closed her mouth abruptly then narrowed her eyes, assessing him. "What do you suggest?" Because if he suggested that they tumble into bed, as much as she'd like that, the answer would be no.

"Art." Allie gaped at him. "I've seen your work, Allie."

"I told you… I don't paint anymore."

"Why?"

"Because I painted to escape. I no longer need that."

"Can you paint for other reasons?"

"Can you leave well enough alone?"

He leaned closer, his hand settling on her shoulder, and she felt the odd sensation of energy flowing from his body into hers. "If you're going to work in a job that doesn't fulfill you, you need to have something in your life that does. It obviously isn't the ranch, so what?"

"I don't know."

"Think about it, Allie."

"I'm tired of feeling like a loser." She shot him a fierce glance. "Don't you dare say, 'Then be a winner.'"

"Why would I say that?"

"Because it's a sports platitude and you're a sports guy."

He smiled and slid his hand on around her neck, easing her closer. "I was this close," he admitted, and after fighting herself for a moment, Allie let her forehead come down to rest on his solid shoulder.

"You are a very frustrating man," she muttered.

"I take after my father."

Allie pulled back before she allowed herself to move closer. "I need to go."

He gave a slight nod. "Think about what I said."

As if she had a choice.

Somehow Allie managed to get herself out of the truck without either kissing Jason or smacking him for saying something else she hadn't wanted to hear. He kept doing that, damn it. Pointing out uncomfortable truths.

Once inside the house, she waited by the door until she heard him drive away, not moving until she could no longer hear the Ford's engine.

Well, this has been an evening.

Allie tossed her coat onto the chair and headed for the stairs, snapping lights off as she went. It was only nine o'clock, but she was done for the day.

She reached the top of the steps and then, instead of going down the hall to the bedroom, she moved the rug so that she could open the attic door. Okay. Yes. She would confront this now. Night of truth and all that.

She stomped up the attic steps, bypassed her canvases and started rummaging through the boxes she'd stored before her relationship with Kyle had started going south—back when she thought putting away her brushes and focusing on her husband would fix everything wrong with her marriage.

She found the box she wanted on the bottom of the stack and after restacking everything, dragged the box out to the middle of the attic, under the slightly brighter light directly beneath the hanging bulb. After putting the lid aside, she kneeled and started sorting through the supplies inside. Her good brushes, bought one at a time with the extra money she'd earned babysitting in high school—money her mother had insisted she spend on herself instead of adding it to the family coffers—were on top, wrapped in newspaper to keep the bristles intact. Allie lifted them out and laid them carefully on the floor. Her oil paints were packed into a flat plastic food container, cushioned with paper towels to keep them from rolling around. The watercolors were similarly packed away. The acrylics, the medium she preferred, were dumped into a larger container helter-skelter. Most of the tubes were half-empty and when she squeezed one, it was hard. Naphthol crimson, of course. The expensive one. Titanium white, burnt sienna, ultramarine blue, cadmium yellow…she might be able to salvage some paint out of those tubes.

Sitting back on her heels, Allie debated, then repacked the paints and brushes. She pulled the string on the overhead light, leaving the box of paints center stage as she walked back to the narrow stairs. Maybe she'd haul it downstairs, maybe she wouldn't.

Allie snapped off the stair light, closed the attic door and put the rug back in place.

Her stomach was in a knot—just as she'd known it would be—and she had no idea whether or not she'd climb the stairs again anytime soon.

CHAPTER ELEVEN

THE NEXT MORNING Jason came downstairs to find Max staring morosely into his decaffeinated coffee.

"So you decided you still live here."

"I think that was your decision," Jason said. Although he could admit to being relieved when he didn't find his stuff waiting for him on the lawn when he got home.

Max gave a grunt of acknowledgment. It had always been this way after their battles. Max acted as if nothing had happened and they were both supposed to act as if nothing hurtful had been said or done. Jason hated that, hated the feeling of unfinished business.

"I made an offer on a place nearby." He figured his dad needed to know that his son wouldn't be there monitoring forever. Max would have his freedom.

Max's gaze came up. "When?"

"Two days ago."

"Something permanent?"

"I may not live there full-time, but I plan to

have a home in the Eagle Valley no matter where I land."

"Where do you think you're going to land?"

Max's tone wasn't nearly as bitter as it had been the night before. Jason poured himself a cup of coffee and sat across the table from his father. "I don't know, Dad."

Silence stretched between them and then Max said in a low voice, "What do you want to do?"

"Million-dollar question."

"I thought you wanted to go to work for Brandt."

"Interview didn't go that well. I need more experience in the real world, it seems."

"Ah." Max nodded without looking at him.

"Seems kind of stupid to be so unqualified at my age."

"You have an excuse. You were…busy with other things."

Yes, he was. And he had the aches to prove it. It felt good to just talk to his dad with neither of them triggering—although that could happen at any minute. He rolled his neck. No tension. Crazy.

"This property I'm looking at. It's a small ranch. I'm thinking of maybe testing the waters."

"You want to be a rancher?"

Jason gave a small laugh as he shook his head. "I like the lifestyle, even though my coworker assures me I have no idea what the life is really like."

"I see his point. Your only ranch experience is tearing down a barn."

"Helped birth a couple calves."

Max's eyebrows lifted. "You didn't do well with the puppies."

"I was six," Jason growled. "Anyway, yeah. I like the Lightning Creek and I like having the animals around, so I was thinking of buying a small ranch and hiring someone to live on the place and manage it."

"A hobby farm?"

"Ranch."

"Huh." Max's mouth worked and then he said, "Not a bad idea."

"And in the meantime, I have to figure out what I want to do with my life." He met his father's gaze, his expression intent. "I'm going to stay in athletics, Dad."

"You could coach here. Volunteer your time."

"It's not enough."

"You can hobby ranch, but not hobby coach?" Max asked darkly.

Jason sucked in a breath, then said calmly, "I plan to work at the collegiate level. For pay. That's my first goal."

"And I know how you are when you have a goal." Max's mouth tightened and then he got to his feet and went for the coffeepot, moving slowly. "And I hope I'm here to see you accomplish it."

Guilt twisted his gut, but Jason refused to let it take hold. He wasn't going to get triggered. Not today.

He glanced up at the clock on the stove. "I need to get going. Ray is meeting me at his office to talk counteroffers." Jason emptied his cup and then went to the sink to rinse it. "You want to come along?"

Max considered for a moment, then said, "I'm a little tired. I think I'll watch the game I recorded."

"All right." Jason didn't know if his dad was being truthful or manipulative, but decided to believe the best for now. "I'll be at the Lightning Creek for the rest of the day helping Zach. Kate—"

Max waved a hand. "I'm fine. Get out of here."

ALLIE FOUGHT A yawn as she packed her tote bag to go home. She'd had a restless night after her sortie into the attic, followed by an unsettled day at school, which had worked in her favor in an unexpected way. While she wasn't exactly an ogre, she was a lot tougher than she'd ever been with kids who pushed the behavioral boundaries, which seemed to confuse her more active students. *What? Nice Ms. Brody was getting mean?* Allie had a feeling she'd dropped a few notches on the favorite-teacher list, but so be it.

Liz had stopped by at lunch to ask about Zach

and Allie gave her a good report. As far as she knew, Zach was doing fine. Jason hadn't complained anyway.

"Good to hear," Liz had said. "He's starting to act a little more like his old self, but he's still so angry."

"Time will help," Allie said. It had helped her, but there were some scars that never fully healed. She wasn't going to mention that. "Do you like teaching?"

Liz's eyebrows lifted at the point-blank question. "I do. There are days I want to beat my head on my keyboard, and swear if I have to zip up one more coat or wipe one more nose, I'm going to go off the deep end, but the other days make up for it." She smiled mistily. "It's the a-ha moments that make everything so sweet."

Allie had smiled at her, more convinced than ever than she was in the wrong profession and that she'd just wasted tens of thousands of dollars. Not the best realization in the world and it darkened her mood through the remainder of the day.

Liz stopped by again after school. Allie thought it was to talk about Zach but instead she asked, "Are you worried about whether or not you'll like teaching?"

"I am. I look at how you guys somehow manage all of these kids, meet their needs, keep your sanity… I don't know if I can do that."

"Younger teachers go in balls-to-the-wall, flooded with optimism and the belief that they can save the world. Older teachers have more of a grasp of reality. Don't let your fears override the possibilities."

"Good advice. Thank you."

Liz waved and headed out the door as Allie closed down for the day. It took a special personality to teach younger kids. Liz was a natural. Allie…not so much.

She said good-night to Mrs. Wilson-Jones as they passed in the hall and then headed out the exit and across the parking lot. Her phone rang as she unlocked her car and she knew from the ringtone that it was Kyle.

Allie tossed her bag into the backseat. Was she to be forever haunted by this guy?

The phone stopped ringing then started again a few seconds later. Allie turned off the sound. Kyle had his own family. She wasn't part of it anymore. He needed to understand that, after five years of cleaning up after him, she was done.

What a winner she'd chosen, yet he had seemed so perfect. While her sisters had all had a rough start to their permanent relationships, she'd had a blissful beginning to her marriage. She'd thought she'd married the greatest guy on earth…then the reality started showing through the veneer.

Sometimes reality really sucked.

But only if you let it. Allie reached for her phone, glad to see that there was no voice-mail alert on the screen. Whatever Kyle wanted, it wasn't urgent enough for him to leave a message.

She scrolled through her contacts and stopped on Jason's number. He answered almost immediately.

"Hey, Allie. What's up?" The deep timber of his voice rolled over her, through her.

"Are you still at the ranch?"

"Just packing up."

"If you don't have plans, would you like to stay for dinner?"

"I, uh…"

"Unless you need to get home and relieve Kate, of course." There. She'd given him an out.

"Kate isn't with Dad. We're letting him fly solo for a while. And, yes. I'd like to stay for dinner."

Allie's heart did a hard thump and she had to remind herself that this was a friends thing. "Nothing fancy," she said.

"I'm good with nothing fancy."

"Great. See you in a few."

The phone vibrated almost as soon as she set it down and after glancing at the screen, Allie focused back on the road. If Kyle didn't stop calling, she'd block his number, except for the fact that she wanted to know if he was trying to get in contact with her. Then she could be on the alert against the possibility of him "bumping into her" and attempting to twist the guilt screws. After all, she had so much. He had so little.

Which was an uncomfortable parallel to the way she'd thought about Jason.

Allie's jaw was aching by the time she turned on the road leading to the Lightning Creek and she made an effort to relax. Kyle couldn't force her to do anything she didn't want to do...but he could drive her crazy.

If she let him.

Jason's truck was parked in front of her house when she pulled into the Lightning Creek, and she could see him sitting on the porch steps, shoulders hunched against the cold spring wind.

"You could have gone inside," she said. Or waited in his truck.

"I spent the day in the weather," he replied as she latched the gate behind her.

"You were moving."

"True." His cheeks were red from the cold, making the color of his eyes seem even more intense than usual. Allie moved past him to open the door.

"Come on in."

"Thanks."

"When I said nothing fancy, I meant it," Allie said as she set down her tote and moved to shrug out of her coat. Jason automatically took the back and then handed her coat to her after she'd slid her arms out. "We can have hamburgers or hot dogs."

"Hamburgers."

"Hamburgers it is." She smiled up at him as if she were totally in control of the moment and then headed for the kitchen, the heels of her dress shoes clicking on the hardwood floor. "Are you wondering why I asked you to dinner?"

"Because of my dazzling personality?"

"Pretty much," she agreed. "And I want to draw you."

His eyebrows shot up. "Draw me?"

"Yes."

"Will I be clothed?"

She almost said, "Your choice," but decided not to tempt fate—or herself. "A portrait." She leaned into the fridge to find the hamburger. "I decided to test the waters. Try something totally new, and I've never done a portrait before."

"Why me?"

"You're the one who told me to go back to my art."

"Revenge, then?"

"Maybe a little. I had my art all tucked away in the been-there-done-that category of life." She opened the hamburger and then pulled wax paper out of a drawer, ripping off a sheet to make patties on.

"I'm not certain I want to go back." She portioned out the meat and started to make patties.

"My art was a lifesaver after my dad died. Painting helped me believe that the world could be colorful again, when it had seemed gray for so long. When I painted, I escaped into this wonderful world."

"Why did you stop?"

Jason had moved closer. Allie shook her head. "I was escaping too much, I guess. I had this idea that I could sell some of my paintings and earn some extra money, but Kyle put the kibosh on it. He hated the time I spent at the easel."

"He sounds like an asshole. No offense."

"He had a point. How much money could I make selling art? It was a risk, while getting a real job was a sure thing."

"And you go for the sure thing."

For once she didn't feel insulted or defensive as Jason pointed out the truth. "Well, the beauty of a sure thing is that it's a—"

"Sure thing," Jason said, finishing her thought. "I get that. But sometimes you should take a risk, when it involves doing something you love."

"That's just it." She turned to face him. "I don't know if I love painting. I did before my dad died. Then it became a lifeline to sanity, but I've been away from it for so long that I don't know how I really feel about it." Her mouth tightened as she looked up at the ceiling. "I can't do garden scenes and still life. It would remind me too closely of what I'm trying to move past."

"Like living here on the ranch does?"

She gave him a startled look. "Yes. I guess so." She went to the stove and turned on the flame under the cast-iron frying pan that always sat on the back burner. "So I decided to try a portrait, since I've never done one." She gave a small laugh. "I don't know if I can do one. You're the guinea pig...if you agree."

Jason shrugged, the movement accentuating the muscles of his shoulders through his shirt. "Sure. Just tell me one thing—will both of my eyes be on one side of my head?"

"No promises. Like I said, I've never done a portrait."

"Guess this'll teach me to butt into your business," Jason said.

"Guess so."

He came up behind her and settled his hands on either side of her waist and leaned down to nuzzle his cheek against her hair. "Can't help myself," he said. Allie leaned back against him briefly before forcing herself to stand upright again.

"Am I going to have to get cranky again?"

Jason laughed against her hair and then stepped back, dropping his hands. When she looked over her shoulder at him, it was to see a faint smile playing on his lips. She shook her head grimly.

"Don't make me become intimidating."

Jason leaned back against the counter, folding his arms over his middle, very much the relaxed male now that he'd gotten over the shock of being a model.

"There's something you should know," he said.

"What's that?" She eased the patties into the pan.

"I have a friend who's so prickly, he makes you look soft."

"Hard to believe," Allie said facetiously. "Yet he's your friend."

"He wasn't always prickly." Jason's voice softened. "He was my mentor and teammate, both in college and the pros."

"What happened?"

"He had issues after he retired from the game."

Allie shot him a look as she moved to the fridge to take out the condiments, the tomatoes and lettuce. She set the tomato on a cutting board next to Jason. "Would you mind slicing?" He took a knife out of the block without comment and Allie asked, "What kind of issues?"

"He discovered he was no longer a hot commodity. That the real world, as you call it, operates differently than that of professional sports. He couldn't get a job he thought worthy of himself." Jason took the tomato to the sink, washed it and brought it back to the cutting board. "Then he had an accident and now he's in a wheelchair."

Allie paused with the spatula hovering over

the hamburgers she'd just rearranged in the pan. "And now he's angry?"

"Very much so."

"And you have survivor's guilt?" A healthy silence followed her words.

"Maybe so," Jason finally said.

Allie set down the spatula and turned down the burner. *Okay...*

Her phone vibrated, stopping her from doing whatever she'd been about to do. She crossed to the living room and pulled the phone out of her purse, muttering a low curse when she saw Kyle's name on the screen.

"What's wrong?" Jason asked from the doorway.

"Just my ex." Allie set the phone down on the sideboard, beneath her garden painting, and went back to the kitchen. "I think he needs money for his medical bills."

"Why come to you?"

Allie smiled humorlessly. "He wants me to co-sign a loan, using an eighty-acre parcel of the Lightning Creek as collateral."

"Tell him no."

"If it were only that easy." She glanced up at him as she passed by him on her way to the stove. "Let's finish dinner, so I can do the prelim work on the portrait."

Jason looked as if he wanted to argue for all

of a second, then he gave an assenting nod and
followed her into the kitchen.

As MUCH AS Jason wanted to pursue the matter
of the money-seeking ex, he didn't. Instead he
sliced tomatoes and tore lettuce leaves. He got
the pickles out of the fridge along with the mac-
aroni salad and helped Allie set the table.

She wanted to draw him. Was it some kind of
twisted punishment? Did she know how hard it
was for him to hold still?

Or was this a way of telling him to be careful how he treaded around her—that she'd find
a way to make him uncomfortable, too?

"This friend of yours," Allie said as she shov-
eled the hamburgers onto the buns. "Does he
have a job now?"

"He's still dealing with his injuries."

"He's paralyzed?"

"Paraplegic." Jason took the loaded plates
to the kitchen table, where Allie had set out
ketchup, mustard and relish. "He's lucky, because he tried to be dead."

Allie gave an audible gasp. "Dear heavens."

"Yeah. He still pretends it's an accident, but
witnesses made it clear that he deliberately drove
into a tree."

"Damn."

"I know. And this isn't exactly pleasant dinner talk."

Allie took the seat on the opposite side of the oak table. "You're right." She poured ketchup onto her burger and plopped the top bun on. "Tell me about the ranch you want to buy."

"It's the Bella Ridge, on the other side of the valley."

"I've heard of the property, but I'm not sure where it is, exactly. Liz would know. Her ex-husband's ranch is in that area."

"It's a pretty piece of property. It'll be a nice getaway." He'd decided before coming that he wasn't going to tippy-toe around his reality. Yes, he could afford a getaway. "And if things go wrong in my life, I can either live there or sell it."

"How will things go wrong?"

"I end up here permanently."

Allie's lips tilted up. "That would be awful, to end up in a place a lot of people dream of living."

"If it had a college football team, I'd be content. So would my father."

"What's your plan, Jason?"

He set down his hamburger and wiped his fingers. "I'd hoped to get an assistant coaching job, but that's not panning out. My next idea was to get on in the athletic department, but I don't have the experience I need." He crumpled the napkin in his fist. "An intern position is opening up that they might consider me for, and I'm quickly learning that I'm not in a position to be proud or picky. If they let me apply, I will."

"Have you ever thought of doing anything else?"

"Allie… I'm trained to do nothing. The world is my oyster."

She gave a small cough, then pressed her napkin to her lips. "You're good at barn demolition."

"I am. And I like being around the cattle and stuff, but I don't think I have what it takes to be a rancher."

"I know I don't." She spoke adamantly.

"Don't or won't?"

Her beautiful blue gaze zeroed in on him and he realized he was doing it again. Pointing out perceived flaws in her approach to life when he hadn't figured out a lot of his own life. "Sorry."

"Here's the deal," she said, setting her napkin on the table. "I don't love the Lightning Creek. For whatever reason, I cannot separate past traumas from the actual physical ranch. When I walk around the place, I think of my dad. I think of how I came here with Kyle to exorcize the memories and ended up making even worse memories. I think of all our mom gave up to keep us on the ranch, because that had been what Dad would have wanted, and how much I wanted her to give up and live her life the way she wanted."

"Did she?"

"Yes. She married Principal Reyes. They live in Florida now."

"Reyes? No kidding."

"Surprised us all," Allie said. "We didn't think

she'd remarry, but she did. She finally escaped the Lightning Creek before it beat her into the ground." She smiled humorlessly. "Not that it didn't come close to winning."

"We're really bad at cheerful dinner conversation," Jason said.

Allie nodded at her plate and picked her burger back up. "We're a pair all right."

Twenty minutes later the dishes were done and Jason was sitting in a hardback chair near the floor lamp, doing his best to hold still while Allie sketched.

"Why don't you just take a photo?" he finally asked.

"That wouldn't torture you as much."

"As I assumed."

Allie gave a small laugh. "I want to try sketching from life. I'll take a photo for the actual painting."

"You're painting me?"

"Don't worry. No one will recognize you."

Now it was Jason's turn to laugh. "Maybe I can buy it from you. Put it over my mantel on the Bella Ridge."

"Because everyone needs a portrait that doesn't look like them over their mantel."

Another half hour passed before Allie let Jason move. Before giving him the go-ahead, she took several photos of him with her phone, then set her sketchbook aside.

"Can I see?" He could tell that she wanted to say no, but instead, she flipped the book open. She'd done several sketches, the pencil strokes dark and bold—slashes across the paper that somehow captured his likeness. Wow.

"Seen enough?"

"They look good."

Allie didn't answer. She got to her feet and stretched, which Jason took as a hint that it was time to go home.

"You'll keep me updated on the status of my portrait."

"I will." She walked with him to the door. "Thanks for coming, Jason." She raised up on her toes, put a light hand on his shoulder for balance and brushed a quick kiss against his lips.

"And that was for...?"

"Being a good sport. See you tomorrow."

Jason sucked in a breath that made his chest expand. He wanted to see more of her tonight, but... He let out the breath. "Yeah. See you tomorrow.

CHAPTER TWELVE

JASON BREATHED A sigh of relief when he walked into the living room and saw the empty recliner. The cell phone was gone and he could hear the Dobes stirring in the room down the hall from the living room before settling again. No parental arguments tonight.

He got a beer and settled in the recliner, popping the top and enjoying the fact that he was drinking it because he liked beer, not to relieve stress. Would his dad still be in a decent frame of mind in the morning?

He hoped so, but right now he wasn't going to waste time worrying about his dad's moods. Nope. He was going to enjoy thoughts of a woman who wasn't really so prickly.

Jason had just turned off the television and was starting for the stairs when the landline rang in the kitchen. He reversed course to grab it before it woke up his father. It had to be Kate or one of his other sisters, hopefully not with an emergency.

"Jason?"

He instantly recognized Zach's voice. "Yeah, Zach. What's up?"

"I, uh, need your help."

"Sure." He spoke as if it weren't at all strange for the kid to be calling him close to midnight.

"I got picked up."

Jason leaned a forearm on the doorjamb. "For…?"

"Drinking." He hesitated, then added, "And resisting. I ran."

"Did you hit anybody?"

"No," he muttered. "I ran on foot."

Thank God. "You know I can't take custody of you, right?"

"I guess I was hoping that you might come down here and calm my mom down when she gets here."

When Jason didn't respond immediately, Zach said, "Please, Jason. She's going to freak over this."

"All right. I'll come down."

Sure enough, a few minutes after Jason arrived at the sheriff's office, Zach's mom showed up looking stressed. She barely seemed to register that he was there as she approached the dispatch window, but Jason instantly recognized her.

She spoke to the woman behind the window, who then disappeared.

"Liz?" Jason said from behind her. "I'm Jason Hudson. I work with Zach."

Her eyebrows lifted. "I know who you are… but why are you here?"

"Zach called me."

"What?" she asked in a stunned voice.

"I'm guessing that it's to take the heat off from him."

"Like that's going to work."

"Are you going to bail him out?"

"Do you think I should leave him here?"

He shrugged. Yeah, he thought she should, but it wasn't his place to say so. He also knew that she was dealing with this alone. "Could I buy you a cup of coffee before you make your decision?"

She stared at him as if he were crazy. "To calm me down?" she asked with a snap.

"Not if you prefer to remain angry."

"I just want to grab my kid and head home and cry." She shoved her hands through her hair, her purse dangling from her elbow. "I don't know if I can down a cup of coffee. I don't know what he's trying to prove." She met Jason's gaze. "I'm rambling."

"With good cause."

"Allie said you were patient."

"I don't know about that, but since Zach's not my kid, I don't have an emotional stake in this."

Liz stared at him again, wearily this time. "Maybe he knew what he was doing calling you. Yes, I'll take a cup of coffee."

"Another half hour won't kill him," Jason said. "And it might do you some good."

She nodded and they walked together down the short hall to the city hall cafeteria, which had two coffeepots and a row of vending machines.

Jason poured two cups of coffee that in all likelihood wouldn't be very good, but would give them both something to do while they talked.

"It's been a long time, Jason." Liz smiled distantly. "You were setting state records the last time I saw you."

"And now I'm tearing down a barn," he said easily.

"What do you think of Zach?"

"He's really angry."

"It scares me," she said. "I know he's done this before, but hasn't been caught.

"Do you think he's driving drunk?"

She shook her head. "He doesn't take his truck at night. He and his friends seem to be on foot for the most part. One of his friends has a dad in prison for third-offense DUI. It left an impression."

"Well, that's something anyway."

"How much do you know?" she asked when they were seated in plastic chairs at a small table.

"I know that Zach had planned to work for his dad on the ranch this summer and it fell through."

"Do you know why?"

"I do."

"So you can see why Zach is bitter and acting out."

"Yes."

She tilted her head as she scrutinized his face. "But you don't think it's an excuse."

"People react differently to things, but frankly, I think he can find a better way to express himself than getting arrested."

"He's going to counseling, but he hates it."

"Because he wants to stay mad."

"Maybe so." She rested her elbow on the table, pushed her fingers into her hair and placed her head in her palm. "I don't know how many times he's done this and not gotten caught," she said. "I just…don't know." She met his gaze. "And I have no idea why he called you. No offense, but I don't think you're his favorite person."

"I gave him some life advice."

"I heard." She let out a small snort. "Something he needed to hear."

"But didn't like."

"Who likes the truth when they're avoiding it?"

An excellent point.

Liz glanced down at the full coffee cup. "I feel better now. A little anyway." She gathered her purse. "I guess I'd better decide whether or not to let my son stay in jail for the night. I'm so sorry he dragged you down here."

"Don't be. I, uh, hope you encourage him to come to work tomorrow."

"Are you kidding? He'll be there if I have to call his dad and have him help deliver him." She quirked one corner of her mouth. "And I never call his dad."

AS IT TURNED OUT, Jason didn't see Zach that night. After finishing their talk, Liz had asked him to go home while she decided how to deal with her son. He did, however, see the kid bright and early the next day when his mom dropped him off for work. Liz had bailed him out, but she'd also taken away his truck.

Zach shot Jason a quick look, but didn't say anything before putting on his hard hat and walking to the toolbox to take out the pry bar.

"I called Allie," Liz said as Zach stalked through the gate. "She knows what happened."

Jason had spoken to Allie briefly when they'd met at the mailbox—her on the way to work, him on his way into the Lightning Creek.

"How're you doing?" he asked gently. She looked as if she hadn't slept at all.

Liz smiled self-consciously and smoothed her hair back. "Okay. I'm going to talk to the school counselor today. Reality check." She smiled tightly and looked past him to Zach. "He's embarrassed and angry at getting caught."

Jason was well aware. He'd had a brush or two

with the law during high school, but the difference was that because of who he was, the coach and the powers that be managed to get him off the hook. Allie was right. He really hadn't lived in the real world.

"Don't worry," he said, knowing even as he said the words that there was no way she wasn't going to worry. "This'll pass."

"I hope so." With a small wave, Liz rolled up the window and started down the driveway.

Jason and Zach worked in silence for most of the morning, maneuvering around the elephant in the room as well as they were able. Finally, when they'd stopped for a water break, Zach said, "My mom said that you wanted to leave me in jail overnight." He sounded utterly betrayed.

"I did."

"Why? To teach me a lesson?"

"I'm a big believer in negative reinforcement."

"Thanks."

"You asked me to help your mom and I did."

Zach grunted something unintelligible and went back to work. Jason joined him and the two of them spent another silent hour busting up foundation before they stopped for lunch.

Jason's phone buzzed in his pocket while he was digging his lunch out of the cooler. He pulled it out, hoping it wasn't Kate with bad news about Max, and was stunned to see Pat's name on the screen. Finally. He'd sent three unanswered texts over the past two weeks and after checking with Pat's sister to make certain he was okay, had all but given up on hearing from the guy in the near future.

"About time," he said instead of hello, a note of dry humor in his voice. "I've been thinking about you." More and more since getting the depressing call from Amanda Morehouse.

"Did you get the job at Brandt?" Pat growled.

Jason rolled his eyes heavenward. One of those calls—the angry calls he used to get whenever Pat OD'd on self-pity or drank too much. Pat sounded dead sober today.

"No, I did not."

"I heard you applied there."

Jason didn't ask how. "I didn't make the cut."

Pat snorted. "You don't want to work for those elitist bastards anyway." Translation—Pat didn't want his protégé working for a place where he hadn't been able to get a job.

"I did," Jason said. He wasn't going to lie and he didn't want to discuss his job search. Pat had helped him with the game and his head and even his women problems, but talking work was not going to help either one of them. "I'm looking elsewhere now. How are you doing?"

Always a loaded question, but Jason found that all general questions were loaded when Pat was in this kind of mood. So if he were going to take flack, he was going to do so for a question that he wanted an answer to.

"Well, I don't have a job."

Because you refuse to train for anything. They'd been over that ground before. Jason wasn't treading it again. His friend had issues and Jason didn't know how to deal with them. He felt helpless—the victim of Pat's anger. Pat had been his hero, then his on-field mentor, then his friend. The guy had been amazing—all-star three times. He'd expected his postfootball career to be amazing, too, and it hadn't been. Pat had been stunned to discover that people forget rapidly. It had almost killed him. Literally.

"Anything new?"

"Still in the wheelchair."

"You know, you could shoot a text every now and then, let me know what's going on."

"Yeah. If anything happens, you'll be the first to know."

"Did you only call to make certain that I didn't go to work for Brandt?"

"I called to touch base."

Bull. "I'll let you know if I hear anything about a job. I've got to go." He paused for a split second, but when his friend remained silent, he ended the call, then set the phone on the tailgate next to his water bottle.

Guilt. Survivor's guilt, just as Allie had said. And this was guilt that he brought on himself.

He couldn't help it if Pat hadn't been able to deal with leaving football. That he'd wanted to be a rock star when in reality he should have looked at being a roadie.

"Is everything all right?" The grudgingly spoken words held an edge of concern and Jason looked up at Zach, who was sitting on the tailgate opposite him.

"Yeah. Old friend. He's having some issues adapting to his new reality."

"How so?"

Reasonable question. "He's in a wheelchair."

"Sucks."

"Yeah." In many ways, the biggest of which was that he wasn't trying to change. "Let's get back at it. I need to leave early. My dad went to the doctor today and I have a feeling my sister will have had enough of him by the time they get back."

Jason spent the rest of the workday putting his back and his frustrations into swinging a hammer and then prying stones out of concrete. At the moment they were simply demolishing. Eventually they'd have to move the material out of the field. And in the meantime, Jason was breaking those rocks. Even Zach, as self-absorbed as he'd been that day, seemed to notice. But he didn't say anything. Jason didn't blame him.

LIZ ARRIVED TO pick up Zach an hour earlier than usual. Jason was good with that. He was feeling low after Pat's call and appreciated the solitude before heading home to deal with whatever Max was going to hit him with. Sometimes they had good evenings and sometimes he had to wrestle the chips and beer out of his father's hands.

Despite Pat's lack of communication, until this call Jason had allowed himself to believe the I'm-fine text. He'd told himself innumerable times that the bitterness would fade as Pat healed.

The bitterness wasn't fading and he was torn as to whether to persevere in the face of adversity, or to simply let go of his connection with his former mentor.

He was stacking smaller rocks in the wheelbarrow when he heard the sounds of straining nearby and walked out into the pasture far enough to see a cow down by the barn. Allie was due home anytime now, and he hoped she got there soon in case the cow had problems.

She didn't. The calf was born with seemingly little difficulty, but afterward, it barely moved. Jason felt a wash of helplessness. He had no idea what to do. He was scrolling through an online search on his phone when he heard Allie's car on the drive and jogged over to flag her down.

"New calf, but it's not moving."

"Right. Was it the cow with the blue tag?"

"Yeah."

"Figures." Allie opened the gate and Jason followed her through. She picked up a short pole that had been leaning against the fence. "I need something to brandish in case Mama gets protective." She looked him up and down. "Maybe you'd better stay here. She doesn't know you."

"So I'm just going to stand by while you head out into the bovine danger zone."

"Yes," she said shortly.

Her ranch. Her rules.

Jason didn't like it, but he stayed put near the gate while Allie started across the field in her flat dress shoes and floral skirt, carrying the brandishing pole in one hand. She stopped several yards away from the cow, who put her head up high and moved so that the calf was on the opposite side of her from Allie. The calf then struggled up off its side and the mother turned back to it and began licking vigorously.

That was apparently good enough for Allie. She took a few backward steps, and then turned and headed toward the gate, glancing over her shoulder every now and again as if worried about being attacked from behind.

Jason felt better when the mama cow took her baby and headed toward the creek. Allie dropped the brandishing stick close to the gate, which Jason held open for her.

"Okay. Only a few more to go."

"What's the deal there?"

"No idea, but it's moving now, so I'll monitor until it gets dark."

"I don't want you going out there when I'm gone."

"All right. I won't."

He narrowed his eyes at her and Allie smiled at him, touching his face briefly with the palm of her hand. "Honest. If I sense something's wrong, I'll call the vet."

"I've never seen you give in so easily." Jason started walking with her toward her car, which was still running.

"Long day. How's Zach?"

"Pissed off, but all right. Liz picked him up about an hour ago."

"She's making him see the counselor."

"Might help...if he feels like listening."

Allie opened her door. "Yeah. That."

She started to get into the car when Jason asked, "Is your ex still bothering you?"

"I think he's finally starting to figure out that I'm not going to answer my phone."

"Good," Jason said. "Stay strong."

"Will do." She closed the door and rolled down the window. "You guys only have another day or two."

"At the most."

She stared through the windshield, then looked back up at him. "I may have to come up with more for Zach to do."

Jason gave a nod. "That'd be a good thing for both of you. And Allie?" He waited until she met his eyes again and then said, "Please leave that cow alone."

IT WAS HARD not to be touched by the fact that Jason was worried about her. Allie was just damned glad that he hadn't ventured near Bahama Mama to see if he could help the calf.

Bahama was not a friendly cow. Allie would have gotten rid of her long ago if she hadn't always thrown such beautiful heifer calves. And sure enough, when Allie checked later that evening, the cow had a perfect little girl by her side. The herd of keepers had increased by one. Jolie would be happy when she got the news.

After feeding, Allie went back to the house and got out the sketches she'd made of Jason, laying them out side by side. The nose was off in one, the mouth in another. She'd nailed the eyes every single time, though. And by putting the three sketches together, she'd have the basis for a painting.

For the first time in forever, she felt a stir of anticipation.

Most of her acrylic paints were beyond saving, so she'd work in oil. She was more comfortable with a water-based medium, but it was time to push her comfort zone. To stop staying with the tried and true. She set a frozen dinner in the oven and then went upstairs to get the box of paints she'd left there and to see if she could find a blank canvas.

She found not one, but three blank canvases—two small and one larger. She was going to start on the large canvas. Go big or go home.

She primed the canvases and then leaned them against the wall to dry, marveling at the fact that even now, with Kyle long gone out of her life, she felt the familiar twist of guilt at doing something just for herself.

Damn it, Kyle.

No...she was to blame. She'd allowed herself to believe his bunk.

Allie sighed and headed out the door to check her garden spot. She'd planted kale, kohlrabi and spinach. Next week she'd put in beets, peas and radishes. Her area of Montana always had late frosts, so she steered clear of anything susceptible to an unexpected cold snap. She leaned down and pulled a weed. Garden started. Canvases primed. She was moving forward. Finally.

So, if she could reclaim the two things that had seen her through hard times, why couldn't she learn to love the Lightning Creek?

Because bad things happened there.

She didn't trust the ranch. Not one little bit. While she'd lived there, she'd woken up every morning with a rush of anxiety, wondering what was going to go wrong that day. What repair would be needed, which animal would get sick? What financial crisis would rear its ugly head?

She had good memories of the ranch, but they weren't strong enough to supplant the bad, to quell the anxiety.

CHAPTER THIRTEEN

ZACH SEEMED A touch friendlier when he arrived at the ranch, actually giving his mom a quick wave before she drove away. Maybe it was because he was no longer hung over, or maybe because he'd come to terms with the fact that drinking too much wasn't going to heal the broken bond with his dad. Whatever the cause, Jason took pains to not alienate the kid.

Most of the foundation was in pieces and instead of bringing in a loader, Zach and Jason put the rocks into wheelbarrows and transported them to a ditch on the other side of the driveway that Allie wanted filled. One of his favorite things about the ranch was that there was always something that needed done, a plan to be made, a goal to achieve.

When they settled on their respective tailgates for lunch, Jason mopped his brow before opening his lunch box. It was getting unseasonably hot and dry for mid-May.

"I've got to leave early today," Zach said. "Meeting with the judge."

"That works for me, too. I'm about to counter a counteroffer on some acreage and I want to look at it one more time." Zach appeared interested, so Jason said, "It was a working ranch once. I'm thinking of hiring a manager and turning it into a working ranch again."

"Which property?"

"The Bella Ridge Ranch."

"That will take a shitload...a whole bunch of money."

Jason stopped unwrapping his sandwich. "How so?"

"They lost their wells about ten years ago. They drilled another, but it was dry."

"Ah." And didn't he feel stupid for not knowing that? Or that it was even something he should have asked about.

"You didn't look into that?" Zach asked curiously.

"I wasn't thinking of that aspect of the place when I talked to the real estate agent."

"Then you probably shouldn't be buying a ranch." Zach took a bite of a cold burrito. The kid had a stomach of steel.

"I like the lifestyle."

Zach laughed. "Well, it won't make you rich, so you gotta love the lifestyle." The less-than-friendly look returned to his face. "Although,

I guess you don't have to worry about the rich part, huh?"

"Not if I manage my business as it should be."

"Must be nice."

Echoes of Allie. "I worked for it."

Zach took another bite. "Not saying you didn't."

"If it makes you feel better, I've been trying to get a job with my former university and not having any luck."

"Why would that make me feel better?"

A smile spread across Jason's face. "Good answer."

Zach shrugged and went back to eating.

They worked in silence for the next hour. How could he, who paid attention to details, have missed the fact that the ranch had lost its wells? He assumed Zach meant irrigation wells, since the house had a water supply—although, he might want to look in to that, too.

He looked up at Zach. "What do I need to know about wells?"

The kid shrugged. "I'd start with gallons per minute."

"All right."

"You might find out how deep it is. When it was drilled. Who drilled it."

Jason tilted back his hat. "You seem to know a lot."

"Naw. I'm just making it up." He smiled a little

as he shot Jason a sidelong look. Jason frowned at him and the smile widened.

"You're cruising for some retribution," Jason said sternly.

"Yeah?" he answered on a disbelieving note. "No. Really."

Zach fought it, but his smile broke through again. He shook his head. "About this ranch thing… I'd steer clear of the Bella Ridge if you want to actually have a ranch. And before you settle on something, you need to have an expert look at it. It wouldn't hurt to check local gossip, too. Ask questions and don't just trust the real estate guy."

Jason shook his head. Schooled by a seventeen-year-old and schooled good.

ALLIE PASSED LIZ'S car on the way home. She'd run errands and shopped for groceries, which meant she was late getting home, which meant not as much time to work on the portrait.

Liz waved, and to Allie's surprise, Zach waved, too—an unsmiling two-finger salute, but a wave all the same. Maybe the day had gone better. She hoped so for Liz's sake. Jason was waiting by his truck when she drove by the work site, so she stopped and turned off the engine.

"Wow," she said. "You're all but done."

"And the ditch is all but full." He nodded at the

tractor with the loader parked next to the arena. "I assume that runs."

"I sure hope so. It ran when Jolie and Dylan left."

"Zach wants to use it to fill the remainder of the ditch and he said something about cleaning corrals for the material."

"I'm good with that."

Jason shifted his weight and Allie instantly said, "What?"

"What happened yesterday has been weighing on me."

Allie frowned, having no idea what he was talking about.

"You had to arm yourself to check the calf? Remember? I hate the thought of you doing things like that when no one's here."

"These are not usual circumstances," Allie said. "Usually there's more than one person living on the ranch."

"Yet you're living alone."

"Like I said, circumstances."

"If there were someone living here full time, then the circumstances would be different."

Allie's heart jumped. "Did you get kicked out of the house again?"

"Not yet. But I was thinking of Zach."

"I can't share my house with a teenage boy," Allie blurted. "And the bunkhouse is in no shape for anyone to move in." Although he did have a valid point. One that she'd downplayed when her sisters expressed concern. Mel had been injured by that cranky mother cow, and she'd been the hardest of the three to convince.

"I thought maybe I could get him a trailer to live in—"

"No."

He cocked an eyebrow, as if to say, "Really, Allie?" Instead he said, "My dad has construction trailers. Some are ready to be decommissioned. It wouldn't cost anyone anything and once your sisters come back, it can go back to the site or be sold or whatever."

She looked down at the ground, lips pressed together. She hated getting hit with ideas that seemed reasonable, yet not. Yes, it was safer to have someone on the place with her, and she wouldn't even mind some company. But a teenage kid?

"I don't know about having a kid here alone all day. Even if he is almost eighteen and a ranch kid."

"This is where part B of my plan comes into play. I was thinking of volunteering my time."

"Volunteering how?"

"I want to learn the rudiments of ranching and I thought that maybe I could be Zach's intern—at least until I get another job."

"So…you'd keep coming here, like you are now, and work with Zach."

"Until either Zach or I get a job elsewhere." He waited for the idea to sink in, then said, "It makes sense. You know it does."

"You're starting to convince me," Allie said slowly. "I might call Liz tonight and see what she thinks about it."

"Call Zach."

"He's a minor."

"He's the one you're hiring."

"You're right." She pulled in a long breath. "Guess I'll see about doing that."

"It'd make me feel a hell of a lot better."

"I'm not your concern, Jason."

His lips curved into a smile that made her breath catch. "Then maybe you can explain to me why it feels as if you are?"

Allie shook her head and made to move past him, but he reached out to take her arm. Allie looked down at his fingers, then her eyes flashed up to his face.

"I think about you, Allie."

"Jason…"

"Can't help myself."

The same thing he'd said when he'd slipped his arms around her when they'd made dinner. Allie swallowed against the sudden dryness in her throat and did her best to ignore the heat building down below.

"I appreciate your concern, Jason."

"You said you needed a friend and not a lover."

"Yes." Allie wasn't foolish enough to try to add anything to the single-word reply. She probably wouldn't have gotten any more words out.

Jason released his grip, letting his hand fall back to his side. "You have no idea how much it's killing me to abide by that."

WHEN JASON DROVE out of the driveway a few minutes later, Allie was still standing on her porch, replaying his words in her head. He thought about her. It was killing him not to get physical.

She hadn't dared say that she felt the same, even though she did. Her body kept trying to convince her brain that getting close to Jason was a good thing. A very good thing.

Her brain, however, had been hardened by adversity. No more mistakes for her. She was going to know exactly what she was getting into before she dove in. Caution was her friend.

After dinner that evening, instead of starting her painting, Allie called her sisters, one after the other, caught up on their news, then told them the Zach plan. All three had been fully in favor, and Jolie had even mentioned the possibility of buying the trailer and using it as a guesthouse. "No hurry there," Allie told her. "Jason will let us keep it as long as we want. We have time to make a decision."

And the decision would then be Jolie's, because she and Dylan would be the people living on the ranch proper. After receiving her sisters' approval, Allie called Liz and asked to speak to Zach.

"All right," Liz said warily, obviously wanting to know why her friend wanted to talk to her son.

When Zach came to the phone, Allie asked him if she could hire him full-time—at least until her sister came home, unless of course he'd changed his mind about college.

There was a long silence, which wasn't the response that Allie had thought she'd get. Finally Zach said, "Is this my mom's idea?"

"She doesn't even know." Allie let out a breath. "If you don't want to do this, just say so. I can hire someone else."

"No. I'll do it."

"Would you consider living here on the property? In a trailer? So that you can handle the calving and stuff?"

"Uh...yeah. Sure."

"Great," Allie said. "Why don't you talk to your mom and we can iron out details tomorrow."

"Sure."

Twenty minutes later, Liz called, just as Allie had expected.

"What do you think?" she asked.

"I felt a little blindsided," Liz confessed.

"Jason thought it was important to call Zach."

Liz gave a small sigh. "He's right. I think this

will be great—as long as Zach isn't sneaking off the place and drinking."

"He can stay at your place at night, if you want."

"No." Liz let out a sigh. "I still hope he might decide to go to college this fall. This'll be good practice. For me, I mean."

ZACH WASN'T AS thrilled with a full-time job as Jason had expected him to be, but it soon came out that it wasn't the job that he had a problem with, but rather the fact that people were getting together behind his back and planning his future. Even though Allie had technically called him, Zach had figured from the get-go that he wouldn't have much say in the matter. It wasn't like he could afford to turn down the job, but he hadn't found it himself. It had been, in essence, thrust upon him.

"Did it ever occur to you that I don't want to do this?"

"Did it ever occur to you to give your mom a break?" *Or that once you broke trust you might not get as much say as if you hadn't?* "You're mad at your dad and you take the shit out on your mom."

"I thought we were watching our language."

"We're friends now," Jason growled. "If you don't want to do this, then what do you want to do? Sneak out of the house and drink while your mom is asleep?"

A flush worked its way up Zach's neck.

"I'm not trying to hurt her."

"It doesn't matter what your intentions are. It's the result that matters. If intentions counted, I would have been on a championship winning team every year." Jason pushed back his hat. "Look. Here's the deal. Allie needs someone to take up the slack and I don't know what I'm doing. I thought maybe you could teach me some stuff."

"Teach you."

"That's what I said."

Zach frowned down at the ground as if trying to figure the catch. Jason knew that at his age, he might have done the same thing, although Jason hadn't partied at Zach's age because he'd been serious about his athletics.

"I want to help Allie and I want to know enough to not be clueless about my own place, when I find one to buy," he added when Zach's gaze came up. "I nixed the deal on the Bella Ridge."

Zach dug the toe of his boot into the dirt as his features twisted into a scowl. Finally he looked up at Jason. "All right."

"Allie will meet with you every morning so that she can line you out and then—"

"I line you out?"

"Pretty much."

Zach gave a slow, considering nod. "Fine. I guess that'll work."

"People are bending over backward for you, so it'd better work."

TRUE TO HIS WORD, Jason had a construction trailer at the ranch within a day of Zach agreeing to live and work on the Lightning Creek. When Allie had left in the morning, the area next to the bunkhouse had been an equipment parking area. When she returned, the equipment had been moved to a different locale and there was a boxy trailer in place.

"That was fast," she said to Jason, who came to meet her at her car.

"Dad's crew set these up all the time. They tapped into the power at the bunkhouse. Joe's coming back tomorrow to plumb it into the bunkhouse water and septic lines."

"Wow. A bathroom and everything."

"Do you want to be the one to tell a teenage boy that he doesn't have ready access to a shower?"

"I would not."

Jason climbed the steps and opened the door, motioning with his head for Allie to follow him inside. The interior was an empty box. There was a row of cabinets with a small sink at one end, a door at the other and nothing in between.

"Zach wanted to move in tonight, but I told him to wait for water."

"Good plan."

Allie crossed the trailer, her steps echoing in the emptiness, and then she opened the door to find a small bathroom with a toilet, sink and shower stall. "Adequate," she said.

"I had to do some fast talking to get a trailer with a bathroom, but I didn't think you'd want a Port-a-John in sight of your house."

"Zach and I both thank you."

Jason smiled down at her, their gazes connecting in a way that felt more intimate than the casual level of conversation called for. Allie tore her gaze away and set her hands on her hips, giving one last look around. "Thanks for doing this."

"Glad to be able to help—you and Zach." His voice was low, sincere and somehow deeply sensual. Allie felt her skin start to prickle.

They left the trailer and then Jason walked with Allie as far as his truck, which was parked next to her front walkway. "Garden looks good."

"What there is, yes."

"Will there be more?"

"A lot more."

Jason didn't move. He studied the garden as if there were an answer to a serious question in the long neat rows of tiny plants. Allie pushed back her hair as she frowned up at him. "I get the feeling that you're in no hurry to go home."

He shifted his attention back to her, a small smile playing on his gorgeous mouth. "I'm telegraphing?"

"Totally."

Jason sighed and leaned back against the front grill of his truck, folding his arms over his chest. "Dad and I have been going the rounds and I'm in no hurry for round, I don't know, eighteen or nineteen." He gave her a wry smile. "I'll probably get kicked out again soon."

"You can move in with Zach."

He grimaced as he shot a look at the trailer. "That would be kind of crowded."

It would be crowded. Jason was a big guy. "Then I guess you could have one of my spare rooms."

"I like that idea better."

"I'm sure you do." Allie sauntered closer, even though she'd felt the need for space in the trailer. Maybe she'd simply needed an avenue of escape. "And next thing you know you'll be trying to worm your way into my good graces so that you can buy the ranch...things like that."

He reached out and took hold of her wrist easing her toward him, until their thighs were almost, but not quite, touching. "I'm still looking for property," he said. "It'll make it easier when Dad kicks me out."

"And the job search?"

"Yeah. That." His lips pressed together. "I've put the search on hiatus for a bit."

Allie's heart rate shouldn't have jumped, but it did, and she wondered if Jason had felt the bump in her pulse through her wrist, which he still held in a light grasp.

"For a bit?"

"A season off won't hurt. It'll give Dad time to heal fully and me time to decide exactly what I want to do and how I need to train. I talked to the high school coach about running a summer camp for the local players and he was all over that."

"I imagine he was."

"I have to accept that things didn't fall into place—"

"As usual," Allie added with mock innocence.

He frowned and then let go of her wrist and brought his hands up to span her waist, pulling her another half step closer. And Allie didn't do a thing to stop him. She didn't want to stop him. Oh, she would at some point, but right now she felt the need to teeter on the edge for just a bit before stepping back. To the safe. To the mundane.

Besides that, she liked the feel of his very large, very solid hands on her body.

"Yes. Me and my charmed life. Right?" he asked mildly.

Allie went with the truth. "Actually, I'm a little jealous that you know what you want. Even though you haven't achieved it yet, you have a goal."

He gave a snort. "Actually, I'm jealous of you."

Allie stepped back and he dropped his hands from her waist.

"How so?" Because she couldn't imagine what she had to be jealous of.

He took hold of her hands. "You live here. You belong."

Allie didn't answer. There was nothing she could say, other than he was wrong. She didn't belong.

"I'd better go," he said in a low voice, raising his hand to gently caress her cheek with a work-roughened palm. Allie allowed herself to lean into his touch before he bent his head and kissed her, a light brush of the lips that left her wanting so much more. "I'll see you tomorrow, Allie."

Allie stepped back, resisting the urge to wrap her arms around herself and hold in some of the warmth that was so rapidly fading away now that Jason was no longer touching her.

"See you tomorrow."

He started the truck as she walked through her front gate and then he was gone, leaving Allie with a whole lot of thinking to do. But instead of thinking, Allie went into the house, changed her clothes, put on her music and started painting.

JASON WASN'T THERE when Allie got home the next day, but Zach was. He was once again driving the truck his dad had bought him—out of guilt, according to Liz—and he'd moved his belongings into the trailer.

"What are you doing for dinner?" Allie asked.

He grinned widely. "Frozen dinners. Mom hates them. I love them."

"Good thing you have a microwave." There were no other cooking implements, but Zach didn't seem to care.

"Jason's going to see about getting me hooked into satellite internet."

"You can hook into mine." Allie wrote the password on a slip of paper and pushed it toward him.

"'I heart Gus'?" Zach said, reading the password.

"My sister made the password. Gus is her dog."

"No one will ever break that code," he said.

"No one is close enough to try. What's on your agenda for tomorrow?"

"We're going to check fences and start spraying." Zach shook his head. "There's a lot of spraying that needs doing."

"I have an account at Culver Ranch and Feed."

"And you said that Jolie used to divide the pastures?"

"She moved the ladies every few days."

"I think I'll call her and see how that worked out."

Allie pulled the paper back toward her and wrote Jolie's cell number on it.

"Thanks." Zach picked up the paper. "I guess I'll see you tomorrow."

"Going to go stir-crazy alone?"

He looked surprised. "I have the internet. I'm fine."

Allie wished it was that easy for her. Her evenings were much better now that she was painting again, indulging in her creativity and regaining her sense of discovery. But even with her artwork to distract her, absorb her, the anxiety was still there, just under the surface. Allie woke up every single morning expecting something to go wrong and went to bed with the same feeling.

And she really, really needed to move past that.

MAX WAS SITTING at the kitchen table with a remarkably pleasant expression on his face when Jason came in through the back door after a fruitless meeting with Ray Largent.

"Hey, I just talked to Mike Czakawski down at the dealership. You're coaching football this summer?" Max raised his coffee cup in a salute.

Jason pulled off his ball cap and hung it on the hook by the door. "Nothing carved in stone, but if I'm here, yes."

"Why didn't you say something?"

"I guess because if Jimmy found out, it'd be all over town."

'Jimmy found out," Max said on a note of satisfaction.

"Then I guess it's a done deal."

"Guess so. Is it such a bad thing?"

Jason took the chair opposite his father and reached out to pour coffee from the carafe. He didn't usually drink coffee at five o'clock in the afternoon, but he needed to do something as he attempted to explain himself to his dad.

'My entire life has centered around football."

"I know that," Max sputtered.

"When I was six, I decided I was going to play pro ball. Everything I did, I did with that goal in mind. When I hit college, I decided that after my pro career, I'd coach college ball. I love college ball, Dad. I don't want to coach in the pros. I don't want to be a movie star or a celebrity like Pat did. I want to coach college ball at a high level. And I can't do that here."

"Nobody's knocking down your door, are they?"

"Because I have no track record." Jason took a sip of lukewarm coffee. His dad needed to get a better carafe. "I can't do anything this coming season. I want you to be fully on your feet before I leave, and I have to figure out where to intern or train to get the experience I need. But,

Dad... I'm going to be involved in college ball, one way or another."

"Because you decided to do it all those years ago? Or because you still want to?"

Jason frowned at his father. What kind of question was that? "Because I want to."

Max gave his head a shake. "Then I wish you luck."

And Jason wished that his father actually meant what he said.

"I'm not going to settle, Dad."

"I'm not telling you to settle. I'm telling you to examine your motivations as well as your goals."

"I'll do that." Jason set down his coffee cup and rose to his feet. He stepped over a sleeping Dobe on his way out of the room. The stress that he'd managed to shed while working on the Lightning Creek came charging back, tightening his shoulders, his neck muscles, his jaw.

Get used to it. You're going to be here for a while.

If not in the house, then in the vicinity.

But what killed him was the fact that his dad had just asked him to do something that he instantly knew he didn't want to do. He didn't want to think about whether or not his goal was still viable.

LIZ WAS WAITING at the library door when Allie got to school the day after Zach moved into the construction trailer.

"Not to play the anxious mom, but how's my son?"

"Good. I have Mike Culver—Jolie's grandfather-in-law—coming over in the afternoon to talk fertilizer and such for the meadows."

"He'll get a charge out of that. He always loved ranching, until, you know…"

"I know." Allie unlocked her door. "I think he likes the idea of working for me now that he's come to the realization that we didn't do this as a form of house arrest."

"Is that what he thought?"

"I heard him talking to Jason just after he agreed to our proposal and that's the impression I got. Jason talked him down."

Liz followed Allie into the library and put her giant teacher tote bag on the library counter. "Regarding Jason, I enjoy telling people, 'Yeah, I knew him back in the day,' even though I really didn't. I knew his sister." Liz shrugged. "Anyway…he's been good for Zach."

"He's a good guy," Allie agreed.

"Are you two, uh…?"

Allie hesitated before answering. Liz was officially single now. And she was attractive and… Allie felt a twinge of possessiveness, which she wasn't going to feel bad about. Jason was good for her, too.

"We've gone out." Not a lie.

Liz gave a faint smile. "I figured, but wouldn't

Jason Hudson be the perfect revenge guy for a woman whose football-loving husband left her for a younger woman?"

"Who then dumped him?" Allie added. It was the one bright spot in an otherwise depressing situation.

Liz smiled darkly. "That was satisfying, but it didn't make up for Derek screwing up Zach's teen years. And it didn't keep him from getting another hottie."

"No." Allie stowed her purse, then draped her cardigan over the back of her chair.

"I heard they're going to fly the third-grade job this week." Liz smiled broadly as she made the announcement.

"I don't think I'm going to apply." Liz's face fell. "I've come to the conclusion that if a person doesn't love to teach, they shouldn't. It's not fair to the students."

"The kids love you."

"And I love them, but Liz… I'm not loving this job. If the job requirements were to have fun with the kids all day and let them run wild, I'd be a shoo-in." She shook her head. "If I'm going to work at a job just to work, it's not going to be one that has such a deep effect on others."

"Allie…wow."

"I know." But she felt good about her decision. "Please don't tell anyone. It's not by any means certain."

"What'll you do, if you don't teach?"

"There're some administrative openings at the community college. Or I can get another book-keeping job. I have experience."

"Those don't pay as well."

"But they pay well enough and I'm not high-maintenance." After a few long nights of soul-searching, she'd come to realize that while she wanted security, she didn't want to pretend to love a job she didn't and in her mind, a teacher needed to love her job. Gnashing her teeth over money lost getting an education degree wasn't going to get that money back, nor was working in the field just because she'd trained for it.

"Think about this," Liz said earnestly. "I swear, the job gets better as time goes on."

"I will think about it," Allie said. "I honestly will."

CUTTING, SPRAYING, CHOPPING. A large portion of Jason's day involved weed annihilation. He'd had no idea that it was such a constant battle. But he could now identify several weeds that had to be eradicated on sight.

It also appeared as if the cows had figured out that they now had a midwife on call, because they started popping out calves. Most of them came easily, but Jason had to help Zach pull yet another large calf two days after his ranch internship had begun. The calf was lethargic and its mother showed little interest in it, barely licking it as it lay in almost the same spot in which it was delivered. After watching for close to an hour, Zach called Allie. He wasn't on the phone long before he disappeared into the house and came back with a tube and a bag of what looked like milk.

"Hold this." Zach handed Jason the bag and then started feeding the tubing up the calf's nose. "You have to be careful to get into the stomach and not the lungs," he said.

"How do you know which is which?"

"Well, he's not gasping for air. This is called tubing by the way. It's important that the calf get the colostrum from the first feeding and if they don't suck then we have to feed them this way."

"Got it."

Once the calf was fed he had more energy and tottered over to his mother, who then heaved herself to her feet. "We need to check on her frequently."

"Right."

They headed back to the work site after Zach had washed up the equipment and stowed it back away in Allie's house. Zach's phone beeped and he checked the message before shoving the phone back into his pocket with a grimace.

"My mom wants me to walk during graduation, even though I finished school in December."

"Why did you graduate early if you didn't plan on starting college early?" Jason asked.

"I couldn't play the game anymore. School didn't mean anything to me and my friends were into stuff I wasn't."

"And your parents' divorce?"

Zach gave a casual shrug.

"You know…it's okay if it rips you up a little."

"I'm seventeen years old, not a little kid."

Jason somehow kept a straight face. If this kid knew that the things that had bugged Jason at sixteen still bothered him now, he probably wouldn't believe it. And Jason wasn't going to work to convince him.

"We need to get back to cutting the weeds."

ALLIE WAS LATE getting home, but Jason wanted to see her, so he busied himself pulling weeds in her garden while he waited. He made no excuses to himself, or to Zach, who was now happily playing video games and eating Hot Pockets, as to why he was staying late. Sometimes, regardless of what his dad had said, one didn't need to assess goals or motivations. They could just go with their gut, and his gut was saying that he should spend time with Allie.

Thankfully, Allie seemed good with that, or so he assumed from the way she smiled after she'd parked her car and approached the garden, where he was straddling a row of kale.

"I'm not going to ask why. I'm just going to say thank you."

"You're welcome" He tossed a handful of weeds into the compost bucket. "After it rains, these things really take off. The weeds, I mean." He stepped over the fence instead of going through the small gate. He'd never gardened in his life, which made him nervous about pulling the wrong plants, so he'd only tackled the obvious weeds on the very periphery of the rows.

"Everything okay at home?" Allie asked. "You didn't—" she shrugged innocently "—get kicked out or anything?"

"Not yet." As was happening more and more, the vibe between them grew stronger as he got closer to her, along with his need to touch her.

"Zach is working my ass off."

"So you decided to stay and weed my garden, instead of going home and recuperating. Good choice."

"Yeah. It was all about the weeds." He smiled down at her and when he looped a casual arm around her shoulders, she leaned into him. There'd been no talk lately of needing a friend, not a lover, and they were touching a lot more. Allie was lonely and she was alone—which Jason had discovered were not the same things— and she trusted him. He was, in a way, honored. Allie didn't trust easily.

"Would you like a beer before you go?"

He turned her in his arms. "Do you remember that first time I came to the ranch?"

"Vividly."

"You had that bottle of Jameson on the sideboard. With the big glass next to it." Allie opened her mouth as if to defend herself, then closed it again and gave a nod. "Well, if there's any left, I'd love a shot."

Allie's eyebrows rose. "If there's any *left*?"

"It was a while ago."

Allie gave him a hard look. "I don't own shot glasses."

"But you do have Jameson."

"And two juice glasses."

"I'm in if you are."

"I'm in," Allie said as she started for the house. Jason caught up with her and they headed up the porch steps together.

"That calf you guys tubed today. It's doing okay?" she asked. "Have you checked it lately?"

"Seems fine. Zach was like a mother hen."

"How'd you do with the tubing?"

"Do you mean did I puke? No." He gave her a wry look. "I'm glad Zach was there to do the tubing, but I think I could do it if I had to."

"You've changed, Jason."

"Ranch life has toughened me up."

Allie gave him a sidelong look. "You haven't seen ranch life at its finest."

"That's what Zach says."

"I like having him here. The ranch feels better."

Jason kept his mouth shut and simply smiled at Allie as she opened the door.

"There's your portrait," she said casually, pointing to the canvas on the easel near the window. Jason walked over to take a look while she continued into the kitchen.

It was indeed him. The work was done in shades of peach and blue and lavender, the brushstrokes loose, yet somehow confident. Gillian, the gallery owner he'd dated for almost two years, would love this portrait.

"This is crazy good, Allie."

"You think so?" She came in carrying the bottle and stood beside him, studying the painting. "I see things I would change, but I always do."

"I want to buy it."

"Not for sale," she said as she went back into the kitchen. "I want something to remember you by."

"Maybe I'm not leaving," he said as the cupboard door squeaked open.

There was brief silence, then Allie said, "But maybe I am."

Jason went to the kitchen where Allie was pouring whiskey into juice glasses. "Ice?"

"Please." He crossed the kitchen to stand close to her, folding his arms over his chest to keep from touching her. "Why might you be leaving?" Even though he fully intended to quit the country, the thought of Allie leaving dug at him for some reason.

"I'm not going to apply for teaching jobs here. It isn't fair to me or the kids. Therefore, I need to find something else. It probably won't be here."

"But it might be."

"It might. I applied to the community college and to a few accounting places. You never know." Allie handed him a glass and he curled his fingers around it without looking at it. She lightly touched her glass to his. "All that money spent, Jason, and I still don't know what I want to be when I grow up."

"It happens to a lot of people." He raised his glass, but didn't drink. "Can you make a living here on the ranch? Hypothetically speaking, I mean."

Allie shook her head. "I might, but I won't. I don't know where I'm going to land, but it'll be in a place where my income comes from a secure job and is not influenced by the whims of nature."

"Income can be affected by other whims."

Allie sighed and put her drink down and Jason had a strong feeling she wanted to take him by the shirtfront and shake him, to make him understand just how serious she was in what she was about to say. "I have had nothing but hard times on this ranch, Jason. I can't get them out of my head. I need to live somewhere else. Away from the memories. I wake up in the morning and wonder what the ranch is going to do to me today."

"It's that bad?"

"I wish it wasn't, but yes. It is. I thought the anxiety would fade with time, but so far...no."

"You don't feel like this elsewhere?"

Allie gave a small shrug. "I do...but not as much. Not nearly as much."

"Then you're right. You need to be somewhere else." And it killed him to think of Allie living on the edge of apprehension, wondering what would go wrong next.

CHAPTER FOURTEEN

HAPPINESS WAS A TRACTOR.

Zach seemed to think cleaning corrals was the worst job on the ranch, but Jason loved it. Maybe it was the novelty of running the front-end loader to scoop the winter's worth of manure up and haul it to the pile, where it would then be used to fertilize the fields, but he enjoyed every minute of the job and he had a hard time believing he wouldn't enjoy it the next time he did it. Jason was definitely buying a tractor the first chance he got.

And even though he was having the time of his life on the ranch, the knowledge that Allie was so unhappy there ate at him. He wished he could fix things. He couldn't. But maybe she'd like a different ranch—one that he owned.

The thought kept creeping back into his brain, the thought of somehow working things so that he and Allie were together, which was kind of nuts, since they'd barely kissed. And she was so busy protecting herself, he didn't know if she'd ever let another guy into her life in an intimate way.

But the thoughts persisted.

"Hey," Zach said when Jason finally turned off the tractor to break for lunch. "All the fences are still standing. Not bad for a beginner."

Zach took his job as intern advisor very seriously and Jason was amazed at how much the kid knew, and how well he could impart knowledge.

Had he known that much about anything, with the exception of football, when he'd been Zach's age? No. The kid was a natural.

He was headed back to the tractor to clean out the last corral when the phone rang in his pocket. He pulled off his glove and checked the screen, then instantly accepted the call.

"Mr. Hudson, this is Amanda Morehouse from Brandt University. How are you today?"

"Good." Jason stopped walking and frowned down at the ground. What was this all about?

"I'm pleased to inform you that we've advanced your application to the second round of interviews for the position of assistant to the associate director of athletics. I'm calling today to see if you are still interested in the position and, if so, to arrange a face-to-face interview sometime next week."

"For real?"

He pinched the bridge of his nose as he realized what he'd just said. Very professional response. *Way to go, Hudson.*

He could hear the smile in Ms. Morehouse's

voice as she said, "Yes. For real. One of the candidates took another position—with Brandt, I'm happy to say. Assistant coach."

His exact career path—the one he hoped for anyway. "I'm not fighting you on this, but doesn't that bump me up to number four?"

"You have an impassioned supporter in the form of Coach Whitmore and, well, you know how he can be."

He must have been great, because Amanda Morehouse was sounding almost friendly, instead of pleasantly polite. Or apologetically polite.

"We're interviewing four candidates for the position. We're still waiting on one, who's flying in from a distant locale, and Coach convinced us that we should interview you, too."

Thank you, Coach.

"I'd very much like to interview," Jason said. "I can come anytime."

"Excellent. We can arrange a flight Monday afternoon, with the interview to commence at nine the next morning and a flight back Wednesday afternoon. That allows time for more intimate discussions and tours of the facilities. Since you are an alum, I imagine the tour isn't all that necessary, although you may not be as familiar with the facilities for the women's sports."

"Not as familiar, no."

"I'll email you the details," Amanda said. "Do you have any questions?"

None that he could think of at the moment.

"Please prepare yourself for a two-hour interview."

"I'll do that," Jason said, even though he wasn't certain what prepping for such a lengthy interview entailed. What could they possibly do for two hours? He'd call Coach to see what to expect—and to thank the guy.

After Amanda Morehouse said "excellent" one more time, she said goodbye. Jason dropped the phone into his pocket and pulled his glove back on. He had an interview and he felt like doing cartwheels—if he could have done a cartwheel without hurting himself, that is. Instead of tumbling, he settled for starting the tractor with a goofy grin on his face.

He had an interview. Still on Plan A. No need for Plan B.

Good thing, because he still didn't know what Plan B was.

GOING TO WORK felt so much better now that Allie had decided not to make education her permanent job. She felt almost at peace, definitely less anxious—which seemed counterintuitive, since she didn't know what she was going to do. But she knew what she *wasn't* going to do and for some reason, that helped.

She wasn't in that bad of shape financially. She could stay at the Lightning Creek for as long as she pleased, dip into her savings if she had to, and, well…she'd figure something out. In the meantime, she'd go home and paint; let her subconscious hammer out the answers to her problems while she dabbed colors onto canvas.

She was actually singing under her breath when she walked out of the school at the end of an unusually pleasant day, only to have the song stall out as she spotted Kyle's truck parked next to her car.

Son of a bitch.

The good feeling evaporated.

As she approached her car with a no-nonsense look on her face, Kyle got out of his truck, stepping down to the asphalt with slow, pained movements.

Allie didn't say, "What in the hell are you doing here?" No, she did not. She stopped a few feet away and waited for Kyle to start the conversation, which he did after another painful limp in her direction. "I, uh, tried to call you a few times."

"I know."

"Why didn't you answer?"

"I thought it might be a continuation of the conversation we had in the hospital."

"Allie…I need help."

"What about your dad?"

"Real estate is in a slump right now. I can't get a job while I'm laid up and I need to pay something on those bills. Soon."

"You just got out of the hospital."

"You know what'll happen to my credit if I fall behind on payments."

Perhaps the same thing that had happened to hers after he'd screwed up the ranch? Everything—all the credit cards, all the utility bills—had been in either her name or under a ranch account. Kyle had walked away from that fiasco scot-free while she had taken the hit.

"Look, Allie, just help me out here and I'll leave you alone."

"You'll leave me alone even if I don't help you," Allie said stonily. Kyle was starting to get red, a sure sign that his temper was rising. Also a sure sign that this conversation needed to be over.

"I should have gotten part of the ranch. I worked it for five years and it was wrong that I got nothing for my labors."

This again? Allie somehow managed to keep her mouth shut.

"It's only right that you help me with these bills, Allie."

There was no arguing with him when he got like this, so Allie simply got into the car. Before she shut the door he yelled, "We'll be talking about this again. You owe me!"

He might think she owed him, but he also knew her well enough to stand back and not try something foolish such as banging on the window.

Allie pulled out of the parking lot and drove home with her teeth tightly clenched together. Every now and again she checked the rearview mirror, but he didn't follow her. Good. Because if he had, then she would have called the sheriff's office.

"You know what to do?" Zach asked sternly.

Jason managed to keep a straight face as he said, "Check the back fence line and finish clearing the ditch."

Zach gave a nod. "And watch the white-face cow."

"Will do."

"How do I look?" Zach asked. He'd borrowed Allie's iron and ironing board to press his shirt and he was wearing slacks and polished loafers.

"The judge will be impressed."

"Hope so." Zach grimaced. "Second offense, you know. He gave me the benefit of the doubt last time and all I got was community service. I was in possession of beer, but blew clean with the breathalyzer."

"And if you'd blown an hour later?"

Zach just shrugged and Jason said, "Yeah." He

wanted to ask him if his dad was going to be at the hearing, but decided against it.

"See you in the morning. I hope." Zach was staying the night at his mom's place, then getting a ride to the ranch with her before she went to work.

"I don't think they're going to throw you in jail, but I imagine you'll be looking at some more community service."

"And I may lose my driver's license and I have to take a course."

"Going to do this again?" Jason asked mildly.

"Hell no."

Jason gave an approving nod and headed to the ditch, pulling his gloves out of his back pocket as he walked. Behind him he heard Zach drive away for what would probably be the last time in a long time. It was going to be hard on the kid to not have a license, but he'd chosen his course of action and now he was paying the price. At least he was able to see his blame in the matter, and maybe now he was done punishing his dad and hurting his mom in the process.

While he cleared muck and debris out of a ditch, Jason practiced interview answers in his head.

What exactly is your job experience off the football field, Mr. Hudson?

Well, I've torn down a barn and managed a

kid who now manages me. Oh, and I've helped birth several calves.

He'd have to come up with something better than that, and he was confident that he would. He'd been doing a lot of research at night, figuring out what he lacked and how he could counter those deficits with his life experiences. He usually did well in face-to-face meetings and he hoped against hope to do well in this one.

And then there was the issue of Pat. Coach had been in contact, and even though he thought Pat had played the prima donna and caused most of his own problems, he was worried. Jason was worried, too, but Pat wasn't answering his calls. At least he was still in contact with their coach.

Jason straightened and tossed a shovelful of wet gunk to the side of the ditch.

He was about to start shoveling again, when he noticed a cow pacing the fence line. She bawled and paced, bawled and paced.

This was not normal cow activity.

Remembering Allie and her brandishing post, Jason put the shovel over his shoulder as he started across the pasture. The cow barely looked at him, and he could see that she'd recently given birth. But where was the calf?

The pasture sloped at that end and Jason started to get the bad feeling that the calf had somehow rolled to the other side. He quickened his pace, eventually breaking into a jog. The cow looked like she was ready to go through the fence by the time he got there. He skirted around her and squeezed through the wires, ducking low, so as not to touch the electric strand at the top.

A small creek paralleled the fence at the bottom of a gentle slope and sure enough, there was a small black calf lying in the creek. Jason sprinted for the animal, scooping it up and pulling it out of the water and hugging it to his chest. It hung limply in his arms.

For a moment he stood, feeling helpless and panicked. The mother bellowed and Jason realized that she truly was going to come over the fence and probably kill him if he didn't get out of there. He started along the creek to the fence that separated the pasture from the meadow hay field. Mom came right long. Praying that she didn't attempt to jump the sturdy pole boundary fence, he started awkwardly jogging through the hay field toward the house, the baby in his arms. It was still warm, but Jason had no idea if it was alive or dead. He just knew he had to get it to the house, where his phone was. Then he'd call Allie, call the vet. Zach. Someone.

The mother cow mirrored him, but didn't come through the fence. He hit the pole fences and squeezed through rather than go to the gate, twenty yards away.

Allie's car was there…

Jason ran across the drive, up the walk, setting the baby down on the porch and pounding on the door before he opened it.

Allie appeared in the kitchen doorway, a shocked expression on her face.

"I have a dead calf that may be alive. I don't know."

Allie brushed by him and went out the open door to the porch. "Get a towel," she yelled.

Jason ran to the bathroom and came back with two bath towels. Allie pulled one out of his hands and started rubbing. Jason stood back, once again feeling helpless. Allie kept rubbing every now and again putting her hand against the calf's nose, then rubbing again.

Finally she sat back on her heels and let her head drop in defeat.

"Too late?" Jason asked softly. She nodded and he crouched down to put a hand under her arm and help her to her feet.

But it had been warm…he'd thought it might have been breathing.

"Not the first time." Allie let out a weary sigh as she stared down at the still body of the little black calf. "Won't be the last."

"Are you okay?" There was a note in her voice that he'd never heard before.

"I'm fine." She pushed her hair back and

turned to look at him briefly. "It's just…been a day. Dead calves. Ex-husbands…"

Jason frowned at her, but she didn't seem to notice.

"We'll put the calf in the barn stall. Zach can take care of it when he gets back."

"I'll take care of it."

"We have ditch we use on the far side of the property. Zach knows where it is." Jason gave her a questioning look and she said, "Animal graveyard."

She went back inside as Jason picked up the calf and carried its limp body to the barn, where he closed in into a stall so animals couldn't get to it. He and Zach would take care of it when the kid got back. In the field the mother still paced, bawling and looking for her baby.

The sound tore at him.

He walked back to the house, went inside without knocking and headed down the hall to the bathroom, where he washed his hands. His clothing was wet and streaked with mud from the calf, but there wasn't a lot he could do about that.

He came out of the bathroom to find Allie standing in the middle of the living room, staring at a painting she'd started. A calf, of course.

"By the way, I really am fine," Allie said, looking over her shoulder as he approached. "It's sad to lose a baby, but it's part of the business. We lose calves every year."

She was schooling him, but it wasn't the calf that concerned him now. It was the other comment she'd made.

"What did you mean when you said something about a dead calf and an ex-husband?"

Allie's gave a careless shrug. "Kyle met me after work to find out why I wasn't taking his calls."

"Your ex is hanging around your place of work?" Jason felt an instant surge of protectiveness.

"He still wants help paying his hospital bills. He never was very good with the word *no*."

"So he's stalking you?"

"I'm calling the sheriff the next time I see him. I don't know how much good it will do, since he used to be a deputy—but he was a bad deputy, so it'll probably be fine."

"I don't like this."

"It's okay, Jason. More of a nuisance than anything."

"Maybe I should stay here. I can bunk with Zach."

Allie's chin lifted. "How about I take care of my issues and you take care of yours?"

She seemed more angry than afraid of her ex, so after a second's pause, Jason said, "Agreed, but…if for some reason you become concerned—"

"I'll call law enforcement."

And judging from the stubborn look on her face, he was going to have to accept that answer. "Any chance you have some Jameson left?"

Allie nodded and silently went into the kitchen. Jason followed her and grabbed the bottle down from over the fridge after she pointed at the cupboard there. She got glasses and he poured a healthy splash in each one. He handed her a glass and said, "I'll be gone next Monday, Tuesday and Wednesday. I have an interview." And he'd hoped to tell her under better circumstances. "With Brandt."

Her gaze flashed up to his. "The job you wanted."

"A candidate dropped out."

"Does Zach know?"

"I got permission to leave." He didn't smile even though it was kind of funny.

Allie pressed her lips together, then took a sip of her whiskey.

"Allie?"

She gave a slight shrug and didn't quite meet his eyes as she said, "I'm going to miss the hell out of you."

HAD SHE REALLY just said that?

Oh, yes, she had.

Damage control.

"It's the truth," Allie said matter-of-factly. "And lately I'm all about the truth, uncomfortable or not. You can't live life well if you're lying to yourself."

He reached out to run a light hand up her arm and then his fingers curved around her shoulder, pulling her closer to him. Allie went without a word, stepping into his one-armed embrace and letting her head rest against his broad chest.

"Any other truths you'd like to share?" he murmured against her hair.

"I don't know if being attracted to you is good or bad." She swirled the whiskey in her glass, then took a sip, keeping her temple pressed against his chest as she drank. False courage was fine with her right now—especially if she were going to start spilling all of her truths.

And damn but he smelled good.

Jason set down his glass on the sideboard and then gently took hers and set it alongside his own. Allie looked up at him, losing herself in the warmth of his gaze as he wrapped his other arm around her loosely and said, "Just to be crazy, why don't we go with good?"

"Then I have to ask myself where it's going."

"And how do you answer yourself?"

"If I'm honest…I have to say that since I haven't figured out my own life, my own self, how can I factor someone else into the equation?" Especially when the results had been so devastating in the past.

He gently tipped up her chin. "You bring up good points."

"Yes. I know." She lifted her eyebrows at him. "I'm great at that. Bringing up points that I don't have an answer to."

He smiled at her—that gentle don't-worry-I've-got-your-back smile that made her want to believe he really did have her back—and then framed her face with his big hands. His fingers were pleasantly warm against her skin and she wanted more than anything to believe that this was a good thing.

If only so many other things in her life had not imploded.

But thoughts of implosions didn't stop heat from flowing through her body. It didn't keep the small tingles from traveling over her skin. And it didn't stop her from just plain wanting.

"Maybe," he said in low voice, "this is a take-it-one-day-at-a-time situation." His mouth was so close. All she had to do was rise up on her toes and touch his lips.

"Could be," she agreed huskily.

The last word was barely out of her mouth when his lips met hers. Lightly. Reassuringly. His fingers pushed up into her hair, just as they had the first time he'd kissed her, and when he raised his head, his lips were still a fraction of an inch away from hers. She slid her hand up around his neck and pulled his mouth back for more.

Jason drew her closer, pressing her body against his long, hard frame. Their tongues touched lightly, jolting her senses, before they tangled and stroked for real, turning her body to liquid fire.

When the kiss ended, Jason raised his head to meet her gaze, his expression so very serious as he said, "One moment at a time. One day at a time. That's how I spent my career, because you never knew when something was going to happen to end it."

She could do a moment. And then another. And another. She could live her life instead of letting fear of consequences rule her world. She'd already made strides forward, deciding to seek out a new career, whatever that might be.

No fear…

Wrong.

She always had fears. Things happened if she didn't.

And they happen when you do.

It was the same argument she'd had with herself since her father had died. The argument she always managed to bury, thinking she'd won, only to have it pop back up at inopportune moments… such as now.

"Allie…do you want me to leave?"

Her eyes flashed up to his. "No. I do not want you to leave."

"Then what?"

"I want you to make me stop thinking," she muttered. "I want you to just make me feel."

"Done," he said, leaning down to touch his lips to her throat. "And done."

He was right. She was done.

She stepped back and started undoing the buttons of his ruined shirt. She'd barely even noticed how wet it was when he'd kissed her, but now...

"I should shower," he said as he helped her undo the buttons, revealing an amazing set of washboard abs. She raised her eyes to his, ignoring what he'd said.

"Why haven't you been working without your shirt?"

He covered her hands with his. "Shower?"

She shook her head. "Later."

"Whatever," he muttered as she took him by the hand and led him up the stairs. Truthfully, she was afraid of coming to her senses if she had time to think, but after he'd taken off his shirt and his jeans, leaving them in a damp heap as he stood before her in his briefs, she realized that wouldn't have been an issue. Not after she'd seen him almost naked.

Her throat went dry. The knit fabric of his underwear hugged him, showing the outline of his erection. And every bit of his body was sculpted, muscled. She'd never seen anything like it. Slowly she reached out to touch him, run her hand lightly over his chest.

"You work out a lot?" she asked.

"Are you going to keep making funny remarks?" he growled.

"I'm nervous." Ridiculously, heart-in-the-throat nervous.

"Aren't we all?"

He was nervous?

As if in answer to her question, he took her hands in his, pulled her a step closer, so that their thighs touched and the hard length of him was pressed against her belly. "This matters to me, Allie."

And, Allie realized, it also mattered to her.

One moment at a time. Time for big decisions later.

"I MIGHT HAVE to invest in a bigger bed." Until tonight, her double bed had seemed quite roomy, but with a football player taking up three quarters of it, not so much so.

"I don't mind this," he said as she nestled against him, totally spent and very, very satisfied. Jason had demonstrated athleticism that she could truly appreciate and now he stroked his hand up and down her back in long, lazy motions. Allie's eyes were just drifting shut when he said, "I'm worried about this guy. Your ex."

Allie raised her head, feeling like she'd been splashed with cold water. "He just wants money."

"You're certain."

"Very." She put her forearm on his chest and propped her chin in her hand. "Trust me on this." He cocked an eyebrow in an if-you-were-me-would-you-let-it-go? expression and Allie gave up. "His plan is to bother me until I get tired of him and pay him off."

"This has happened before?"

"Not exactly." Allie sighed. "But kind of."

"How so?"

"When we divorced, he wanted a piece of the Lightning Creek in the settlement. Montana is not a community-property state and the ranch was never in my name, but he wanted part of my share. When he didn't get what he wanted... he started taking things from the ranch. A few of the things, like my grandfather's old tractor, we got back. The rest he sold. Some of the stuff, I encouraged him to take in an effort to get rid of him."

"Did he leave you alone?"

"After he lost his deputy job and moved."

"Now he's back."

"Apparently so. I don't know what happened with his job, but I wouldn't be surprised to find that he lost it due to his massive sense of entitlement. Anyway, now he has medical bills."

"And he wants you to co-sign a loan."

Allie lifted her chin from her hand. "He actually said to me that I owe him because he put five years of his life into this ranch and got nothing for his trouble. The only problem was that he all but destroyed the place over those five years."

"And I used his father as my real estate agent."

Allie made a dismissive gesture and settled back against his chest, stretching her leg out over his thighs. "I have nothing against Ray. He spoiled his son, but that's his only crime."

"Caused you some misery by doing that."

"As much my fault as his." She was quiet for a few seconds, then said, "I have never gotten over feeling stupid for falling in love with Kyle. I've spent a lot of time feeling bitter."

"At him or yourself?"

She shot him a surprised look. "At myself. Kyle is who he is. I should have seen that."

"At the ripe old age of twenty-two?"

"I expect more of myself, even at twenty-two—and don't say you're not the same. I know you are. You have high personal expectations."

One corner of his mouth curved. "And how do you know this?"

"I watched you from afar during high school. Watched you power through your classes. Did my best to keep up with you."

He shifted a little so that he could see her face. "Wait a minute... I was being intimidated by you and you were admiring me from afar?"

"I didn't say 'admiring,'" she said with a little sniff.

Jason hauled her all the way onto his chest,

cupping her ass with one hand. "How could you not admire me?"

Allie laughed and kissed his smiling lips. "All right. I was right there with the legion, admiring. But I also despised you for getting my scholarship."

"Sorry about that," he murmured as he traced the curve of her butt, making Allie shiver as his fingers dipped pleasantly lower.

"You've made up for it."

She felt him growing hard again against her thighs. He stroked the hair back from her face with his free hand and said, "Any chance I can make it up to you again?"

Allie closed her eyes as his fingers dipped even lower. "Yes," she finally said, her voice barely audible. "You definitely should make it up to me again." If she'd known how good he was at making things up to her, she would have started his penance a long time ago.

CHAPTER FIFTEEN

ALLIE WOKE WITH a start when Jason rolled over in his sleep, then she sighed and curled into him, enjoying the warmth of his big body and the feel of his firm ass pressed against her thighs. She slipped an arm over him and a moment later he took her hand in his, holding it loosely against his chest for a few seconds before slowly pulling it down to where he needed some attention. Allie smiled against his shoulder. The man was pretty much insatiable. As was she. Apparently they'd both had a long dry spell, although hers had been exponentially longer and drier.

Half an hour later, she was still smiling as Jason headed downstairs.

When he came back, he was carrying two cups of coffee. Allie propped herself up against the headboard and took both cups, carefully balancing them as he got into bed again. She handed him his cup and slowly sipped hers, closing her eyes as the coffee hit her tongue. Perfect.

"It's been a while since I started a day like

this," Jason murmured, pressing the length of his leg against hers.

Allie couldn't imagine how. Women had to be all over this guy. But she wasn't going to question the situation. She was simply going to enjoy, and the beauty part was that she could talk to him, let him know when she was starting to feel uncertain, and he would understand. Let her do what she needed to do. Maybe even talk things through…if she felt like talking. Allie had never been much of a talker. So much easier to hold it all in and carry on.

But for right now, she was taking Jason's advice. She'd handle matters moment by moment. Day by day.

That way she would never truly lose control of her life, her direction.

JASON HAD JUST gotten out of Allie's shower when he heard the car pull away and realized that Liz must have delivered Zach…and his truck was at the ranch a lot earlier than usual, parked in front of the house. The last thing he needed was for the kid, or his mom, to put two and two together and deduce that Jason was sleeping with the boss. But when Jason left the house fifteen minutes later, wearing a too-small hoodie that he'd borrowed from Allie, the kid didn't act as if he'd noticed anything.

He was waiting at the barn with the sprayer

and weed-attacking tools at the ready, looking chastened and preoccupied. The judge must have had a few words to say about the kid's actions.

"Did court go okay?" Jason asked, still trying to work the sleeves of the hoodie into a comfortable position over his biceps. Allie had washed his shirt earlier that morning, but it was still in the dryer. First chance he got, he'd head back to the house and put it on, so he didn't feel as if he were wearing a wetsuit.

Zach gave a small shrug. "As well as could be expected. It isn't going to help my scholarship chances any."

"So you're thinking about college?"

"Eventually."

Jason clapped him on the shoulder and left it at that. Sometimes it wasn't necessary to hammer a point home when it was sinking in all by itself.

Allie left for town shortly after Jason and Zach started working in the field. She still hadn't returned when lunch rolled around, but she'd said something about going for coffee with Liz and a lot of errands, so Jason tamped down his impatience to see her again. He went into the house to get his shirt out of the dryer and fill his water bottle while Zach went to his trailer to microwave a Hot Pocket for lunch. A car pulled in as he topped off the bottle and he headed back outside without changing his shirt, stopping on the porch when he realized that Allie's car wasn't the only vehicle in the yard. There was also a blue truck and Allie was having a standoff with the owner, her hands on her hips, her chin jutted out.

Instantly Jason was on his way down the walk toward the face-off. The guy, who had to be the infamous Kyle, jerked up his gaze as Jason's boots hit gravel.

Yeah, asshole. She's not alone.

He couldn't tell if Allie was glad to have backup or not, but regardless of her feelings, she had it.

She smiled tightly. "Kyle, this is Jason Hudson."

Kyle shifted his weight as he looked Jason up and down, then he gave an unsmiling nod.

"Hello, Kyle."

"Is there anything else?" Allie asked pointedly. Kyle shifted his gaze to her as Jason stepped closer. He didn't presume to touch her, but he got near enough that Kyle would get the message—he was dealing with two people, not just one.

"No." He turned and got into his truck, revving the engine after starting it and swinging into a wide arc.

Jason settled his hand on Allie's shoulder once Kyle was partway down the driveway.

"He followed me home," Allie said in a deadly voice. "Just to argue money again."

"This has got to stop."

"Agreed. I may have to see about a restraining order."

Jason's eyes narrowed as he watched the truck turn onto the road. "Maybe that won't be necessary now that he knows you have backup."

"I hope." Allie turned to him just as Zach came out of his trailer and started toward them. "Want to have dinner tonight?"

"I promised my dad pizza."

"He can eat pizza?"

"As long as he follows the salt restrictions. Special sauce and cheese. No meat."

"He must love that."

"Oh, trust me, he does." Allie laughed and Jason raised a hand to indicate to Zach that yes he would meet him at the gate. "The boss is coming. I'll try to stop by to see you before I go."

He started across the drive to where Zach was waiting for him, but he couldn't help shooting another glance at the plume of dust from Kyle's truck. As he'd said to Allie, this had to stop.

As IT TURNED OUT, he didn't get a chance to see Allie before he left. She was on the phone with one of her sisters and Kate called to ask Jason to pick up the pizza early. He waved at Allie from the porch, signaled that he had to go, then headed for his truck. Forty minutes later he was home and his dad was being remarkably well behaved.

"What happened?" he asked Kate in an undertone as he dropped ice cubes into glasses.

"I think he's realized that you may not be around for much longer."

"I haven't gotten the job yet."

"He's concerned."

"So now he behaves."

"Just like a little kid." Kate got out the plates and carried them in to set the TV trays in the living room. She called the Dobes and put them outside, since they had a habit of knocking over the trays and then devouring whatever hit the floor.

"Hey, Dad," Jason said as he came in carrying the drinks. He usually drank cola or club soda now when he watched TV with his father, since his dad couldn't drink until his medication was changed, and often wished for alcohol because of the effect hanging with his dad had on him. Oddly, he didn't feel like having a stress-reducing beer tonight. Apparently good sex had the same effect, only it lasted longer.

"JD." His dad automatically reached for the glass and took a long drink.

"How was your day?"

"About the same. Except I saw the shrink."

"Did you make him cry?"

Max slowly turned to meet Jason's innocent gaze and his lips twitched. "No. Not this time. I'll try harder next time."

Jason smiled broadly and then went back in

the kitchen to help Kate bring the pizza. They served Max, then the three of them settled in front of the baseball game.

"When do you think you'll hear about the job?" Max asked after almost two innings.

"It took them weeks to let me know I made the cut, so I don't know."

"Be sure to ask," Max said.

"I will." They watched another scoreless, rather boring inning, then Jason said, "You know, I can still fly home on long weekends. I'll do my damnedest to be here at least once a month. And you can come down to San Diego."

Max only nodded and Jason felt a stab of guilt, which he did his best to tamp down. This was a great career move and they both knew it.

Just as the game was ending, the Dobes went crazy outside and Kate went to look out the window. "Uncle Jimmy," she said.

Jason hoped that his dad and uncle hadn't cooked up one final double team, but apparently they hadn't. Jimmy settled in the extra chair, declared the pizza miserably bland and then started talking about the business to Max. He was only a couple sentences in when he looked up at Jason and said, "Don't worry, kid. We're not going to try to tap you to fill in anywhere. Besides, I hear you're leaving."

"I have to get the job first."

Jim waved his hand dismissively and Jason

took that as his cue to escape. He helped Kate haul the dishes back to the kitchen and load the dishwasher, then said, "I'm heading out for the night."

"Have fun," she said in a way that indicated she had an inkling of where he was going and why. But since he didn't talk to his sister about such matters, he simply nodded and headed out the door.

JASON CAME HOME late that night and he was surprised to see that Jim was still at the house... until he came inside and found his father and uncle sleeping in the side-by-side recliners. He let them be and went on down the hall to bed, wishing he could have stayed with Allie.

He woke up the next morning to the smell of bacon cooking. Uncle Jim was manning the stove and Max was sitting at the table.

"I don't think this is on your prescribed menu," Jason said as he poured himself a cup of coffee.

Max merely waved a hand and Jason let the matter drop.

"Two eggs or three, JD?"

"Three," he answered automatically. "So did you guys solve the world's problems last night?"

"Most of them," Jim said. "I still need to find a detail guy, since my guy quit yesterday, but other than that, I think we worked through things pretty well. Did you know that I'm going to run for city council?"

"I did not, but that's a great idea." Why his Uncle Jim hadn't thrown his hat into the political ring earlier was a mystery, since he had the perfect politician mindset.

"I thought so. It might help business, too."

Jason dug into his breakfast when Jim set it in front of him, eating as his dad and uncle talked campaign strategy, then an idea struck him.

"Hey." Both men turned to look at him. "I have something I want to run by you guys. Unorthodox, but it might help both of us—" he moved his finger between Jim and himself "—solve a problem."

Jim gave the scrambled eggs a stir, then said, "Shoot, kid. I'm all ears."

IT TOOK JASON a good half hour of driving around town before he spotted Kyle's truck in one of the many places Allie had told him her ex frequented. He finally found him at the café, where he was unlocking the door to his truck. Jason parked close by and got out of his truck. Kyle started fumbling for the door when Jason said his name.

"I understand you need money for medical bills," Jason said before Kyle could get the door open.

"I, uh…"

"That you're harassing Allie, hoping she'll pay you off to make you go away."

An indignant look crossed his face. "Did she say that?"

"I said that." Jason folded his arms over his chest. He had to give Kyle credit for standing his ground after taking that first backward step. "Do you want money?"

Kyle looked confused, as if he thought that Jason might be offering him money. He was. In a way. "Like you said, I have medical bills and no insurance to speak of."

Jason reached into his pocket and pulled out a card. "If you want that taken care of, meet me here."

Kyle hesitated, then reached out to take the card. He glanced down at it, then back up at Jason, looking bewildered.

"I'm heading over there now. I expect you to be right behind me."

Kyle did as told, following Jason to Jim's car lot. Once there, Jason gestured for Kyle to get out of his truck and walk with him to the dealership showroom.

"Jim!" Jason bellowed as soon as he was inside the glassed-in room. His uncle appeared from a pine-paneled office.

"Jason. What a surprise."

"Meet your newest detail man. This is Kyle Largent."

"I know Kyle," Jimmy said with a smile. He'd agreed to take on Kyle on a contingency basis earlier that day and now he held out his hand to welcome him aboard.

Kyle slowly extended his hand and Jimmy gave him a hearty handshake.

"Good to have you. Now, you'll start in the detail department, but after a few weeks we'll cycle you into sales and see how you do. You can make some good money in commissions, win trips and such."

Kyle perked up at the words *good money*.

"You'll have to kiss some ass, of course, but that's the sales game." Jimmy beamed at him. "I think you'll do well."

Kyle straightened his stance. "Uh, how much does the detailing pay?"

"It's decent. Come on into the office and I'll show you the salary scale, the benefits and you can fill out your W-2."

"Uncle Jim? I'd like to speak to Kyle for just a quick minute before I take off."

"Sure thing."

Jimmy went to the nearest show model and wiped a few smudges with his handkerchief.

"Here's the deal," Jason said to Kyle in a low voice. "This job will pay your medical bills easily. And you can make a lot of money, but if you screw up and get your ass fired, if you start harassing Allie again, there will be hell to pay. Do you get me?"

Kyle swallowed. "I get you."

"I'm doing you a favor, man. One you probably don't deserve. Do not make me regret it."

"No regrets. Got it."

Jason gave him a stern look then raised his hand at his uncle. "I gotta run, Jim. I'll see you soon."

"Bye, Jason."

Jim gave him a wave and then gestured for Kyle to follow him into the office. Jason got into his truck and started the engine. Hopefully this was one problem solved. All it had cost him was Kyle's first two months pay and a smiling photograph of himself in his jersey that Jimmy planned to use as part of his new pull-'em-in-off-the-streets campaign. Jimmy wasn't as happy as he would have been had Jason come to work full-time, but he was satisfied. And hopefully this would keep Kyle busy until Allie left the Lightning Creek.

ALLIE HAD DINNER almost finished when Jason showed up at her door. He walked in and kissed her lips, then asked, "Spaghetti?"

"And meatballs. Garlic bread. Salad."

"Great last meal," he said on a dry note.

"Worried about your interview?" Stating the

obvious after his first experience with the phone interview, but Allie wondered if he needed to talk.

"A little," Jason said in a voice that made it clear he was grossly understating the matter.

Allie poured two glasses of red wine. "You'll do well. You have charisma."

"I think they want experience."

"And you've come up with ways to make up for lack of experience. Right?" She handed him a glass as she spoke.

"Yeah. Coach and I have been communicating, coming up with ideas. We'll see if they work, I guess." He pulled in a breath that made his shoulders rise and then fall. "I saw Kyle today."

Allie stiffened as her gaze flashed up. "You did?"

"Sought him out, actually." He set his wine down on the counter, untouched. "Found him gainful employment."

"You what?"

"Got him a job with Uncle Jim. He's going to detail cars and work his way into a sales position."

Allie let out a sputtering breath and set her own wine down. "He'll never last."

"He'll last until he gets those bills paid. We, uh, had a talk."

Allie wasn't going to ask about the talk. "I don't like this, Jason."

He seemed genuinely surprised. "Why?"

She exhaled and said, "This is a matter for me and Kyle to work through."

"You and Kyle and the sheriff from the sounds of things."

"I appreciate what you're trying to do, but I don't need a white knight."

His expression clouded. "Couldn't you just say thank you, Allie?"

She pushed the hair back from her forehead in a distracted gesture, then let it fall again. "I could, yes. But..."

He settled his hands on her shoulders. "I didn't want him bothering you while I was gone."

"If you get this job, you're going to be gone permanently." Her mouth quirked. "Except for the long weekends you promised your dad," she muttered.

"Allie, look at me."

She did. Big mistake. His expression was so damned sincere as he stared down at her. "Don't say you did this for me when you did it for you."

"I did it for you and I think you're secretly glad, but you freak if you think anyone is taking control of any part of your life."

"I'm not freaking."

His grip tightened ever so slightly on her shoulders. "And I'm not taking control."

She arched an eyebrow at him. "Next time ask me, okay?"

He dropped his hands and looked past her for a

moment. When he looked back, he said,
You're right."

Allie stood stiffly for another few s
then took a step forward and slowly wra
arms around his waist, letting her cheek
rest against his solid chest. "This is a g
tion, Jason. Thank you. But next time,
in the loop."

Because the one thing she couldn't handle was
to have someone directing her life without her
input. She'd put up with that for way too long,
and she wasn't going there again.

Jason's arms closed around her. "I have a big
learning curve with you."

She nodded against his shirt. "It's not that
hard. Before you throw money at a situation to
make it go away, check with me first."

"Throw money?" She leaned back and met his
gaze, saw the conflict there, the urge to argue
with her, and then he gave a small nod. "I guess
you're right."

"Yeah," she said simply. "I am." And what she
wouldn't give to be able to throw money at a situation and make it go away—however, she wanted
to decide how she was throwing that money and
what her expected outcome would be.

He stroked a hand over her hair, then put her
away from him and looked down at her. "I don't
want to argue tonight."

"Arguing would be a bad way to spend this

night," Allie agreed. A very bad way. Especially when she had no idea how many more nights she was going to have with this man. She rose up on her toes and met his lips. "So let's consider the matter settled."

THE MATTER MIGHT have been settled, but as Jason sat in the small Bozeman airport, waiting for his flight to San Diego, he kept thinking about Allie's allegation that he threw money at problems to make them go away.

Not totally true, because if so, he would have hired a full-time caretaker for his dad long ago.

But it was a little bit true—okay, a lot true— and the realization bothered him. He had money, why not use it to fix problems?

He put aside the newspaper he'd been reading.

Good question. Maybe because that made it easier to dodge the problem than deal with it?

Well, how the hell was he supposed to have dealt with Kyle and get him off Allie's back? Rehabilitation? He snorted at the thought and the older lady sitting across from him looked up, then did a double take.

"Are you Dolph Lundgren?" she asked, wide-eyed.

"Dolph who?"

She gave her head a shake. "Sorry. You're too young." She smiled and went back to reading her phone.

Jason looked up Dolph on his phone and decided to feel complimented, then he turned his thoughts back to Allie.

If he had run his get-Kyle-a-job plan past Allie, she would have balked. But she was right—he couldn't say he'd only done it for her, when he felt so much better after getting the guy out of her hair.

Life with Allie was complicated and he sensed it was about to get more so.

His flight was called and Jason followed the lady who'd mistaken him for Dolph to the boarding line. She looked over her shoulder at him and then made an O with her lips.

"You catch pizzas."

Jason gave the woman a weary smile. "Yes. I catch pizzas."

One of his many talents, but probably not one that would get him this job.

SHORTLY AFTER ARRIVING at his hotel, and before he'd had time to open his suitcase, Jason got a call from his former coach, who was waiting downstairs in the bar for their planning session. They'd emailed back and forth over the past week, but Jason not only wanted to buy dinner for the guy who'd guided his college football career, he wanted face time.

He wanted to talk about Pat.

"Pat is in a place only he can get himself out

of," Coach said when Jason brought up the subject before they started their strategy session. "You can't do that for him."

"I think if he would let me talk to him, that maybe we could at least get to a point where he'd call me when he needed to. Or I could call him." As he used to do.

The coach speared the loose olive at the bottom of his glass. "I don't think so. He's bitter and he's jealous."

Jason massaged his forehead. He wasn't ready to let go. Pat had helped him so damned much. Yes, he'd gone seriously off the rails during his first year of retirement, but that was what frustrated Jason. He was in a position to be there for his friend, who didn't want anyone there.

"He's not the same guy who helped you with your career."

"And my personal problems."

"Not the same guy."

"Then maybe I can get to know the new guy."

"You won't like him."

"We were friends for ten years." The coach had only known Pat for four. They'd been intense years, but still, less than half of Jason's time with the man.

"What do you want to do?"

"I want you to take me to his place."

"And what? Join you in an intervention?"

That had been one of Jason's ideas, but it

seemed too much like ganging up on the guy. "Or maybe wait in the car?"

"I'll give you his address," Coach finally said. "But you're on your own. Pat wants to stew in his misery, and experience tells me that no one can change a person in that frame of mind." Coach popped the olive into his mouth and chewed before downing the last of his drink. "Right now, we need to focus on other things." He met Jason's gaze. "You belong on that coaching staff, so you need to get this job to work into it."

Jason wanted to be on that staff...he wanted Pat there, too. Like old times. The two of them working together. His mouth twisted sardonically. When had he become such a fairy-tale kind of guy?

Allie would have said it was because he'd led a fairy-tale life.

"I've been meaning to ask...have you done any volunteer work with the local football programs or anything? That would be a plus."

Jason shook his head. "I spent my free time on the ranch after my dad got back on his feet."

Coach gave his head a bemused shake. "I know your family is in Montana, but I never thought there were cows involved. My uncle had a dairy. Smelly business."

"It's not a family ranch," Jason explained. "It belongs to a friend." A woman who was now so deeply under his skin that he was having a hard imagining life without her. "She needed help demolishing a barn and I had free time, so I helped her out." He tapped the sides of his glass with his fingers. "One thing led to another and I eventually learned a lot about the operation, although they assured me I'd only been exposed to the tip of the ranching iceberg."

"Did you like it? I never saw you as an animal kind of guy."

"I spent more time spraying weeds than tending to animals..." Although he'd seen them both into the world and out of it. "But I did help with the calving to a certain extent. There was a lot to do. A lot to learn. It was kind of cool not knowing what was going to happen day to day, what with the weather and the animals." And Allie.

"Huh. So tell me—did the place stink?"

Jason choked on his drink. "No. It smelled pretty good."

"Dairies stink. Silage, I think."

"I'll avoid them."

Coach narrowed his eyes at Jason. "What do you see yourself doing in five years, Jason?"

Another practice interview question, one they'd covered previously. But it took Jason a split second too long to answer. "Coaching Brandt football."

The coach's gaze remained both narrowed and thoughtful. "Amen to that."

Jason took a slow sip of his drink. The coach

wanted him at Brandt and until that very moment, Jason had been utterly convinced that
he wanted to work there, too. Why this crazy
moment of doubt? Because they'd been talking
about the ranch, which in turn made him think
of Allie. He'd finally broken through, and now
that he had gained her trust, he wanted more time
with her. A lot more time.

It could be done. One hurdle at a time.

"Whatever you do—" the coach's voice jerked
Jason back to the present "—do not see Pat before the interview. You don't want to go in all
pissed off."

"I agree."

Coach pulled out his phone and flipped through
his contacts, then held the phone out for Jason to
see. "This is where he lives now. He moved a few
weeks ago. His sister is living with him now."

Jason keyed the address into his phone.

"I'm glad to hear he's not by himself."

"He's alone," Coach said abruptly, making
Jason wonder if he really were wasting his time.
Regardless, he had to give it a shot. Coach signaled the server for another round and Jason figured what the hell. He didn't actually interview
until the next day and alcohol would help him
sleep.

After the drinks arrived, Coach pulled a paper
out of his pocket and unfolded it, placing it on the

table between them. "This is the lineup," he said. Jason leaned closer to read the list of six names.

"Now Laurel's going to be your biggest hurdle. He's all about hard-line experience. However, he has a weak spot…"

CHAPTER SIXTEEN

WHEN JASON WALKED under the stone arch at the entrance of the Brandt campus, he felt as if he were walking into the locker room before a play-off game. Mentally, he was ready. Beyond ready. The coach had lined him out, helped him plot strategy. He knew how to address Laurel's concerns and those of the other committee members. He knew who was most likely to favor him and who he needed to be on guard against.

He'd shoved all thoughts of his dad, Pat and Allie out of his head as he walked into the athletic department offices. He was here to win and that meant focusing on the goal.

"Mr. Hudson." A tall woman with short dark hair came out from behind her desk and offered her hand. "Amanda Morehouse."

"I recognize your voice," Jason said.

"Excellent." She smiled and waved him to a seat. "It'll be just a minute or two and they'll be ready for you. We have one committee member on video conference and the rest are here in person."

"Any advice?" he asked, more for something to say than anything.

Amanda thought for a moment, then said, "Your strength is in your offense."

It always had been. Jason smiled. "Thank you."

A moment later the doors to the inner sanctum opened and Amanda motioned for him to go inside.

Jason's two-hour interview lasted only an hour, but not because he'd done poorly. Thanks to the coach and his own late night online research, he was well prepared to answer all questions, counter all objections to his lack of training and make suggestions on improving the efficiency of the job he was applying for. His college GPA didn't hurt, either. He'd managed to be a student and an all-star, which spoke to his ability to multitask and tackle new challenges.

He'd even managed to work his volunteer ranch experience into the conversation, using it as an example of his adaptability. He didn't know how effective that was, but every little bit helped when a guy had no work history, and, strange as it was, the ranch was his first job experience ever. Before that, training and practice had filled his time from junior high through college. When other kids had been working at McDonald's, he'd been lifting weights or running.

So his privilege paid off in some ways and hampered him in others.

Just another hurdle to cross.

"As I see it, Mr. Hudson," Dr. Laurel had said just before the interview ended, "as a former professional ball player, you're used to doors opening easily." He let the words hang between them, watching Jason closely. Jason had no idea what response the guy expected, but after dealing with Allie, this attitude was nothing shocking or new.

"Those days are long gone," Jason said. "I have to make up for lost time in the professional world and right now I'm working hard to do that. I have no qualms about starting low and working my way up."

A couple of the committee members exchanged glances, then Dr. Laurel thanked him for his time and handshakes ensued.

A moment later, Amanda told him that he'd hear from them in a matter of days and said goodbye. Once the office door closed behind him, Jason drew in a deep breath and then checked his watch. A little too early to call Allie, so he'd head back to his hotel and prepare for his last obstacle before heading home the next day—ambushing Pat and trying to talk sense into him.

EVEN WITH ZACH on the ranch, happily managing everything that he could find to manage, the place felt empty. Allie missed Jason. A lot. But she was not going to panic because she missed the guy. He was her first lover in years and he'd been a daily fixture on the ranch for the past couple of months. Of course, the place seemed empty without him.

She planted more of the garden while he was gone, changing up the rows from the way she'd always had them before. Corn was no longer on the north side of the garden and beans were no longer on the south. Small changes, unimportant changes, but changes all the same. Allie needed to become more comfortable with change, and that was her frame of mind when she called her mother in Florida late Tuesday afternoon.

"Is all well on the ranch?"

"The ranch is fine."

"I guess I meant are you doing well on the ranch?"

"Better than when I lived here before," Allie said. "A lot better."

"Good to hear."

Her mother was well aware of Allie's feelings about her childhood home, and Allie had long suspected her mother's feelings mirrored her own. It wasn't as if Anne Brody Reyes had had a great time there, losing her husband and barely hanging on through the rough times that followed.

"Mom, I'm not going to pursue teaching." There. It was out.

"What?"

"At least not unless I can find a secondary art position and right now that seems nigh impossible."

"But...you got your elementary degree so that you could work in education."

"I'm painting again."

"Lovely, but—"

"I think I'll be happier if I work at a job that requires less of a personal commitment and pursue my art career on the side. At least until I hit a point where I might be able to pursue it full-time."

A long silence ensued and Allie found herself squirming. "It isn't like my education degree will go bad. It's just... I'm not an elementary teacher. Maybe secondary, but not elementary. And now, while I have no commitments, seems like a perfect time to pursue a reckless venture."

Yes. She was going to take a risk—just as soon as she got a steady job.

"Well...I guess. I mean, it isn't like you're running off to join a cult or something."

Allie gave a small laugh. "I'm feeling good about this decision."

"In that case, I wish you well."

And was probably going to wait and see if Allie came to her senses rather than waste her breath right now. Allie knew her mom well because they were very, very similar.

After ending the call, she poured a glass of

wine and had just taken the cover off her palette when the phone rang again. She knew without looking that it was Jason.

"How'd the interview go?" she asked as soon as she heard his voice.

"I think I have a shot."

"Congratulations."

"Thanks." He cleared his throat and changed the subject. "How are you doing?"

"Everything's the same as when you left." Two whole days ago.

"Kyle?"

"Haven't seen him. How's San Diego?"

"It feels like a different planet here. A different world."

"One you like, I hope."

"Oh, yeah. I like it. It's just...different."

"Well, you know what they say about going home."

"I think Montana is home."

"No. You only lived here for two years before taking off for college. You're a California boy."

"You're a snob, Allie."

"Guilty," she said with a smile. "And now you can tell me what's bothering you."

There was a brief silence, as if he were going to deny that there was a reason for his flat tone of voice. "I'm going to see Pat tomorrow before I catch my plane home."

"Good luck with that."

"Yeah. Coach told me not to go."

"Then why are you?"

"He's dealing with stuff, Allie."

"Jealousy?" She knew all about that.

"Among other things."

Allie tamped down her frustration. Jason had to handle the matter in his own way, but having dealt with a bitter person, namely Kyle, she had little patience. Even if said bitter person was in a wheelchair.

"I'm with Coach on this one, but if you must go, don't let him guilt-trip you."

Because even though Jason was about as centered as anyone she knew, from their brief discussions on the subject, she knew that this Pat character was his weak spot. And Jason was a rescuer.

"I'm just going to open the door to future conversations."

"Great. But if he gets difficult, you might just give him that speech about heads and asses."

"Thanks, Allie. I'll keep that advice in mind."

PAT'S GROUND-LEVEL APARTMENT was part of a well-manicured cul-de-sac neighborhood. Jason parked in front of the building and double-checked the apartment number before ringing the buzzer. A moment later the door swung open and Delia Madison frowned at him. Then she smiled. "Jason."

He gave Pat's sister a quick hug. "How are you?" Delia had also attended Brandt and they'd spent a lot of time together back in the day.

"Doing okay. You must be here to see Pat? He didn't say anything to me."

"Because he doesn't know."

Delia's smile faltered. "Out back," she said, waving toward the patio doors leading out into a private garden. It was a nice place, but nothing like the mansion Pat had once owned.

"Hey," Jason said as he slid the door open.

Pat's head jerked around and then he scowled. "What the hell?"

"Yeah. Good to see you, too."

Pat's mouth clamped shut and Jason felt like telling him to stop being so fricking proud, but he didn't. Instead he said, "I interviewed at Brandt."

"Thought that wasn't going to happen."

"A guy dropped out."

Jason sat in a white wrought-iron chair next to Pat's wheelchair. A towel was draped loosely over Pat's lap, but Jason could still see how atrophied his friend's once powerful legs had become.

"If I got the job at Brandt, and can arrange it, would you consider doing an internship there?" One of the perks of the job, or maybe it was one of the duties, was that Jason would select and train interns to help the coaching and administrative staff.

"Little premature, isn't it?"

"I said *if*, and since you don't answer my calls or texts, I figured I'd see you face-to-face before flying home."

Pat looked very much like he wanted to tell him to go to hell, but he didn't. Instead he shook his head. "Go there and have people looking at me? Saying there's the guy who couldn't handle real life? I don't think so."

Jason sucked in a breath. "When I had difficulties with my head on the field, when I was missing my catches, you helped me straighten things out."

Pat gave a small shrug.

"When I was drawing into myself because, for the first time ever, I wasn't the best, you told me to get a grip and stop feeling sorry for myself."

Pat's eyes widened angrily. "I know where this is going and don't you dare."

"I'm daring. This is your life. You made it. Now do something with it and stop hiding."

"It's none of your business what I do."

"Yeah, it is. Because I owe you."

"You owe me nothing. We're even."

Jason stood and walked over the chair, then crouched down so they were at eye level. "I am not the enemy, Pat. I think we both know who the enemy is. When you want to face reality, give me a call."

He stood then and headed for the door to the house, which was cracked open. Delia was just inside, openly eavesdropping. She slid the glass open and after Jason walked into the air-conditioned room, she shut it behind him.

"Good try," she said. "Coach tried, too." Her jaw tightened briefly before she said, "*I'll* try to knock sense into him, but no promises."

"Yeah." Jason smiled grimly, then lightly kissed Delia's cheek. "You're a good sister, Del. Call me if you need anything."

ALLIE WAS ON her knees in the garden when Jason's truck pulled into the drive, shooting to hell her plan of looking great when he showed. It wasn't as if he'd never seen her dusty and disheveled before.

He parked the truck and came to meet her at the garden, taking her into his arms and kissing her long and hard.

"Any new calves?" he asked.

Allie laughed. "One. Now we're done for the season." She smoothed a hand over his face, then kissed him again.

Jason tilted his head toward the garden. "Looks good."

"Yes. Better than it looked the last time I planted it, but I didn't properly care for it then."

One corner of her mouth quirked. "I was fighting to survive." She turned back toward him. "When will you hear?"

"A matter of days."

"Did you talk to Pat?" His expression clouded over, giving her the answer. "That bad?"

"He has issues."

Which were hurting Jason and she hated seeing that. They started for the house with Jason's arm still loosely slung over her shoulders. "Is Zach around?"

"He's at that class he was ordered to take. Liz's dropping him by later tonight. Have you been home yet?"

Jason stopped on the porch and took her face in his hands, leaning down to first kiss her, then lightly nip her lower lip, sending a stab of need slicing through her. "I thought I'd stop here first. Say hello."

"Yes," Allie said as she gently nipped him back. "Hello is definitely in order."

JASON SHOWED UP for work early the next day and life on the Lightning Creek continued as it had before he'd left for the interview. Zach lined him out and Allie went to school and Jason realized as he strode out into the field that if he couldn't eventually coach football, he'd be quite comfortable working on a ranch. Not just owning one, but working on one.

Of course, he'd have to have a manager to tell him what to do, because he didn't have a clue. But the actual work—he loved it.

And he was beginning to suspect he loved Allie, too. What had started as an attraction and a challenge had grown to feel like a partnership and...something more. That something more, he suspected, was love, plain and simple. Which made him glad that she didn't want to stay on the Lightning Creek, because that made it all the more possible that she might go with him if he got the job. Together they could test the waters. She was at the perfect point in her life to do that.

Yes, things could easily fall into place and he felt pretty damned good about life.

He felt even better later that day when the call came in from Amanda Morehouse, offering him the job of assistant to the associate athletic director of Brandt University. The pay would be less than advertised, due to his lack of experience, but he would get full benefits and a yearly bonus.

"I accept," Jason said. He'd just realized his goal while standing in the middle of a Montana cattle pasture. Life was funny sometimes.

"I'll send you the paperwork."

"Excellent," Jason said, beating Amanda to the punch. He hung up and dropped the phone into his pocket. He was looking forward to telling Allie the news.

WHEN ALLIE GOT HOME, Jason had the Jameson bottle on the sideboard along with the fancy crystal on-the-rocks glasses he'd bought in the airport on the flight back from San Diego. The woman he loved couldn't continue to drink whiskey from a juice glass.

Allie walked into the house and stopped, her gaze swinging from him to the new glasses and back to him. "You got the job, didn't you?"

"Yeah."

"I knew you would." But even though she smiled back, she didn't look all that happy. He hoped that was a good sign—a sign that she didn't want him to leave. "I thought a toast was in order."

"I'm all for that." She dropped her tote bag next to the door and crossed the room to take the glass he offered. "Nice."

"They're yours so that you can retire the juice glasses."

"Thank you." She gingerly touched the rim of her glass to his. "Congratulations."

He gestured with his head and Allie followed him out onto the porch, where they sat side by side on the sun-warmed top step. Jason sipped and looked out over the ranch he'd once tried to make his own. A ranch he'd truly come to love, even though Allie didn't. Every couple had their differences.

"I'm going to miss this place. You should have let me buy it."

"My sisters would have killed me. Besides, aren't you supposed to be back frequently?"

"Supposed to be. But it won't be the same as it's been while I was working here. Practically living here, really."

"You did spend a lot of time here."

He gave her a long serious look. "I wonder why?"

"It wasn't me to begin with."

"It was always you."

Her eyes narrowed. "Really?"

"No other reason."

"Except escaping your dad."

"I could have done that in other ways."

Allie leaned her shoulder against his. "True."

Jason set his hand on her knee, enjoying the feel of her silky skin under his fingers. "I know these are early days, but I thought I'd throw something out for you to think about."

"And that is…?"

"Eventually moving to California with me." Her muscles instantly tightened beneath his hand. "I'm not talking instantly. I know you have a commitment here on the ranch, but I was thinking…eventually."

She leaned back, putting space between them. "You know that would be difficult for me."

"Why?"

"Because it's expensive to live there."

"I thought we would live together."

"If we live together, then I have to be dependent on you until I get a job."

"So?"

"I can't get into a situation where if things go bad, I'm helpless. I've been there before. I can't do it again."

"If things go bad, you can fly back to Montana. Live on the ranch." It seemed so sensible and easy, but he'd been ready for Allie to balk. And she was.

"I'm...not ready for anything like that."

"So that leaves us..."

She gave him a cool, almost perplexed look. "With you taking this job you worked so hard for and me figuring out life here." He started to shake his head and she touched his lips lightly. "Jason, I'm not ready to start a serious relationship. If I move with you, that makes it serious."

"I've been reading things wrong here? I don't think so."

"How are you reading them?"

"I'm reading them as you once again letting your past stand in the way of your future."

Allie stood. "Read it as you will." She turned then and walked into the house, letting the screen door bang shut. He got to his feet and followed, leaving his glass sitting on the opposite side of the step from hers. Allie could run, but she was not going to hide until they sorted this out.

ALLIE DID HER best to keep her game face on as the screen door opened and shut behind her and she turned to face a very angry Jason. She raised her chin, ready to do battle. Of course, her past was keeping her from moving forward. People learned from the past and avoided future errors.

Right now, during early days, as he'd called them, everything felt right about being with him. But she knew about the bliss of early days, and she also knew that she couldn't move to California and be dependent on him this early in their relationship. She was too cautious for that and she didn't see how he could blame her for being that way.

"This is too much at one time. Moment by moment, remember?"

"Screw moment by moment. That's no longer the point."

"What is the point?"

"I want to hear why you think being with me would be a repeat of your relationship with Kyle."

"Because of me. I'm afraid to need you, all right? I love being with you, but I am terrified of needing. Needing means that I'll do things out of character. I *needed* Kyle. *Kyle*, for pity's sake. I put up with things out of fear that I should never have put up with."

"That was Kyle. This is me."

"It wasn't Kyle. It was *me* and *my* needs and *my* fear of loss clouding *my* judgment. Moment by moment I can do. Anything else…" She shook her head. "You're asking for too much, Jason."

"Well, this was one hell of a homecoming," he said, rubbing a hand over the back of his neck.

"I'm sorry." And she was. Sorry that push had to come to shove so soon. She'd thought they'd have more time to simply enjoy one another without real life butting in.

"Me, too." There was weariness in his voice and Allie felt the gulf between them widening as he fell silent. But what could she say?

It was Jason who broke the silence. "I need to go. I'll…catch up with Zach later. Explain things to him."

"I understand." Allie swallowed the lump in her throat, told herself that this was merely the two of them facing the truth. It was. Sometimes the truth hurt.

No. It did more than hurt—it tore you apart inside.

Jason went out the door without a word. Allie stood where she was until she heard the truck start, then she sank down onto the sofa and let the tears come. A few tears now were better than days' worth later.

MAX TOOK JASON'S new job a lot better than Allie had. But Max didn't have the baggage Allie did; he had different baggage that was easier to work with. Still, it was a difficult conversation, convincing his stubborn father that he wasn't abandoning him forever.

"I know you hate California, but there are some great golf courses. I'll fly you down when I can't make it home. You and Jim, if you want."

Max let out a long sigh and muted the television, which had been playing in the background. "You didn't make it home all that often while you were playing."

"Gee," Jason said dryly, "I wonder why."

"I know why," Max snapped. "I was just hoping that once you retired I'd see more of you."

"We'll spend a lot of time together, Dad. I promise. I want to spend time together, too." He smiled a little. "Someone's got to take the heat off Kate."

Max waved his hand dismissively. "You still looking to buy property here?"

"Investment property."

"Not living property?"

"I'm going to take things slowly right now. Concentrate on the job. One thing at a time."

"You always were a goal-focused kid." Max turned the volume back up on the television.

"Learned from the best. And when I come back, I thought I could stay here with you."

"That would work."

Jason stayed in the recliner next to his father until Max fell asleep and then he made his way out to the kitchen to make a sandwich. Kate had taken refuge in the garage while Jason talked with Max, supposedly going through storage boxes, and she'd yet to surface. Jason made two sandwiches anyway. Hiding could build an appetite.

He was on his way to the garage when his cell phone rang. Pat.

Wonder of wonders.

"Yeah," Jason said.

"Coach told Delia that you got the job."

"I did." And since Pat wasn't growling out his words, maybe he'd called to congratulate him.

"You said something about an internship."

Jason's tense muscles relaxed an iota. Maybe something good would come out of the evening.

"Yes. I have the opportunity to bring an intern on board to work with me as part of the program I oversee and I thought you might be interested."

"Yeah?"

It was the first positive note he'd heard in Pat's voice in a long, long time. "You'd shadow me and when something permanent opened up, you'd have a shot at it."

"How much will I be paid as an intern?"

"Uh…it's not a paying position. It's a way to get a foot in the door."

"What?" The word dropped like a stone.

"It's a start, Pat. A way to work into a job." Because right now he was fairly certain that Pat didn't have a job.

"It's a way for them to get my expertise for free."

Jason's temples were starting to pound. "That's not what it's about."

"Not interested," Pat said coldly.

"Think about it." Jason spoke from between gritted teeth to keep from giving Pat more helpful advice regarding his head and his ass.

"Done thinking."

"Me, too." Jason hung up the phone, then turned to see Kate leaning against the doorjamb.

"Rough night?"

"You have no idea."

"Want a drink?"

Jason almost said no, then realized he might not have all that much sharing-a-drink time with his sister in the future. "Sure."

She opened the junk drawer and dug around until she found a key, which she held up.

"The good liquor?"

"Desperate times. Besides, Dad isn't supposed to be drinking the stuff." She went into the living room and came back a moment later with one of the better bottles of Scotch. She pulled the stopper and took a deep sniff. "Oh, yeah. This will do the trick."

She poured a generous two fingers, then touched Jason's glass with her own. "To spilling your guts."

"I'm not—"

She raised a hand. "Don't even try to resist. Just...spill."

"Spill. Right." Jason took a drink, barely noticing the excellent after notes of the eighteen-year-old Islay Scotch as it slid smoothly down his throat, warming him. "Where to begin?" he hedged.

Kate watched him over her glass with a sisterly no-nonsense expression.

"I got the job."

"I know that."

"I asked Pat if he'd be interested in interning, and as soon as he discovered it was unpaid he refused to consider it—even though it would put him in position for a paid job in the future."

Kate made a face. "Pat is his own worst enemy. Nothing you can do about that."

Jason shook his head. Kate didn't know how many times Pat had helped him through.

"What about Allie?"

Jason gave his sister a hard look, took in her mild yet determined expression. She wasn't going to let this go—not unless he got tough. What the hell? Why shouldn't she know? "I asked Allie to come with me, so that we could continue what we started. No go."

"It is a little early."

He set his glass down and leaned back in his chair, assuming a relaxed position even though every muscle in his body was tight. "I know what's going to happen. I'll go down there and get buried in the job—"

"Because that's the way you do things."

"It is. I won't lie. And I want Allie there with me, so when I do have time, we can spend it together."

"And she..."

"Has issues with that."

Silence hung for a long moment, then Kate said, "And that's all I'm getting?"

He raised an eyebrow at her. "That's it."

Kate swirled the Scotch in her glass, staring thoughtfully at the amber liquid. "This thing between the two of you, it seems to have gotten serious fast."

"It did."

She raised her gaze. "Is it possible that it might get un-serious just as fast?"

Jason shook his head. "I don't see that happening."

CHAPTER SEVENTEEN

THE WEEKS CRAWLED by after school let out. Allie did not apply for either of the two elementary jobs that were posted, and she didn't make the cut to interview for the community-college administrative-assistant positions. She sent out another round of applications and it was once again a waiting game. Ironically, Kyle was still working at the Hudson dealership—thriving there, actually, and hadn't bothered her once since Jason had gotten him the position. Allie could only wish him luck in his new job. As long as he was employed, he'd leave her alone.

Now that Jason was gone, she helped Zach around the ranch during the days, and in the evenings she painted. She'd secured a space in a small Bozeman gallery and put five paintings on commission there. One sold within a week for what seemed like an obscene amount of money—although it was a much more reasonable amount once the gallery took its cut—and Allie began to feel as if she could actually make some extra money doing what she loved.

Now she just had to find something steady to pay the bills and she'd be okay. And until then, she had the ranch—the ranch that felt so empty without Jason there.

She missed him. Ached for him.

Was afraid to contact him.

How fair would it be to start something again, only to find that she was incapable of following through? She'd skewered him once. Damned if she'd do it again. She was flawed when it came to relationships. Afraid to commit. Afraid to need. Knee-jerk, gut-level fear was hard to overcome. She knew because she was trying.

So she took out her frustrations by working tirelessly around the ranch—not in the way she'd done when she and Kyle had lived there, and she'd been trying to keep up with his unfinished projects and new ideas while working a full-time job to bring in enough money to keep him from draining the ranch account. And not in the way she'd worked when she'd been propping up her mother and caring for her sisters while the ranch refused to produce enough hay or cattle to provide a viable income in a sliding economy.

She was no longer working out of a sense of desperation or in a bid to sidestep disaster. She was working to work, to keep her hands and her mind busy. And she couldn't say she was unhappy doing that—for the first time in a long time, the ranch did not feel like an enemy. It gave her something to focus on other than what she was going to do for a living and what had happened between her and Jason.

She and Zach fertilized, weeded, cleaned and painted from dawn to dusk, and, despite the lack of rain, the place was starting to look more as it had when her dad managed it.

Thankfully, her long days exhausted her to the point that she fell asleep quickly every night. Now if she could only stop dreaming.

That was probably asking too much.

THE BEAUTY OF being single was that Jason had a lot of time and energy to pour into his new job. Good thing, because there was a big learning curve. Ironically, even though he'd come to Brandt to work his way into the football program, he seemed to be involved in every sport except football. They were stacking on the work and if Jason didn't have his evenings free, he would have been drowning. He needed to hire his intern soon, but had been putting it off in the futile hope that Pat would come around. He'd called Delia, told her that he could probably delay hiring for another week or two, but then he had to fill the position. He still wanted Pat.

The down side of being single was that Jason didn't want to be single. He wanted a woman by his side; a very specific woman who needed to learn to trust herself. It was hard to accept, but there wasn't a lot Jason could do about that. This was all on Allie.

Jason told himself to give her time, even though he suspected that she was never going to move to California. Maybe that was part of the reason why, even though his new position was challenging and interesting, he wasn't feeling his usual drive. That and the fact that he was still in learning mode, struggling to keep his head above water. It hadn't taken him long to discover that nine to five could be brutal in a way that football never was.

So many things had changed in his life in a short period of time and he'd yet to deal with all of them. Once he found his footing, he'd be able to focus on the goal, regain his drive. Take care of other areas of his life that he was neglecting. He hadn't even furnished his apartment yet beyond a bed, a sofa and an entertainment center. Who had time to do this stuff?

When he wasn't working on schedules or athlete eligibility or compliance, he was down on the field, watching the low-key summer practices, getting to know the players, reconnecting with old coaches and getting to know the new ones. Everyone knew why he was there, and most were good with it, but some of the younger offensive coaches kept an eye on him, as if expecting him to jump in with unwelcome suggestions and comments. Jason kept his mouth shut and his demeanor respectful and some of the more standoffish guys were loosening up. He went for beer with them on Fridays and then he'd go home to his lonely apartment and watch tapes or catch up on the news. He talked to his dad and Kate a couple times a week and thought about getting a dog.

Most of all he missed Allie.

And hell, he missed Pat, too. They lived in the same city and the guy wouldn't even see him, which tore him up; but just as with Allie, there was little he could do about it. He was going to have to hire an intern soon and if Pat wouldn't do the job, then he was going to have to accept that, too.

He seemed to be doing a hell of a lot of accepting lately.

Jason walked out onto his balcony and stared off at the distant Pacific. The air was different than in Montana. Warmer, moister, even though the city edged up to a desert, and there were none of the pungent ranch odors that he'd come to appreciate. The air wasn't the same. Not as full of hope and promise and challenge.

Shaking his head, Jason went back into his living room and turned on his laptop. His boss expected preliminary schedules tomorrow and he would have them.

JUNE HAD BEEN brutally dry and there didn't appear to be any relief in sight during July.

Welcome to ranching.

Allie grimaced as she thought about all the many times she'd said that to Jason. Bitter words that at the time had come from the depths of her soul. But right now the drought didn't seem as personal as it would have when Kyle had been pretending to work the ranch. It was a drought. The same drought her neighbors were suffering through.

Meanwhile, Jason's area was getting record rainfall, thanks to El Niño.

So how was he doing with the rain and with his new job?

That question was answered in mid-July when Allie ran into Jason's younger sister, Kate, in line at the grocery store. Allie, who had alleged to her sisters more than once that she did the hard thing when necessary, wished she would have noticed Kate in line before she wheeled her cart up behind her, because she so would have gone to another line.

Kate smiled tightly at her. "Hi."

"Hi."

Awk. Ward.

So Allie jumped in. "How's Jason?"

Kate's eyes narrowed slightly, as if she were trying to read the motivation behind the question. "Good. Loving his job."

"Glad to hear that." Allie stared off over the top of the check stand for a moment. She didn't owe Jason's sister any kind of an explanation. She did not.

"Look." Kate turned toward her and Allie continued in a low voice, hoping no one else was listening. "It's a small town and we're going to see each other, so I want you to know that even though things didn't work out between us...I think the world of your brother. He's a good guy and I want him to be happy."

Kate blinked at her and for one wild second, Allie wondered if Jason's sister was unaware that she and Jason had been involved. She'd simply assumed...

"Thank you," Kate finally said. "I wish all of his friends had the same attitude."

"How so?"

Kate let out a soft sigh and glanced around just as Allie had done. "Has he ever talked about Pat?"

"Yes."

"He's the problem."

"Why does Jason keep trying?"

"Because Jason doesn't give up on friends just because they give up on him. Or themselves. And, no offense, but you didn't help matters."

"I stopped things before they went too far," she said in a near whisper, checking again to see if anyone was listening. No. Their conversation was their own.

Kate regarded her for a long moment. "Yes. I guess you did. Thanks for that." She wheeled her cart into the check stand, leaving Allie to debate the sanity of an idea that came out of nowhere.

"Kate." The woman looked at her over her shoulder. "Do you have Pat's phone number?"

"Why?"

"Do you really want to know?"

Kate's eyebrows came together. "You aren't going to double-team Jason, are you?"

"No. But I think Mr. Madison needs to think about what he's doing to a guy that's trying to help him."

"Is this really your business?" But even as she spoke Kate was pulling out her phone. She showed Allie the number when she found it, and Allie typed it into her contacts.

"No. Not my business at all." Allie dropped her phone into her purse.

And that's what she kept telling herself for the next few hours…right up until she dialed the number Kate had given her. There was a very good chance that the guy wouldn't answer an unknown number, but after a few rings a deep male voice said hello. Allie sent up a silent thank-you.

"Pat? I'm a friend of Jason's."

"He's not here."

"I know."

"Then why are you calling?"

"I'll tell you why I'm calling—I think you need to give Jason a break." She did her best to keep her voice even, when all she really wanted to do was to yell at the guy.

After a beat of brittle silence, Pat said, "Who the hell are—"

Allie drew in a breath and said calmly, "I'm a person who's watched Jason get turned inside out because of you."

"Look—"

"No, *you* look. Look at what you've done to a guy who cares about you. He was trying to help you."

"Would you stop interrupting?"

"Yes." The word came out on a snap.

"Who are you and how did you get my number?"

"Allie Brody." She wasn't about to tell him about Kate.

"You're the one."

"The one?"

"Allie. The woman who wouldn't go to California with Jason."

"This call isn't about me—"

"Why not, if we're talking about turning Jason inside out?"

"Now, wait a minute—"

"No. You wait."

A silence fell and then hung for a tense moment.

"I'm waiting," Allie said from between her teeth.

"Waiting to interrupt me."

"Fine. Talk. I won't interrupt."

"You're certain."

Allie gave a small snort instead of answering.

"All right, then. For your information, I have been talking to Jason."

"Good talk or bad talk?" Allie asked suspiciously.

"Middling."

"He cares about you, you know."

"Yeah. I do."

"As near as I can tell, he cared about you when you didn't care about yourself."

"We covered this."

And they were getting nowhere. "Here's why I called—Jason wants to repay all the stuff you did to help him."

"And…?"

Allie gritted her teeth. "Reach out to him, would you? In a positive way. A supportive way."

"I could say the same to you."

"He's still trying to make a relationship with you," Allie said through gritted teeth, frustrated that the guy kept trying to sidetrack the issue. "Why are you so hard on him?"

"I'm not trying to be hard on him...but he just doesn't get it." Pat's voice changed, shifting toward quiet frustration. "Doesn't get what I'm facing. Have faced."

"Then explain it to him." Allie sighed and pushed her hair back from her forehead. "I know he comes from a place of privilege."

"And I don't?"

"I looked you up." Pat had been raised in one of the poorer neighborhoods in Atlanta. Football had saved him and ultimately, in a way, destroyed him.

"Oh."

"What I'm saying is that he has a big heart. He tries to help everyone...why don't you accept his help? Or at least decline in a way he can accept. You know—be a friend?"

"Good question, missy. And, I might ask, why you can't do the same thing?"

"Because—" Allie hesitated, then murmured the truth "—I'm really afraid of messing him up."

"You don't have much faith in him then." Allie opened her mouth, then closed it again. "The boy's strong," Pat said. "Stronger than you give him credit for."

"Strong enough to put up with you dissing him for a year," Allie said. "I don't know why I called you."

"Yes, you do. You care about Jason and you

think I'm hurting him. The only problem is that you didn't want to have the same finger pointed at you."

THE GRASS CRACKLED beneath their feet as Allie and Zach walked back across the pasture toward the barn. The reason they were able to clean the ditch was because no water was flowing. It was the driest summer they'd seen in a decade, but even though she was fighting the whims of nature, Allie no longer muttered to herself about hating life on the ranch. She had a mission now—to bring the Lightning Creek through the drought. For her sisters. For herself. And, in a way, for the Lightning Creek itself.

The tables had turned and the ranch needed her.

In a crazy way, she was starting to need the ranch. Focusing her energy there took her mind off Jason.

Allie hadn't spent productive time on the Lightning Creek in years, and even though the drought was taking its toll, she and Zach were managing the place as well as they could. Fields were drying up, but she'd adjusted by selling five cows to a neighbor. The herd Dani and Jolie had worked to build was smaller, but she wasn't feeding as many head. They'd replenish stock when the drought ended.

They would get through and she'd be stronger

because of it—stronger than she'd been when she'd used the ranch as a scapegoat for her grief and sense of loss, which was exactly what she'd done. She couldn't blame her dad for dying, or her mom for being totally focused on providing for her family, or her sisters for needing her help and care, so what could she blame?

The ranch.

A few years later she'd returned, armed with new hope and a husband, and experienced even more loss.

She blamed the ranch again.

Then Jason and Zach had come on the scene. Good things started to happen. And even though Jason was gone, the memories of his time there were good memories, uplifting memories. Memories to cling to.

Because she hadn't been brave enough to cling to the man himself. And she really wished she hadn't called Pat the previous evening, to straighten him out, because he'd said things that were still eating at her.

"I'm going to do my rain dance tonight," Zach said as they parted ways at the barn.

"Let me know if you need help."

"Will do."

But if Zach did a rain dance, he was doing it in town. He left with a friend just as Allie was eating a lonely dinner. He didn't drink anymore. He'd explained that to Allie as they'd worked.

And he was going to start community college in the fall, eventually transferring to U of M so that he could study Ag Econ and manage Jason's ranch someday. He was kidding about Jason's ranch, but Allie found that she wished he wasn't. If Jason had a ranch, he would come back.

She walked out to the porch and sat on the top step, exactly where she'd sat when she and Jason had discussed California. Or rather when he'd suggested and she'd reacted.

Fear had motivated her for the longest time. And what had it gotten her?

She could say exactly what it had lost her— time with a man who was now building his life elsewhere.

THE CALL CAME just before midnight. Jason was going over intern applications when his phone vibrated on the sofa beside him.

"It's me," Pat said without a hello. "I couldn't sleep."

"And wanted to make sure I wasn't sleeping, either?" Jason set his laptop aside and got to his feet.

"Maybe." Pat blew out a breath and then fell silent. The seconds ticked by while Jason studied the carpet, waiting. "I want my life back," Pat finally said on a weary note.

"Yeah." Jason bit back the platitudes. Pat wasn't getting his old life back and they both knew it.

"I screwed up."

Jason waited. No sense agreeing with the obvious.

"Delia's all over me. I tried to kick her out. She won't go. And that woman of yours…"

Jason's gut tightened. "What woman?" Had Amanda contacted Pat? That didn't seem likely.

"Your Montana woman."

Allie? "I don't understand."

"She called me."

Now he really didn't understand. "Why?"

"Because she wanted me to treat you better." Pat snorted. "I told her to do the same. She didn't like that."

"She called you." Suddenly this phone call was about him, not Pat.

"Can I be any clearer?"

"No. Sorry. I'm just…surprised."

"Surprised me, too," Pat grumbled. "Until then I didn't want to think about you. I wanted you to leave me alone. Go live your life." He cleared his throat. "She told me to be a better friend. Then Delia jumped me. Hard." Pat's voice was barely audible when he said, "She told me that if I was going to spend my days in a puddle of self-pity, that I may as well finish what I started. Said she'd help me. Woman was pissed."

Jason closed his eyes. This was the first time Pat had come close to admitting that his car accident wasn't an accident. "But she didn't leave," he said.

Another long silence. "That's what made me understand—it wasn't all about me. People who cared for me were hung up in my limbo, too. They don't know my pain, but they felt pain. Because of me."

Jason massaged his forehead. "So what now?"

Pat cleared his throat. "That job you mentioned. The unpaid one... I've been thinking about that."

"Do you *need* a paycheck?" Jason asked quietly.

"I need to face that I'm afraid that people might think I hit that tree on purpose."

Which was probably why he'd spent the last year hiding out.

"Pat...why would they do that when you're trying to change things? You spend too much time in your head, man."

"I gotta learn to deal," he continued as if speaking to himself.

Yeah, you do. "I'll talk to Amanda and my boss, and get back to you tomorrow. Say around ten o'clock?"

"I'll be here."

"I'm glad you called," Jason said.

"Yeah." Pat cleared his throat again, then said a gruff goodbye and hung up.

Jason stood for a moment holding the phone, a

little stunned and a lot grateful at what [...] transpired. He knew Pat well enough to [...] stand that it wouldn't be all roses from h[...] out, but at least his friend was moving forw[...] That was huge.

Jason set down his phone and walked over to the window to stare at the lights of the city. Not a constellation in sight.

He missed the stars, which were so bright at the Lightning Creek. He missed the ranch. Missed Allie. The fact that she'd called Pat only reinforced his belief that she cared for him. Cared, but was too cautious to do anything about it.

He'd definitely made a tactical error by asking her to come with him when their relationship was still so new. But what else could he have done? Try to build a relationship long distance? Oh, yeah. That always worked so well.

Asking her to come with you hadn't worked any better.

Jason turned away from the window and headed for bed. He wasn't going to solve anything by staring at the skyline and wishing he could see stars.

ALLIE WAS POURING coffee into her travel mug when her phone rang. She stepped over to the table, still holding the pot, then froze when she saw Jason's name on the screen. It was early, st after dawn. Too early for a casual call—as if there could be such a thing between them. She fought with herself for two more rings, then set down the pot and picked up the phone.

"You called Pat," Jason said immediately after her hello.

Her heart thumped hard at the sound of his voice. "I did."

"Why?"

She tightened her grip on the phone, thought about hedging, then went with the truth. "I talked to your sister and she told me that neither Pat nor I were doing you any good."

"So you yelled at Pat."

"I did." A horrible thought struck her. "Please tell me he's okay." Because he'd sounded okay, and maybe even a touch protective of Jason, when she'd ended their call.

"He wants to become my intern."

Allie felt a rush of relief. "Glad to hear it."

"Since you had something to do with it, I thought I'd let you know."

"Thank you." She didn't say anything else, but she hung on to her phone as if it were a lifeline. The silence crackled between them.

"How's it going there?" she finally asked.

"My job's challenging. I like it. How's it there?"

Lonely.

"Dry. Really dry."

"It's not dry here."

"I've been envying your weather." And wasn't this a ridiculous conversation? Two people skirting the real issue, because there was no immediate remedy for the problem they faced.

"I miss you."

Allie's heart hit her ribs. Okay…maybe they were going to tackle an issue or two.

"I wish things were different, Jason." So cool. So distant. He'd never guess that she was fighting to keep from infusing heavy duty emotions into her words.

She was certain he was going to say something along the lines of, "They could be," but he didn't. In fact he said nothing at all.

So what now? Should she chat about the weather some more? Pour out her guts?

"I'm glad you're happy there."

"Like I said, I like my job."

"I'm beginning to like my job, too."

"What job?" Jason asked.

"The ranch. I couldn't land anything else, so now the Lightning Creek is my job. And it isn't bad, even though the place isn't in the best shape."

"That's good, Allie." He sounded like he meant it. She closed her eyes as she realized that she didn't want to break the connection—that now that she was talking to him, she didn't want to let him go.

"I guess I needed some one-on-one time with

the land to come to understand that I'd been through a hell of a lot of stress on this place, but the ranch itself wasn't to blame."

"It bothered me that you disliked it," Jason said. "It's a beautiful ranch."

"I'm starting to appreciate—" A knock on the door startled her, then she sighed. "Zach's here. I have to go. We're driving to Missoula to look at bulls and he has to be back in time for his class."

"Allie…"

She heard the door open as Zach let himself into the house. He called a hello from the living room.

"I have to go." She hesitated, then said, "I'll call you. Maybe not tomorrow, but…I will call."

"All right, Allie. Take care."

"I will."

After ending the call, she fastened the lid onto her travel mug and set the coffee pot back on the stove, doing her best to appear normal when she felt anything but.

Zach stopped just inside the kitchen doorway. "Ready to go?"

"Oh, yeah." She was ready for just about anything except for figuring out how to deal with her feelings for Jason and her fear of needing him way too much.

ALLIE HAD MADE peace with the ranch. That was a good thing…or so Jason kept telling himself over the days that passed after their phone call. Days? It had been almost two weeks since he'd heard from her. She'd said she'd call, and he believed her—but that didn't mean he wasn't getting antsy waiting.

A low curse brought him back to the present. Pat was still working his way through the intricacies of his computer program, but Jason knew better than to offer assistance. Pat would ask for help when he was ready, which was usually when he was approaching the end of his rope.

At least he was asking now. The first few days had been hell as Pat had battled intimidation, ego and a healthy lack of computer knowledge. Amanda had been great at ignoring his aura of bristling defensiveness and offering help in a way that Pat could accept.

"He's just nervous," she'd confided in Jason, before Jason could tell her the exact same thing.

Eventually Pat began to relax, and on the Friday of his first week, he'd asked Jason if he could accompany him to the football field. They'd watched the end of a low-key passing practice from the stands and Pat had actually smiled as he watched a particularly beautiful catch.

That had been a good day.

"I'm supposed to ask you if you want to come over for Sunday dinner," Pat said when he finally stopped grumbling at his computer.

"Sure. Tell Delia thanks for the invitation."

"You need to get out more."

"What?"

"You used to have a social life," Pat said as he maneuvered his chair away from the computer desk.

"I haven't had any time."

"You used to make time," Pat said.

"Fine. You and I can go out sometime."

Jason expected Pat to decline the offer, but he said, "It might be good for you."

Jason rolled his eyes, but inwardly he smiled. It felt good to ease back into their old roles. At least one of his relationships was working out. He still had no idea what he was going to do about a certain other one.

ALLIE HAD BEEN so sure that once she and Jason were apart, her life would eventually drift back to the way it'd been before he'd shown up. It hadn't, and the odd sort of limbo in which she found herself was worse now that they'd spoken.

She thought about him during the day as she worked around the ranch, thought of him in the evening when she painted. Most of all, she ached for him at night. She wanted him close and he wasn't there.

So what was she going to do about that? Hide out and hope that she'd eventually feel normal again?

That strategy hadn't worked so far, and she didn't see it working in the future.

She hadn't had a lot of control of the other losses in her life, but this one...this one was all on her. She hadn't been ready to commit to a big move when Jason had sprung his plan on her—more accurately, she'd allowed knee-jerk fear to overwhelm her—but she'd had time to assess her fears. Talk herself through the potential benefits and consequences of trying a relationship.

They didn't need to move at lightning speed. As long as she took things slow, as they'd once done, she'd be fine. No need to feel like her stomach would turn inside out.

Who was she kidding?

She was scared to death, but something had to give. So late one evening, after trying and failing to focus on her painting, she finally reached for the phone.

When Jason answered, her pulse jumped, but she took a breath and dove in.

"Hi. I told you I'd call. Sorry it took so long." *I just wanted to be sure of my next move.*

"How are you?" The sound of his deep voice almost did her in.

I'm conflicted. Scared. Determined.

"Thoughtful," she finally said.

"In what way?" She caught the edge to his voice, buried beneath the casual tone of the question.

"I have been considering your previous offer.

I'm not ready to move, but maybe I can visit in the near future."

A few silent seconds ticked by.

"I'd like that," Jason finally said, and she realized then that she needed to exhale. He'd probably been waiting for her to lay down conditions.

She had no conditions. She just wanted to see him. Test the waters. Figure out her next move.

"I'd like it a lot," he added, and now she could hear the smile in his voice. More than that, she could visualize it, the way it creased his cheeks and lit his eyes. Damn, but she'd missed him. "When would you like to come?"

"Why don't you look at your schedule, let me know a good time, and we'll work from there."

"I'll do that and call you tomorrow."

"All right."

"Are you sure you're ready for this?" he asked.

"I'm pretty sure I can handle a visit," she said in a dry voice. It was time for her to man up and look at the reality of the present instead of reacting to the past. "We'll take it from there. Try not to rush things."

Now she sounded like she was trying to convince herself, so she stopped talking.

"This will be good, Allie. I promise. I think you'll love it here."

"It'll get me off the ranch." But even as she spoke she knew she wasn't as anxious to leave the Lightning Creek as she'd once been. She couldn't use wanting to escape the ranch as an excuse to visit Jason. Not if she were going to remain honest with herself. "Actually, I want to see you and I don't mind the ranch so much."

"Still growing on you, eh?"

"Like I said, I've made peace. It was just a long time coming."

"I'm glad, Allie. I'll check into things and call you."

After saying goodbye, Allie walked out onto her porch and stood leaning against a newel post looking out over the ranch. She'd done some good here. Dealt with her painful memories. Actually come to feel as if she belonged again.

She'd eventually have to learn to belong somewhere else, because no matter what, she didn't feel complete without Jason.

"WHAT'S EATING YOU?"

Jason looked over at Pat with a frown. "Nothing."

Pat shook his head and focused back on the field. "So your lady is coming to visit."

"We worked out the details yesterday." Allie was flying in at the end of the next week for four days.

"And you're good with that?"

Jason's eyes narrowed. "Of course I am. Why wouldn't I be?"

"That's what I'm trying to figure."

"What the hell are you talking about?" Because Jason had had enough hints that all was not well.

"You're deep in your head, JD. You only do that when things aren't right and you're figuring how to make them right."

Jason blinked at him. "Things are great."

Pat rolled a little closer and jabbed his finger at Jason. "Then why are you so closed off and preoccupied? You've been that way since I started here."

"Because I'm in transition. Working my way into a new life. You know...kind of like you are."

"Only I'm excited about what I'm doing." Jason raised his eyebrows and Pat flushed. "All right," he grumbled. "I didn't want to do this in the beginning and I started out a little intimidated, but I like it. You watch—I'll be on the payroll by the end of the year."

"You're welcome," Jason said, hoping to sidetrack his friend. It didn't work.

"But you...you're going through the motions. I've never seen you like this."

Jason opened his mouth to protest, then closed it again when Pat gave him a dangerous look. "So now your lady will come here and things will work out and you'll make a life."

"That's what I hope happens."

"A happy suburban couple."

Jason scowled at his friend. "What are you getting at?"

"I don't know," Pat said. "Things just seem... off."

Jason muttered a curse and sank down onto the bleacher bench beside Pat's chair. "It'll work out. I belong with Allie."

Pat shifted his chair a quarter turn to fully face him. "But do you belong *here*?"

Jason stared at him. What kind of question was that? "Yeah. I do."

"Then act like it. If you expect her to adapt to your world, then you'd better be sure you love what you're doing."

"I do love it," Jason said. He was in position to start working his way into the postfootball career he'd dreamed about, and, damn it, he was going to make it happen. Allie would come to love San Diego and they'd be happy.

Things were going to work out.

TWO NIGHTS BEFORE Allie was supposed to leave for San Diego, a series of thunderstorms started moving in over the mountains behind the Lightning Creek.

Rain. Finally.

Only it didn't rain. The thunderstorms shook the house and lit the windows, but stubbornly refused to release any moisture. Eventually the thunder rumbled into the distance and Allie nodded off, only to wake up a little after midnight to the feeling that something wasn't right.

Smoke. She could smell smoke, and the odor was too strong to be from a distant fire.

Allie jumped out of bed and raced downstairs to the front door, her heart pounding as she shoved her arms into her robe. Acrid smoke hit her lungs when she threw open the door and she could hear the cattle milling around restlessly in the darkness.

This fire was close. Too close.

She was about to head back into the house to grab her phone to call dispatch when she heard the siren and spotted the flashing lights in the distance. Okay, nix dispatch. Now she had to see how close the fire was, how much time she had.

She ran into the yard and started around the corner of the house, then stopped dead in her tracks. The fire wasn't on the mountain as she had thought.

The fire was at her fence line, less than a half mile away.

JASON SETTLED IN his chair and clicked through the television channels trying to find something to catch and keep his attention since he couldn't sleep. The phone vibrated on the table next to him and he answered it without looking at the screen.

"Jason...?" It was Allie and her voice had cracked as she said his name.

"What's wrong?"

"The Lightning Creek is on fire."

Jason nearly dropped the phone. "On fire?"

"Not all of it, but the house...we're about to lose the house. We're moving the livestock now. The fire crew is working on saving the barn and the arena."

Jason didn't care about the barn and the arena. "Where are you? Are you safe?"

"I'm just leaving with a trailer load of animals that I'm taking to another ranch."

"Stay there. At the other ranch. I'll get there as soon as I can."

"I... Thank you."

She didn't argue, and that was major. "I'll be in touch," he said. "Promise me you'll stay away from the fire."

"I promise you I'll stay safe. I have more livestock to move."

"Allie—"

"Keep me posted," she said. "I've got to focus on my driving." She hung up and Jason stood holding his phone, feeling like he'd just been knocked sideways by a charging linebacker.

What first? Call Amanda, tell her he needed a few days' emergency leave, then call Pat.

The call to Amanda went to voice mail, because of the hour, no doubt, so he called Pat. "I have an emergency. I have to leave town."

"For how long?" Pat asked on a stunned note.

"A day or two. Allie's ranch caught fire. I need to get there."

Pat let out a low whistle, then said, "Is it possible for me to cover for you?"

Jason stilled momentarily, then said, "Yes. Totally possible." He shot a look at the clock, thanked God for the internet, texting and video chat, then said, "I can talk you through everything. I just need to bring Amanda into the loop…"

Two hours later, he was on the way to the airport, glad that travel from San Diego to Bozeman wasn't all that popular on a Tuesday morning. He'd get there by midday. Kate would pick him up at the airport.

He'd talked to Allie twice and not once did she say, "Don't come. I don't need you."

Which meant she did need him…maybe even as much as he needed her.

She didn't talk long either time. She was busy with her livestock and propping up her sisters and mother, who were also on their way to Montana. Story of her life—propping up a family who didn't need propping up. But that was the way she was wired—protectiveness was second nature to her.

And to him. Which was going to make for an interesting future.

THE FIRE WAS out when Jason's truck came roaring down the road leading to what was left of the

Lightning Creek. Her mother and sisters were due later that evening—all of them, even though there was nothing any of them could do. Except mourn.

She'd once wondered what could be the worst that could happen while she was on the ranch and now she had her answer. The ranch could be destroyed, and wasn't it ironic that it had happened after she'd made peace with it?

Jason pulled to a stop at the edge of the burn and got out. The two firefighters who were still there, tending the ashes, looked up to see who had arrived, then went back to their jobs. Allie started walking toward him, her steps becoming quicker as she neared him. He looked like hell with circles under his eyes and a day's worth of scruffy growth on his chin, his hair sticking up. But he was here and even though she'd promised herself not to fall apart when she saw him, as soon as he was near enough, she wrapped herself around him, holding him close, breathing in his scent.

He held her against him, his lips pressing against the top of her hair, which probably reeked of smoke. He didn't seem to care, because he nuzzled his cheek against her head, kissed her again.

"Thank you for coming," she said.

"Not coming wasn't an option." He put her away from him and then put an arm around her shoulders, pulling her to his side. "I'm so sorry, Allie."

She simply nodded in response. At this point, she felt a surreal detachment from what had happened.

The smoke was still rolling off the ashes of the house she'd grown up in. The house she'd mourned in after losing her father. The house she'd brought her husband home to, and then left after the divorce to start a new life.

The house where she'd fallen in love with Jason.

She blinked back tears. Looked away.

Jason nodded at the fire guys, then steered her toward the barn and arena. The barn had singe marks on one side. The arena was remarkably unscathed.

"How on earth did it escape?" he asked.

"They drenched it when it became obvious they couldn't save the house. The canvas held the moisture, I guess. So did the barn."

He started walking again, stopping at the half-burned fence posts that edged the barn. "Did you get all of the animals out?"

"Cows, goats, horses. All of them."

"Thank heaven for small blessings."

Allie gave a small shudder and Jason looked down at her. "Let's get out of here."

"I... Yes. Please." The tone of her voice made her cringe a little. She was stronger than this. She didn't need to go to pieces just because Jason was there to prop her up.

Why not?

She allowed everyone else she knew to go to pieces. Why not her?

Jason wrapped an arm around her even tighter and steered her toward the truck.

Another small shudder went through Allie as they walked past what had once been her garden. The plot was now a smashed mess of tire tracks from the trucks that had parked there trying to save the house.

"Jason?"

He stopped walking and turned her in his arms. "Yeah?"

"I'm so glad you're here."

"Me, too, sweetheart." He pulled her closer, enveloping her in warmth and comfort. She laid her cheek against his chest, suddenly, over-whelmingly glad that he was there when she needed him most. She, who didn't allow herself to need.

Well, she needed him now, and he had traveled for almost twelve hours to get to her.

"I want to go to the Staley house."

"You bet." He leaned back to look down at her. "Why aren't you there now?"

"I had to come back." She stepped away from him. "Look at this, Jason. Look at my ranch."

Her ranch.

She heard him inhale deeply. "Come on. I'll take you ho...to the house." He'd almost said *home*, but she no longer had a home, temporary or otherwise. He helped her into the truck and they drove in silence to her brother-in-law Gabe's beautiful cedar, stone and glass house. The fire had missed it by one small mile.

Allie opened the unlocked door and Jason followed her inside.

"Some place."

"If you like quartz and hardwood and stainless steel and a whole lot of stone and glass." Her voice broke a little on the last word. "I kind of like beat-up flooring that's raised a few generations of kids. And squeaking stairs and faucets that turn the wrong way because someone put them on backwards."

"Allie..."

She stepped into him then, wrapped her arms around him and pressed her cheek against his chest. The tears came before she could stop them, spilling down her face and soaking Jason's shirt. His arms closed around her, holding her to him until the tears slowed, then stopped.

"I don't usually cry," she muttered against his shirt.

"You don't usually lose a ranch."

"True." Allie let out a long shuddering breath. She felt drained. More than drained. And she had to look like hell, all grimy and smoky, but she didn't care, because Jason didn't seem to care. He was there for her, and despite feeling disoriented and exhausted and all cried out, she realized that that was huge—not that he was there for her, but that she could *accept* him being there for her.

She stepped back away from him then, keeping her hands at his waist as she met his gaze and realized just how much she loved him.

"Do you want to eat?"

She almost laughed at the incongruity of their thought paths. "No, but I'm tired of smelling like smoke." And her face was sticky from tears. "I need a shower in the worst way."

"Okay. You shower. I'll light that pretend fire over there." He pointed at the propane fire place flanked by the leather sofas. "When you're done, we'll sit and watch the fire and not talk."

"Not talk?"

He shook his head. "We'll just hang out."

"What if I want to talk?"

"Later."

"Are you giving me orders?" she asked mildly.

One corner of his mouth twitched. "As if you'd let me get away with that." He smiled and gave her a gentle nudge toward the hall leading out of the great room. "Give a yell if you need anything."

True to his word, Jason had the fire lit when she came out of the bathroom wearing her sister's

robe and then they snuggled silently on the sofa.
Not talking felt good. They'd talk later.

ALLIE WOKE UP in Jason's arms. She raised her
head to look at him and he smiled down at her.
Satisfied that all was well, she nestled her cheek
against his chest as he slowly stroked her hair.
"How long was I out?"

"About an hour," he said.

Her eyes were drifting shut again, but she
didn't want to sleep. "Is silent time over?" she
asked.

He laughed softly. "Yeah."

"How long can you stay?"

"A couple days…and then pretty much forever." Her head jerked up, and when she met his
eyes, she saw a hint of uncertainty there. "I…
uh… I want to help you rebuild."

"Are you quitting your job?"

"Yeah."

"The job that's going to help you build your
career?"

"I'm changing careers."

"Not because of me, you aren't."

"Because of us," he said gently. "You. Me. Us."
He tilted her chin up and kissed her, ending the
kiss before it got away from them. "I don't belong
there, Allie. Maybe I would have if I'd taken the

job right after I walked off the field for the last time. Before I came home. Before I met you."

"You're saying you belong here?"

"I belong where you are. And yeah. I belong here. I like it here."

The sincerity in his expression as he stated the simple words made Allie's heart swell.

"Maybe you can get us a deal on materials."

"Maybe."

"It'd be nice to have a house big enough for everyone to have their own bedroom when we got together for Christmas."

"Five bedroom?"

"Pipe dream?"

"Totally doable."

She wrapped her arms around him more tightly. "I love you, you know."

"Good thing because you've changed my life, my career, my everything." He kissed her again, and as Allie splayed her fingers across his broad chest, felt his heart beating low and slow beneath her palm, she knew that she'd found where she belonged. With him, wherever that might be. And the best part was that it didn't scare her to need him. Not anymore.

"Before we get carried away here," she said huskily, "and trust me, I have every intention of getting carried away, I want you to know that I love having you in my future."

Jason pulled her the rest of the way onto his lap and wrapped his arms around her. "In that case, babe, why don't we settle in and make some plans?"

* * * * *

LARGER-PRINT BOOKS!
GET 2 FREE LARGER-PRINT NOVELS PLUS
2 FREE GIFTS!

◆HARLEQUIN®

INTRIGUE

BREATHTAKING ROMANTIC SUSPENSE

YES! Please send me 2 FREE LARGER-PRINT Harlequin® Intrigue novels and my 2 FREE gifts (gifts are worth about $10). After receiving them, if I don't wish to receive any more books, I can return the shipping statement marked "cancel." If I don't cancel, I will receive 6 brand-new novels every month and be billed just $5.49 per book in the U.S. or $6.24 per book in Canada. That's a saving of at least 11% off the cover price! It's quite a bargain! Shipping and handling is just 50¢ per book in the U.S. and 75¢ per book in Canada.* I understand that accepting the 2 free books and gifts places me under no obligation to buy anything. I can always return a shipment and cancel at any time. Even if I never buy another book, the two free books and gifts are mine to keep forever.

199/399 HDN GHWN

Name _____ (PLEASE PRINT)

Address _____ Apt. #

City _____ State/Prov. _____ Zip/Postal Code

Signature (if under 18, a parent or guardian must sign)

Mail to the **Reader Service:**
IN U.S.A.: P.O. Box 1867, Buffalo, NY 14240-1867
IN CANADA: P.O. Box 609, Fort Erie, Ontario L2A 5X3

**Are you a subscriber to Harlequin® Intrigue books
and want to receive the larger-print edition?
Call 1-800-873-8635 today or visit www.ReaderService.com.**

* Terms and prices subject to change without notice. Prices do not include applicable taxes. Sales tax applicable in N.Y. Canadian residents will be charged applicable taxes. Offer not valid in Quebec. This offer is limited to one order per household. Not valid for current subscribers to Harlequin Intrigue Larger-Print books. All orders subject to credit approval. Credit or debit balances in a customer's account(s) may be offset by any other outstanding balance owed by or to the customer. Please allow 4 to 6 weeks for delivery. Offer available while quantities last.

Your Privacy—The Reader Service is committed to protecting your privacy. Our Privacy Policy is available online at www.ReaderService.com or upon request from the Reader Service.

We make a portion of our mailing list available to reputable third parties that offer products we believe may interest you. If you prefer that we not exchange your name with third parties, or if you wish to clarify or modify your communication preferences, please visit us at www.ReaderService.com/consumerschoice or write to us at Reader Service Preference Service, P.O. Box 9062, Buffalo, NY 14240-9062. Include your complete name and address.

REQUEST YOUR FREE BOOKS!
2 FREE WHOLESOME ROMANCE NOVELS
IN LARGER PRINT
PLUS 2
FREE
MYSTERY GIFTS

⁂⁂⁂⁂⁂⁂⁂⁂⁂⁂⁂⁂⁂⁂⁂⁂⁂⁂⁂

H E A R T W A R M I N G™

⁑⁑⁑⁑⁑⁑⁑⁑⁑⁑⁑⁑⁑⁑⁑⁑⁑⁑⁑⁑⁑⁑

Wholesome, tender romances

YES! Please send me 2 FREE Harlequin® Heartwarming Larger-Print novels and my 2 FREE mystery gifts (gifts worth about $10). After receiving them, if I don't wish to receive any more books, I can return the shipping statement marked "cancel." If I don't cancel, I will receive 4 brand-new larger-print novels every month and be billed just $5.24 per book in the U.S. or $5.99 per book in Canada. That's a savings of at least 19% off the cover price. It's quite a bargain! Shipping and handling is just 50¢ per book in the U.S. and 75¢ per book in Canada.* I understand that accepting the 2 free books and gifts places me under no obligation to buy anything. I can always return a shipment and cancel at any time. Even if I never buy another book, the two free books and gifts are mine to keep forever.

161/361 IDN GHX2

Name	(PLEASE PRINT)	
Address		Apt. #
City	State/Prov.	Zip/Postal Code

Signature (if under 18, a parent or guardian must sign)

Mail to the **Reader Service:**
IN U.S.A.: P.O. Box 1867, Buffalo, NY 14240-1867
IN CANADA: P.O. Box 609, Fort Erie, Ontario L2A 5X3

* Terms and prices subject to change without notice. Prices do not include applicable taxes. Sales tax applicable in N.Y. Canadian residents will be charged applicable taxes. Offer not valid in Quebec. This offer is limited to one order per household. Not valid for current subscribers to Harlequin Heartwarming larger-print books. All orders subject to credit approval. Credit or debit balances in a customer's account(s) may be offset by any other outstanding balance owed by or to the customer. Please allow 4 to 6 weeks for delivery. Offer available while quantities last.

Your Privacy—The Reader Service is committed to protecting your privacy. Our Privacy Policy is available online at www.ReaderService.com or upon request from the Reader Service.

We make a portion of our mailing list available to reputable third parties that offer products we believe may interest you. If you prefer that we not exchange your name with third parties, or if you wish to clarify or modify your communication preferences, please visit us at www.ReaderService.com/consumerschoice or write to us at Reader Service Preference Service, P.O. Box 9062, Buffalo, NY 14240-9062. Include your complete name and address.

HWI5

LARGER-PRINT BOOKS!

◆ HARLEQUIN

Presents®

PASSION GUARANTEED SEDUCTION

GET 2 FREE LARGER-PRINT NOVELS PLUS 2 FREE GIFTS!

YES! Please send me 2 FREE LARGER-PRINT Harlequin Presents® novels and my 2 FREE gifts (gifts are worth about $10). After receiving them, if I don't wish to receive any more books, I can return the shipping statement marked "cancel." If I don't cancel, I will receive 6 brand-new novels every month and be billed just $5.30 per book in the U.S. or $5.74 per book in Canada. That's a saving of at least 12% off the cover price! It's quite a bargain! Shipping and handling is just 50¢ per book in the U.S. and 75¢ per book in Canada.* I understand that accepting the 2 free books and gifts places me under no obligation to buy anything. I can always return a shipment and cancel at any time. Even if I never buy another book, the two free books and gifts are mine to keep forever.

176/376 HDN GHVY

Name	(PLEASE PRINT)	
Address		Apt. #
City	State/Prov.	Zip/Postal Code

Signature (if under 18, a parent or guardian must sign)

Mail to the **Reader Service**:
IN U.S.A.: P.O. Box 1867, Buffalo, NY 14240-1867
IN CANADA: P.O. Box 609, Fort Erie, Ontario L2A 5X3

**Are you a subscriber to Harlequin Presents® books and want to receive the larger-print edition?
Call 1-800-873-8635 today or visit us at www.ReaderService.com.**

* Terms and prices subject to change without notice. Prices do not include applicable taxes. Sales tax applicable in N.Y. Canadian residents will be charged applicable taxes. Offer not valid in Quebec. This offer is limited to one order per household. Not valid for current subscribers to Harlequin Presents Larger-Print books. All orders subject to credit approval. Credit or debit balances in a customer's account(s) may be offset by any other outstanding balance owed by or to the customer. Please allow 4 to 6 weeks for delivery. Offer available while quantities last.

Your Privacy—The Reader Service is committed to protecting your privacy. Our Privacy Policy is available online at www.ReaderService.com or upon request from the Reader Service.

We make a portion of our mailing list available to reputable third parties that offer products we believe may interest you. If you prefer that we not exchange your name with third parties, or if you wish to clarify or modify your communication preferences, please visit us at www.ReaderService.com/consumerchoice or write to us at Reader Service Preference Service, P.O. Box 9062, Buffalo, NY 14240-9062. Include your complete name and address.

HPLP15

LARGER-PRINT BOOKS!
GET 2 FREE LARGER-PRINT NOVELS PLUS
2 FREE GIFTS!

HARLEQUIN®

Romance

From the Heart, For the Heart

HRLP15